BETRAYED BY ASH

STEPHANIE E. DONOHUE

Published by Never and Ever Publishing https://neverandeverbooks.com/

Edited by Meg Dailey https://thedaileyeditor.wordpress.com/

Map created by Hannah at Centaur Maps https://linktr.ee/centaurmaps

Cover by S.E.D Creations

https://sedcreation.com/

UCHEN
Dunbar
Ashborne
Norhall
Furness
Thorne
Lenwick
IDRIL
Detha
Onryx
Lundy
Exeter
DAIGH
AECKLAND
Solaris
Oakwell
Keld
Nascombe
NERDANEL
Kalo
APRA
Mortham
Salkire
ECHA
SAKAR
Mulnigan Sea
VATRA
Muirin
Darfield
Kilerth
Laewaes
Harthwaite
Vaporia
Swindon
VICTARION
Ilragorn
Pantmawe
Niall
Hadleigh
NETHERIDGE
Glenarm
Bullmar
Marren
Sanadrin
Lamex
Ecrin
Emall
Aramore
Dalry
Haran
Cullfield
Jabbart
Sharpton
Sanlow
MARACH
Alryne
BAFRUS
Mirfield
Pella
Pirn
Landow
Berkton
Merton
Cynerik
Fallholt

Contents

Content Warning   vii

Previously on...   1
1. Norhall   5
2. Control   17
3. Ramiel   27
4. Raven   39
5. Invitation   51
6. Departure   61
7. Barbarians   69
8. Teeth   81
9. Icarus   91
10. Predator   103
11. Quinn   113
12. Waterfall   125
13. Joy   139
14. Tragedy   149
15. Raphael   161
16. Betrayal   175
17. Cheriour   185
18. Flame   195
19. Oath   205

Acknowledgments   209
About the Author   211
Other Books by Stephanie E. Donohue   213
Fires of the Forsaken   215
Ashes of the Earth   217

Content Warning

This book contains scenes of violence and descriptions of blood/gore, scenes discussing the loss of family members/loved ones, and scenes showcasing mental health issues, including (but not limited to) anxiety and depression.

There are also mentions of abuse to a minor, and a relationship with a large age gap that veers into grooming territory and eventually turns violent. I have tried to handle these topics carefully and with respect, but the contents may be disturbing.

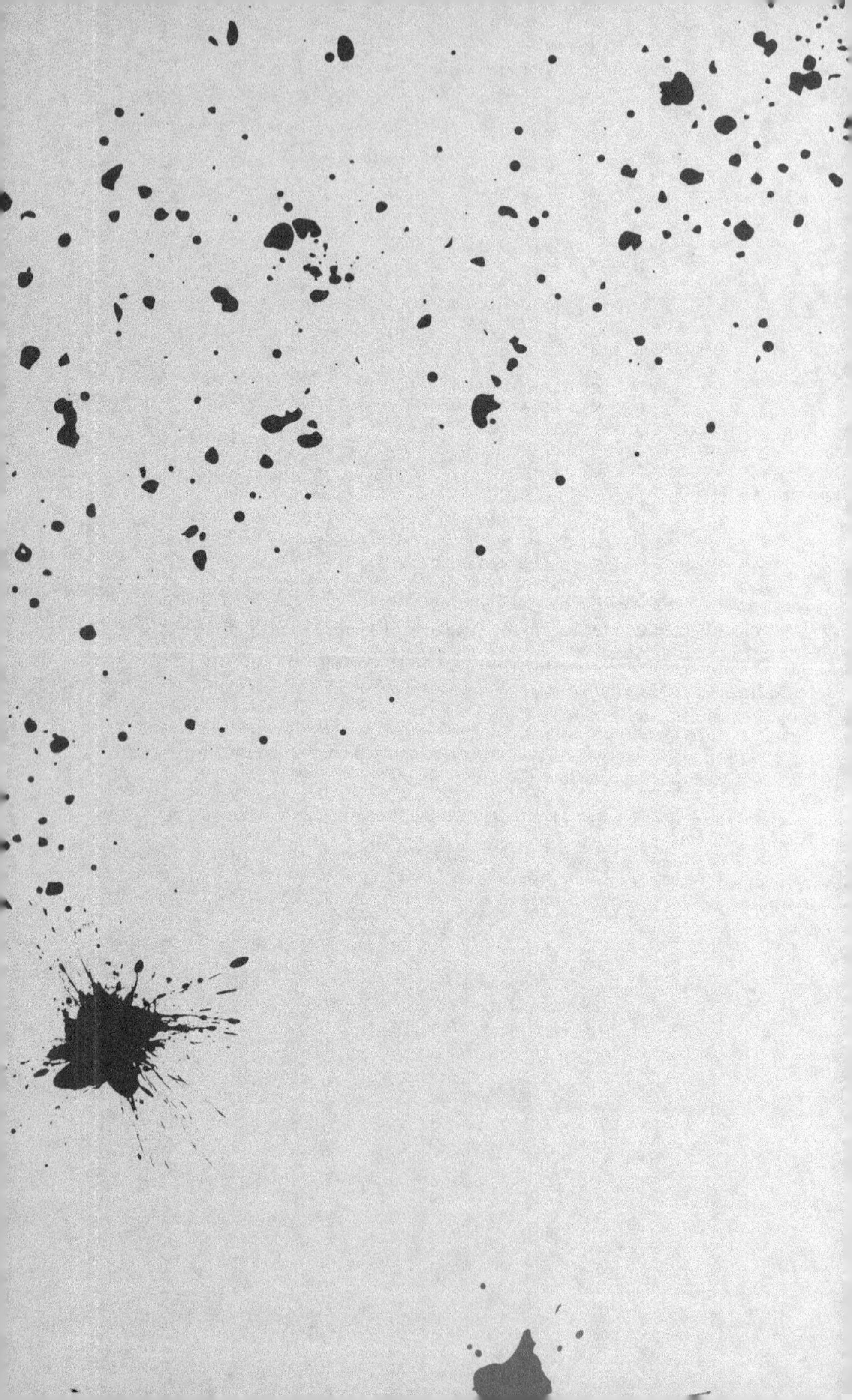

HUNTED BY FIRE

At six years old, Lass is orphaned and sentenced to death.

Her mother's demise leaves Lass unable to gather The Offering, which all residents of Detha are required to collect for their Celestial rulers. So the Wraiths, enforcers of Celestial law, arrest her. She is "rescued" by the infamous Firestarter Celestial, Seruf, and turned into a hybrid. As the transformation completes, a second Celestial steals Lass away from Seruf and drops her into the human-ruled Sakar.

But fire now courses through Lass's veins, and it riots at the slightest provocation. During one of these rampages, a terror-stricken Lass accidentally plunges into a lake, nearly drowns, and is rescued by an aging Concealer hybrid named Terrick. When he realizes Lass is orphaned, he takes her to his home in Swindon, where she lives with him for several peaceful years. But as she grows, the fire within her grows as well. Although it remains dormant for much of her childhood, it takes only a spark of fear, which Lass experiences when she witnesses a traumatic assault, for the fire to rage again.

The humans of Swindon, unwilling to tolerate having a volatile Firestarter in their midst, drive Lass and Terrick from the town. They seek refuge in the seaside city of Darfield. While exploring her new home, Lass has multiple encounters with an impish blue-eyed boy, a hybrid soldier who shirks his responsibilities and dreams of becoming a musician. Amused by his mischievousness and charmed by his kindness, Lass finds herself falling for him. But her fire, once again, torments her.

The more the fire grows, the more Lass fears it. The more she fears it, the more she strengthens it. Soon, Terrick is forced to make a hard decision: to confine Lass and feed her a tonic to dull her emotions and keep the fire contained. This barbaric arrangement works for many years, until Terrick's heart fails him, and the fire takes control of a grieving Lass. Hunted once again by the humans who fear her, Lass finds an unexpected ally in the blue-eyed boy she'd met as a child, who helps her escape Darfield and finally gives her his name as a parting gift: Quinn.

But her freedom does not last long. As the rumors about her power spread across Sakar, Lass is tracked down and taken to a town called Lamex, where the Manipulator hybrid, Byron, tortures her for information about Seruf. Upon realizing she has no information to give, Byron banishes her. An increasingly frightened Lass tries to find refuge in the woods, but humans continue to pursue her, ignoring her pleas to be left alone, and her fire continues to kill them. This vicious cycle repeats until Lass arrives at the ill-fated Vaporia.

In the ruins of the once-thriving town, Lass finally meets the Celestial who had made her: Seruf. But the meeting is not a happy one. Lass mistrusts Seruf, dislikes the new name she bestows upon her (Lasair), and scorns her offer of help. But when Quinn and other soldiers draw Seruf's ire, Lass hastily strikes a bargain to protect them: if Seruf agrees to spare the humans, Lass will depart from Sakar with her.

And thus, Lass begins her life with the Celestials.

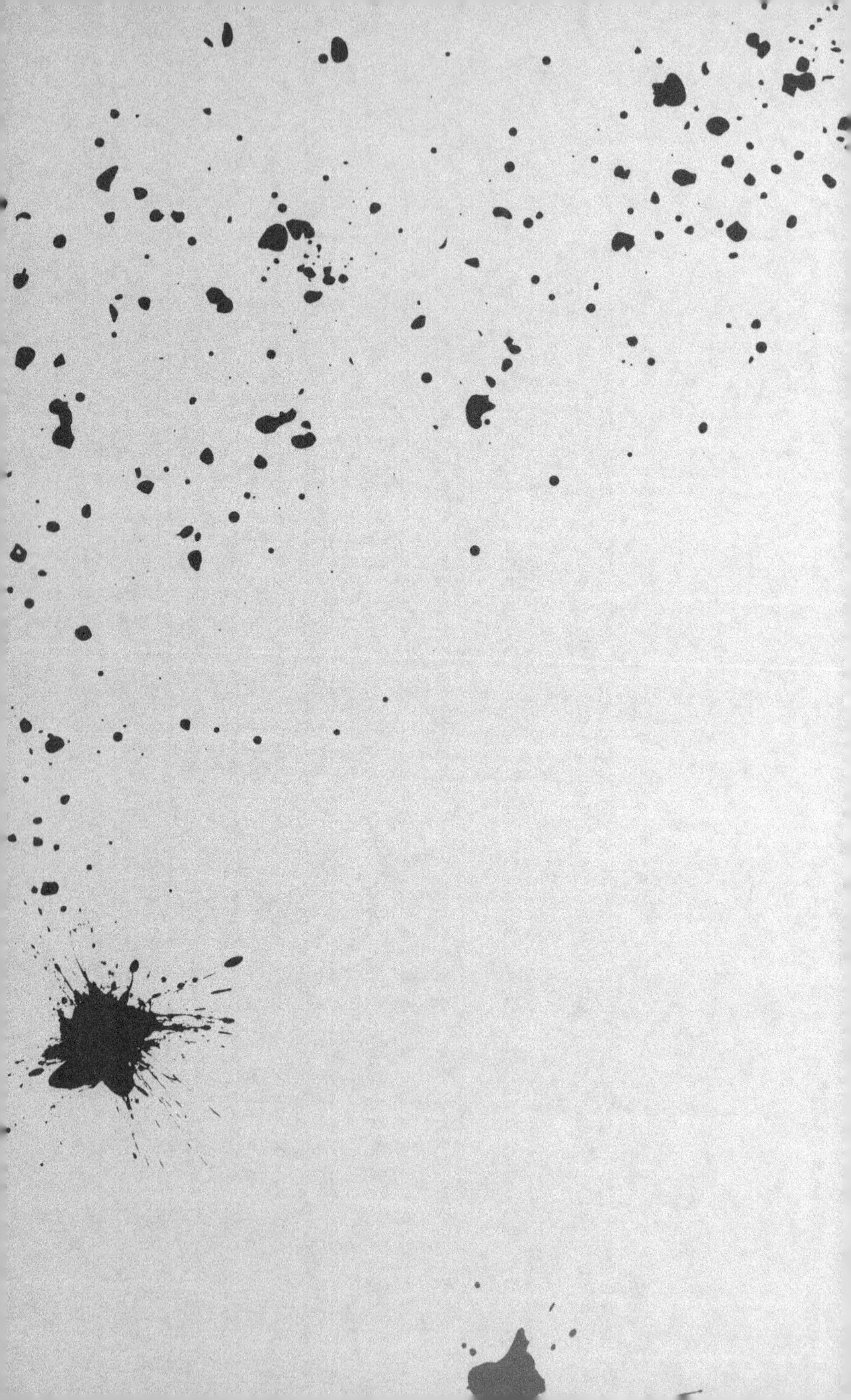

Norhall

Ziiing. Snap.

Whips create a beautiful, lilting whistle when they are loosed. An alluring tune, even if the brutish crack of the weapon striking its target turned the song into a ~~macabe~~—macabre one.

Ziiing. Snap.

"Keep close, darling," Seruf called over the cacophony of whistling music. "And gather your skirts as you walk. You don't want to get blood on your new dress."

I scowled. For I, indeed, wore a freshly made garment. And I *despised* the wretched thing.

The delicate fabric was a dreary shade of pale blue. So pale, in fact, that it was more akin to a sheen of snow disfigured by the wanderings of animals and people than any blue flower or sky I'd ever seen. The fit of this dull garment was as impractical as it was uncomfortable. The tightly laced bodice squeezed my bosom and compressed my stomach, making it difficult to breathe. The skirts, meanwhile, were far too loose and entirely too long. They billowed about my legs, coiling around my ankles, making it difficult to walk without stumbling.

Seruf claimed the tight cut of the gown was *"fashionable"* and the color *"complimented my complexion."*

She had a poor eye for beauty.

The garment looked—and felt—absolutely dreadful.

A few specs of blood might've improved upon its drabness.

But at Seruf's behest (this is a word, yes? I've heard it used before), I gathered the ripples of skirts in my hands before I trod in the trickling river of crimson liquid. A river that originated from a dark-eyed man, who now lay dying in the street, his back cleaved from the near thirty whiplashes he'd been forced to endure.

His crime had, no doubt, been a piddly offense. In Wraith-governed towns, humans could be stricken for sitting too long, speaking too loudly, breathing too rapidly, making an odd noise, or having an unappealing look on their face.

Wraiths needed little excuse to wield their whips.

I paused beside the man's prone body as his breath hitched and stuttered.

Nearby, the Wraiths who had beaten the man laughed and flicked droplets of blood from their whips as they monitored the other pale-faced humans shuffling about the town.

I'd seen countless grim days like this one during my childhood in Detha.

But I gazed upon my bleak surroundings, at the city Seruf called Norhall, with older, hardened eyes.

"Come, darling." Seruf was now several feet in front of me, clutching the evergreen skirts of her similarly tight-fitted garment. "We'll leave the Wraiths to their work."

Instead of heeding her call, I turned away, stepping closer to the man. The stench of his unwashed skin rose to my nostrils, mingling with that of my own rose-scented flesh—courtesy of the odd, bubbling liquid Seruf forced me to bathe in each morning. "Human you may be," she'd say as she scrubbed her bubble-coated hands over my bare back, "but you need not reek like one."

To which I'd respond, "The odor of humans is not so offensive as this." And then I would slosh warm water over my body, removing the rose-scented foam.

But now, as I stood before a dying man and stared at a town of enslaved humans, I realized Seruf was right. Humans *did* reek. The rank stench wafting from their unclean flesh turned my belly to rot.

"Darling..."

I startled when Seruf's silken hand closed around my bare wrist.

Even after spending weeks in her care, I had not managed to dispel the odd sensation that accompanied her touch, as though each brush of her fingers sent a legion of insects burrowing into my flesh.

"Oh, poor darling." Seruf grasped my wrist more firmly, drawing me against her side. "This must be *terribly* traumatic for you, given your origins. I would do away with them if I could." She used the toe of her high-heeled boot to nudge the man onto his side, turning him away from me. "Sadly, they must dwell here. But pay them no mind! You need not see them after today." She strode forward, pulling me alongside her.

The humans watched me as I traversed their soiled streets at Seruf's side. Many of them were ill, suffering from the same cough that had long ago stolen Mama from me. Many more bore deep wounds that seeped blood or yellow fluid. Angry wounds, Mama would have called them. All were emaciated; food was a scarcity in places such as this. For the humans, at least.

These people were my kin. Theirs was a suffering I knew well.

Their hateful, cautious, and frightened stares were also familiar. Humans had regarded me with fear for much of my life. And doubtless these humans, upon seeing me enter their village under the protection of their ~~barberous~~—barbarous master, despised and feared me more than the humans of Sakar ever had.

In Sakar, I'd been Seruf's hybrid—a despicable creature but one that could be captured, tortured, and killed. In Norhall, I was Seruf's ~~protojay~~—protégé. An untouchable monster whose presence would bring more misery to those already suffering beneath the Celestial's rule.

But I did what I'd always done beneath the weight of so many hateful stares.

I ignored them.

Or rather, I tried.

"We're nearly there now, darling," Seruf said. "I'll place you in a west-facing room, where you'll not be bothered by any of this vile mess..." As she spoke, she navigated me around a large pile of human feces.

I shuddered and forced myself to keep my eyes forward, allowing the sorrowful humans to fade into the blurred edges of my vision.

Before us sat a resplendent castle. The oblong structure was comprised of eight cylindrical towers, which stretched toward the heavens, disappearing into the damp mist that shrouded the land. Despite the dullness of the day, the castle's gray walls rippled like a pool of water beneath a cloudless sky. Wide, arched windows were dotted sporadically about the building, each splashed with every color imaginable: pinks, reds, blues, greens, and many shades I did not recognize.

Seruf's dwelling was magnificent, and she took great pride in it. As we drew closer, she sang its praises, assuring me I would forget the vile human village as soon as I set foot indoors.

"The entrance is around the other side." She pointed to the arched column of the west tower. "Fret not, darling, the humans will go no farther than this. They certainly do not *dare* to loiter by the entranceways." She sniffed. "I would hardly wish to step outside my door and smell their filth. Should you ever wish to visit the ground, you may do so in peace."

My skin prickled. "The entranceway does not overlook the village?"

"It does not."

So why, then, I pondered, had we walked through the village? Surely this path was not the only one that led into her dwelling? Even if it was, she held a clear abhorrence for the humans. Would it not have been more palatable for her to simply fly us over the village and into her dwelling? Although she was loath to fly over water—we'd traversed the sea on a wooden vessel that had left my stomach quite unsettled—she had not yet hesitated to fly over land.

So why had we walked?

I stared at her voluminous black and red wings, which fanned elegantly behind her as though she were wearing a cloak. "You wished me to see this," I murmured.

"To see the magnificence of my castle from a distance?" Seruf laughed. "Of course. Is it not stunning? Sadly, the sun has forsaken us this day." She raised her arm to the cloud-laden sky. "But when it shines, these walls will show their true turquoise color. This is stone from the *Celestial City*, darling."

"There must be other places on your land which provide scenic views of your dwelling," I said. "You did not trek this path merely so I could stare upon this building. You wished me to see the humans." An uncomfortable itch danced across my skin. There were no flames yet, but they roiled beneath the surface, readying themselves. "I spent my childhood in a place such as this. I do not wish to be reminded of my origins. Or my humanity."

Seruf angled her head, allowing me to glimpse her smile. "You are tempestuous, darling." She paused, turned, and cupped my cheek in her palm.

I fought the urge to pull away.

"I'd hoped you would be," she continued. "Ever since I saw you as a child, watching your kin bleed in the streets with those marvelous and calculating eyes of yours..." Her nails gently scratched my skin. "You're correct, darling. I *did* want you to see this place. But not to remind you of your humanity—you are *far* superior to this filth. No. I wanted to see if your gorgeous gaze," her thumb caressed my cheek, "remained as shrewdly unsympathetic as it was all those years ago. And I'm *delighted* that it has!"

* * *

Outside, humans toiled.

But inside the castle were pleasures and comforts that defied all rational expectation.

Seruf led me across reflective floors and through glistering hallways. Each door was embossed with silver jewele (I never spell this dratted word correctly on the first try) encrusted handles. Gold chandeliers hung from the ceiling. *Magikal* chandeliers that required no flame.

"Ah, yes!" Seruf exclaimed when I twisted beneath one such chandelier, admiring the beads of silver which hung from its artfully twisted arms. The structures were quite high. Even Terrick would not have been able to reach them, and he'd been a man taller than most. And although they hung from cords of gold chain, there seemed to be no way to lower them. I'd just begun to wonder at the arduous task it must've been to light those candles when Seruf spoke.

"I forgot you wouldn't have seen this before!" She strode to the doorway we'd come through and touched an ornate gray square that hung suspended on the silver walls just inside the room's entrance. "Mind your eyes, darling," she cautioned.

I turned to her, the question dancing upon the tip of my tongue, but it was stolen by a baffled gasp as light filled the room.

'Twas not the soft, warm glow of a flame. This illumination was sharp and bright—more akin to the haze of the sun on a cloudless summer day. But it was harsher; my eyes immediately began to water. And staring at the chandelier as it glowed with this vivid sheen made my temple pulse with pain.

I lowered my gaze to the floor, blinking the tears away.

"Ingenious, isn't it?" Seruf asked.

"I-I couldn't say." The throbbing in my temple was slow to fade. "It seems...treacherous."

"Only if used incorrectly." Seruf seemed entirely unaware of my discomfort. "It's called elektricity, darling. We use it to light my castle." Her fingers tapped against the wall.

The space was suddenly, *mercifully*, cast once more into the dull pallor of a foggy afternoon.

I stared around the room again. The gray daylight streaming through the wide windows fell gently upon the gleaming floors of marbled stone and swaddled the plush chairs and benches which occupied the space. "Would a flame not suffice to illuminate your rooms?"

Seruf tutted and walked toward me. The heels of her impractically shaped boots made sharp clicks against the reflective floors. "They would suffice, yes. But our elecktrik lights are far more practical. You'll grow accustomed to them, darling. Your kin were once capable of creating such things on their own. Did you know that? No, it's likely you didn't." She waved her arm, dismissing an answer I hadn't given her. "They lost such knowledge two generations ago. Perhaps three." She pursed her red-painted lips. "How long would you say an average human lives, darling? Thirty or so years? Oh, I suppose it doesn't matter." Again, she rejected a response I did not give. "Humans misplace great swathes of information while they are still living. It takes naught but one generation to lose an entire way of life. They're not the most intelligent of beasts, are they? Come now, darling, we'll discover the other splendors your kin have long since forgotten."

Elektricity.

It was the first of many new words I learned during my time with Seruf.

Although, even after all these years, I still don't grasp what elektricity is. I've been told a flame travels through *wyres*, but I know not where it originates from or how it burns so brightly without melting everything around it.

Perhaps, as Seruf implied, my human brain was too dim-witted to understand.

Seruf continued leading me through the castle. We climbed steps lined with lush, velvety carpeting. I had to pause midway up one such stairwell to touch the fabric, marveling at its softness. We journeyed through wide, sun-speckled hallways adorned with more elektric chandeliers and bold, colorful paintings, then through a large room were columns (I remembered to add the "n" onto this word!) of leatherbound parchment stretched from floor to ceiling.

"The library," Seruf supplied when I paused. "Many of these texts would be ill-suited for you, darling. They're written in old tongues; ones humans have never been acclimated to. But I do believe one of these shelves contains an array of human writings."

My throat burned as I stared at the dizzyingly tall rows of books. There were so many. Hundreds. Nay, *thousands*. The books consumed every sliver of wall space.

Terrick would have adored this room.

But his awe would have been mingled with disappointment, for Terrick would have not wished to see me in the Firestarter's domain. Nor would he have wished me to ignore the humans outside the castle walls.

Guilt tasted like ash on my tongue. I swallowed it and continued following Seruf.

The castle had rooms in abundance, and each was designated for a different activity. One was evidentially not meant to think quietly in a space crafted for reading, nor could one read in a room designed for quiet reflection. Meals were eaten in an enclosed space far from where they were prepared, and the meal preparation rooms were a labyrtinth—labyrinth of confusion. Meats were stored away from vegetables and fruits. And there was meat in abundance: no less than thirty skewers filled the icy room (kept cold with the magikal elektricity). It was enough food to nourish each member of Seruf's human village for weeks, perhaps months.

Lastly, after what seemed like hours of exploration, we arrived at the space designated to be mine.

"It's *marvelous*, is it not?" Seruf entered the room with her arms outstretched, beseeching me to behold its splendor.

This singular room was larger than Terrick's dwelling and bookshop at Swindon. Larger, even, than the entirety of the tannery at Darfield. Larger than any dwelling I'd ever known.

The reflective floor stretched to all four walls. Six windows encircled the room, each shuttered with sheets of colored glass, which obscured any view I might've had of the grounds. This might've set me bristling in annoyance, for I oft enjoyed sitting by a window and watching the world below, if the pale sun streaming through the glass hadn't looked so radiant. The dappled rays of light cast bold, vibrant, colorful swirls over the floor akin to the smudges of color seen in the sky after a hard bout of summer rain. *Rainbows*, Terrick had called them.

"Come, lass! Quick! Look to the sky. It's a rainbow! *Do you see all the colors? It's the heavens' way of telling us the storm has passed."*

The memory of Terrick's deep, warm voice left my heart aching. I turned away from the windows, looking instead to the fireplace on the farthest wall. The expansive structure was wide enough to stable a large bull within its hearth. A dozen plush chairs and five elegantly crafted tables cluttered the area around the fireplace—far more than a singular person would ever need. I only had one set of buttocks, after all. The canopied bed in the center of the room could have accommodated several full-grown men. And the armoire, which sat several paces to the left of the bed, could have provided an ample dwelling for a small family.

"Ah, yes!" Seruf, as though noticing my gaze, moved to the afore mentioned (is this meant to be one word or two? Aforementioned?) item of furniture and flung its doors open. "I've sent some of my old gowns for you." She shifted through the layers of fine fabrics. "And I'll have more made. You'll soon fill this armoire with gowns in whatever colors you wish."

"It's already quite full," I said.

"Quite full? Oh no, no, no, my darling..." Seruf pushed all the gowns to one side. "These take less than half the space. And the colors will not do for you." She clicked her tongue and stroked her red-tipped fingers over a crimson gown. "This will clash *dreadfully* with your eyes. But *yellow*...yellow is quite complimentary, wouldn't you agree?"

I said nothing. Truthfully, I could scarcely keep from screaming.

I turned away from her, shaken, and found myself facing one of the color-painted windows. This one boasted glass panels of azure blue.

Like Quinn's eyes.

Quinn. The blue-eyed boy I'd long dreamed about. The friend I'd abandoned to journey here with Seruf.

My feet moved of their own accord, pulling me closer to the window, and my fingers trembled as I traced them over the glass.

"Lasair?" Seruf spoke my name for the first time since we'd arrived on her lands.

My *new* name. A sophisticated title. It sounded elegant as it rolled off Seruf's tongue.

But it would never truly be my name.

I closed my eyes. "I am tired," I said to Seruf.

She cooed. "Oh, *darling*."

I flinched when she closed the space between us.

"Yes." Her fingers traced my cheeks. "You have become quite flushed, haven't you? Perhaps I should have spared you the tour— you've barely recovered from your fever! Forgive me. I forget how slow mortals are to heal. You may rest now, my darling." She kissed my brow.

I was stricken with an urge to cry. But I held my emotions steady until well after she had left. For I would not allow someone I mistrusted to see my tears.

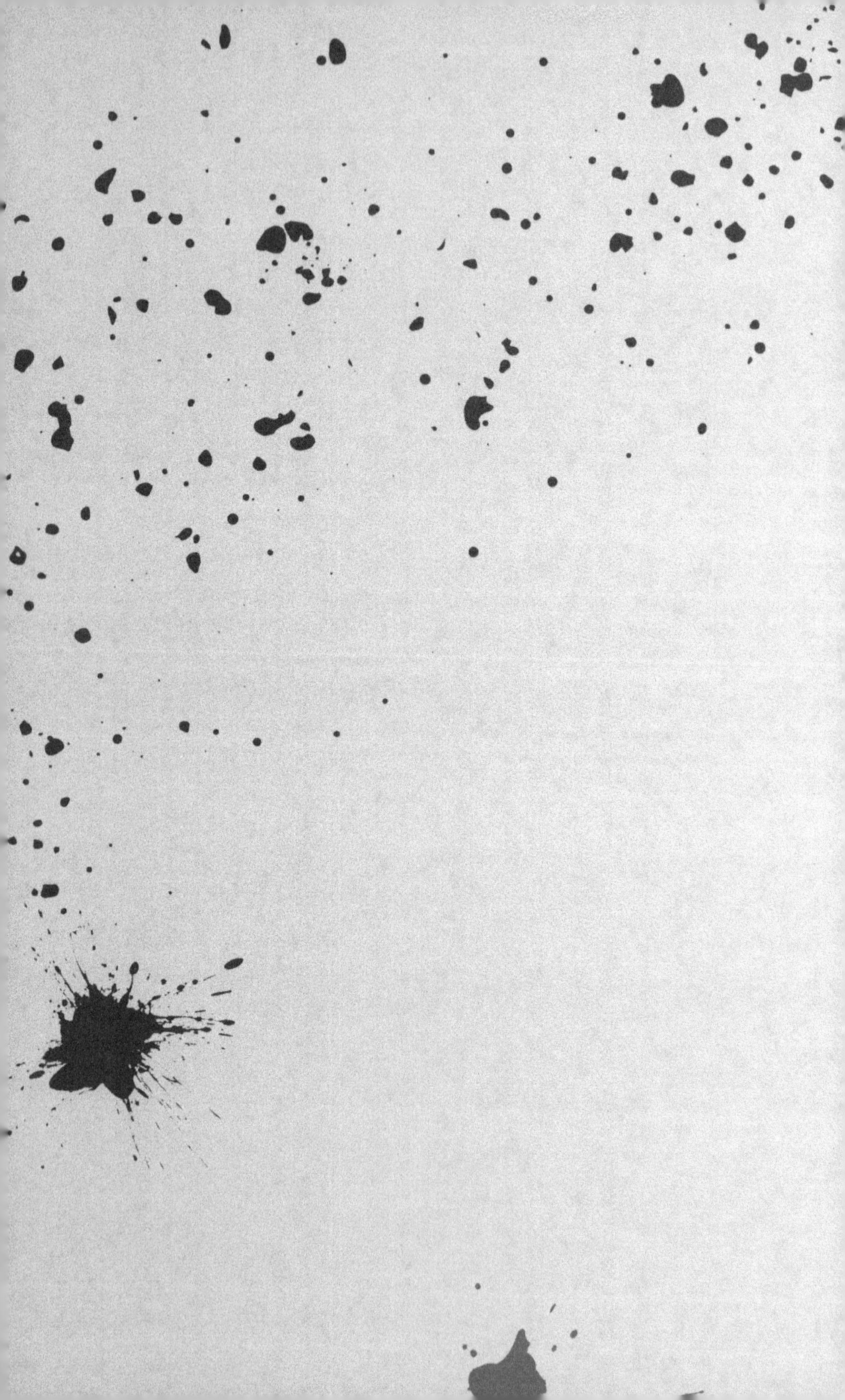

Control

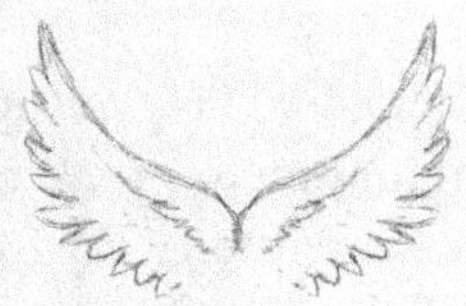

Supper that evening was an extravagant affair.

After my afternoon of rest, a portly boy led me to a dining hall, where a long table stretched lengthwise across the room. An excessive number of chairs curled around the table—far too many to count.

Seruf sprawled in a chair at the far end, facing the wide, arched windows. Her chin rested on her palm, and her wings pooled lazily on the floor about her feet. The red light from the dying sun cast a fiery glow upon her hair.

"Ma'am." The boy's gaze remained trained on his boots, even as he addressed Seruf.

She turned. "Lasair! Come sit with me. I have a *tremendous* feast prepared for you this evening. Oh, darling, this *hair*." She tutted when I ungracefully lowered myself into the chair on her right side, taking care not to tread on her wings. "Oh no, no, no...this will not do. These frayed ends look *dreadful* in this light." She dragged her long nails along my scalp. "We'll need to have this cut. First thing in the morn—goodness, child." She laughed. "There's no need to look so horrified. I'll not shear it all."

I had, indeed, sulked at her words. An expression Terrick would have called *haughty*. Had he been here, he would have told me to "kindly remove that haughty look from your face or risk losing your supper this evening."

Seruf only fretted over the state of my hair, which caused my scowl to deepen. I was not, as she believed, upset at the prospect of losing my hair. I merely found her touch unpleasant, as it oft left my skin prickling with unease.

"Oliver!" Seruf curled her fingers along the side of my neck as she trilled the boy's name. "Be a doll and inform the kitchens we are ready to dine."

Oliver, who had not yet raised his gaze, nodded and left.

I had an urge to plead for him to stay. Perhaps his presence would have drawn some of Seruf's attention away from me.

For in the moments following Oliver's departure, Seruf's hands wandered restlessly over me. She stroked my hair, fretting over the snarls I had missed in my wayward attempt to comb it. Then she coiled an arm around my shoulder, her apple-scented breath tickling my nostrils as she told me to *behold the view.*

"There is nothing to *behold*," I said. Even though these windows were not shuttered in colored glass as the ones in my rooms were, I saw naught but trees and mountains.

Seruf's claw-like nails dug into my shoulders. "Do you not see the sun setting, my darling? Perhaps your eyes are worse than I feared..."

I drew away when she reached for my chin, no doubt preparing to cup my face and peer into my eyes. She had already lamented at the damage done by Jaxon and Darragh and had considered forcing me to wear glass *spekticles.*

"They'll strengthen your vision," she had said. "*Supposedly.* Celestials have never had a need for such things, but humans have suffered from poor vision for much of their existence. I'm certain I can find a human with some knowledge of this practice."

The notion of putting shards of glass into my eyes sounded horrid. So, I maintained the lie that my vision was a minor inconvenience.

"The colors are dull." I turned my gaze to the deep orange sun as it dipped over the mountains.

"Dull?" Seruf repeated incredulously. "They most assuredly are not. Do you have difficulty perceiving colors, darling?"

"The sunsets were far more resplendent over the ocean at

Darfield." Not, of course, that I'd ever witnessed an oceanic sunset, but Terrick had told me of their splendors. *"Ah, lass, I will take you there one eve. You have my solemn promise. There are no sights in this world as magnificent as the sun setting over the ocean."*

"Well," Seruf said as she gave my cheek a severe pinch, pulling me away from the memory, "you have high standards."

Moments later, a dozen children, including Oliver, entered the room. Each carried a silver platter piled with all manner of foods, most of which I'd never seen before.

"Ah, yes." Seruf's voice was little more than a purr as she surveyed the children. "I did not know your tastes. And as you've been trapped amongst those horridly uncouth humans, I thought it likely your palate would be unschooled. So we shall sample a bit of everything!"

The dishes smelled delectable. Sweeter than the creamy cheese Quinn had once won for me. Saltier than the pork Terrick used to smoke for our morning meals. There were other aromas too, spices I had no name for at the time. Cinnamon. Basil. ~~Time thime~~ (curse this dratted word...there's an h and a y in it, yes. Thyme? I'll never understand why it's spelled in such a way). Things I had never tasted. Odors that tickled my nostrils and made my stomach twist with hunger.

But the dread within me was not so easily quelled by the tantalizing food.

For in that moment, as pastries, meats, cheeses, and fruits were placed before me, my mind was filled with images of Mama: starving, sick, and unable to eat the tomatoes she had spent many hours nurturing.

I thought of my kin at Detha—many of whom had likely long ago succumbed to starvation and sickness. Even the children in Seruf's dwelling, finely dressed and well presented as they were, appeared nearly as underfed as those toiling outside.

Shame and anger foamed inside my belly. There was food enough to satiate the entire human village at Seruf's doorstep twice over. Yet those humans would return to their dwellings with empty bellies and hunger-weakened limbs.

Seruf gave my hair an affectionate tug. "What do you wish to try first? The turnover is simply delightful...*Apple* turnover, darling," she amended with a clicking laugh, for I had lifted one of the shimmering plates, believing I had to "turn it over" to reveal the food she spoke so enthusiastically of.

"Here..." Seruf leaned forward and lifted a triangular pastry from its tray. "Oh, and you'll *adore* these delectable little things!" She plucked a handful of berries from a bowl. "Grapes," she informed me as she deposited them onto my plate. "Those are sweet. But these"—the next handful of berries tumbling onto my dish were the color of pale, dying grass—"can be quite tart. And *these*..."

More food was piled upon my dish, and Seruf declared each *more* delicious than the last. I didn't know where to begin. I stared at the mound of delectable delights before me, my stomach hollow with hunger but bursting with regret and revulsion.

"There's no need to wait, darling," Seruf encouraged.

The food—what little of it I could bring myself to eat—did not taste sweet or tart or savory as she'd promised. It all left the same ashen flavor on my tongue.

* * *

That night, I dreamed.

I heard Terrick's baritone laughter as he sat in front of the fire with me, tapping the open book in my lap. "Slowly, lass," he said. "Take your time. Words are not meant to be rushed."

I'd been a child then, full of life and vigor. Learning to read had seemed painfully boring. The letters were too still for my rapidly roaming eyes. The process of connecting those tangles of symbols into a sentence, or even a singular word, required too much inactivity for my restless legs. I was a poor pupil.

Hence why I didn't learn to read properly until later in life.

But I loved listening to Terrick read. He folded the words easily around his tongue, drawing emotion from me with a mere wisp of a sentence. If I were being truthful, hearing him regale me with the tales from his fiction books made me *less* inclined to learn to read. For I feared if I was capable of consuming the stories on my own, Terrick would no longer have cause to recite them to me.

In my dream, which was also a memory, Terrick was teaching me to read my favorite tale: the one of Dorothy and her dog. I grew frustrated and uneasy, as I always did during these sessions, and Terrick pulled me into his chest to calm me. "We'll read it together, lass." He took my hand, pressing my fingers over the words as he spoke them.

The dream changed.

The fire beside us burst from the hearth, consuming the room, Terrick's beloved fiction books, and us, although the flames did little more than nuzzle my skin.

Terrick's steady voice pitched into a wail of agony as he burned. The more I attempted to douse the fire, the quicker he was incinerated.

"Stop!" Flames encircled my arms, like a lover embracing their partner. But it was a grim and suffocating embrace. "Go away! *Please*!"

"Lasair!"

My eyes opened, and a howl tore from my throat as I glimpsed the flames engulfing the canopy above my bed.

"Lasair, calm yourself." Seruf perched beside me, her flesh and clothing unaffected by the fire.

"Don't touch me!" I screamed when she stroked my cheek.

"*Tssk*, there's no use making a fuss." Seruf idly twirled her finger through the flames, seemingly unbothered by the destruction they were causing.

When the canopy above my bed collapsed in a plume of smoke and ash, Seruf merely cast the ruined furnishings aside. "There really is no need for such theatrics," she said. "If you calm yourself, you'll be able to stop this."

"I *can't*." The flames devoured my clothing next, leaving me bare before Seruf's cool gaze.

"You *can*."

"If I could control it," I seethed, "I would have done so before."

Seruf sighed, stood, and thrashed her palm against my left cheek.

The sudden movement and stinging pain brought tears to my eyes. As I raised a hand to probe the tender area, the fire stuttered and stilled. As did my heart.

But once the agonizing echoes of her blow faded, the fire resumed its consumption of my bed and clothing.

"Darling..." Seruf grasped my chin in her right hand. I whimpered when her nails ~~purforated~~—perforated my flesh. "*Hush,*" she said. "This isn't your fault. If my loathsome brother hadn't snatched you from me...Well, this power would have been much more pliable in your youth. Now it's grown into a petulant young adult, quite like yourself. But it *can* be reined in, if you learn not to fear it. Fear"—Seruf's nails caressed the underside of my jaw—"is a wicked human emotion that only serves to make mortals easier to kill. Or control. In inhibits clear thinking, you see. For if you *were* thinking clearly, you'd realize your terror fans the fire."

She spoke in a slow ~~cadance~~—cadence. Like Terrick's voice when he'd tried to teach me to read, assuring me that the seemingly insurmountable task was simple, if only I'd be still and take the time to learn it.

But Terrick had been patient and kind, even when faced with my petulant frustration.

Seruf's melodic voice held no such warmth. Hers was a placid tone with teeth skimming beneath the surface, ready to devour.

Even as she turned away from me and reclined on the ruined remnants of the bed, feigning a careless indifference to the fire raging around her, her wings twitched, betraying her agitation. "Control it, Lasair," she said. "Bring the fire to heel."

"I *can't.*"

The tip of Seruf's wing collided with my face.

When angled correctly, her silken feathers had a ~~barberous~~ barbarous edge. They weren't sharp enough to fully puncture flesh, but they left flaring welts across my face.

When I touched my temple, the blood drizzling from the shallow wound made a ~~gastly~~—ghastly hiss as it dripped onto my flame-wrapped fingers.

"Control it," Seruf repeated.

Irritation prickled my skin, making the flame burn ever hotter.

Again, I felt the sting of Seruf's wing as it flogged my face.

"Anger, *especially* unbridled anger," Seruf chided, "will also incense the fire."

"Perhaps if you would cease striking me, I would not be angered."

Her wing lashed me a third time.

"Had you a shred of discipline, I would have no need to chastise you."

I turned my nails into my forearm, raking my flesh, wishing I could claw the fire out of my blood. "*I hate it*! And I've no desire to control it. I want it to *leave*—"

Seruf's feathers whipped me yet again, this time creating a deep fissure on my lower lip. Blood pooled in my mouth.

"Lasair, you mindless girl..." Seruf shook her head. "*Calm your-self*, and the fire will leave."

But 'twas not an easy thing to accomplish.

The more the fire raged, the more my chest and belly became filled with an odd emotion. Not fear but a similar agitation. A gnawing restlessness. An urge to scream or thrust my head against the wall until darkness consumed me.

I was not afraid of the fire. Not on that night. I was *annoyed* by it.

My fear now cowered from a different enemy: the black and red feathers of Seruf's wings. Every time she moved, I recoiled. She struck my face, my arms, my legs, and each swat was punctuated by a cold, "*Control it.*"

But the fire only grew. When the remnants of my bed dissolved, Seruf rose to her feet and watched me tumble to the ground.

I cried then. A weak and childish reaction, perhaps, but it was the only thing my body could do. I could not restrain the fire as Seruf wanted me to. I could not flee—Seruf undoubtedly would not have allowed me to leave the room. Even if she had, running would not have helped me. The fire, clinging so adamantly to my skin, would follow.

So, I sobbed.

The blood welling from my lacerations bubbled and hissed.

The fire rampaged over the floors and walls, eagerly searching for flesh but finding only stone, cloth, and wood.

Seruf battered me several more times before she moved to the corner of the room, perching herself on the sill of a nearby window.

The fire encircled her, dancing along her legs and arms and coiling around her delicate throat like a band of flickering gold. She remained poised, her posture relaxed, as though she was observing a spectacle she found only mildly interesting. But she could not mask the darkening of aversion in her eyes.

After an hour, perhaps two, the fire finally abandoned my weary body.

I lay on the floor, my muscles sore from trembling, and watched as Seruf strode across the room, idly shifting the rubble from her path. She lowered herself into a crouch before me, reaching for my cheek. Her fingers were cool against my fevered, bleeding skin. I had not the energy to pull away. "Surely you don't want to live the rest of your life like this?" she asked.

I said nothing. My tears were answer enough.

"Wouldn't you be more content if you simply learned to control your silly human emotions? Instead of allowing them to rule you?"

I nodded.

"If you open yourself to my teachings..." Seruf's eyes roamed over me. "You shall learn to bring the emotions to heel."

Unease rippled along my flesh. Although I'd never felt shame in my nakedness before, I'd never felt as bare as I did beneath Seruf's stare.

"In the meantime, we shall need to fit you with a proper wardrobe." Seruf's rich blue gown, unmarred by the fire, whispered around her legs as she stood and walked to the door. "Oliver." She pushed the door open, frightening the portly boy, who'd had his face pressed against the keyhole. "Don't eavesdrop, Oliver," Seruf said. "It's unbecoming."

"Sorry, ma'am." Oliver stepped back, dropping his gaze to his feet.

Seruf combed her fingers through the boy's hair, cooing when he shivered. "I'm sure you realize our guest has a unique problem, yes?" Seruf cupped Oliver's chin, forcing him to look at her.

"Yes, ma'am."

"She'll be needing more durable clothing. As most of the Celestial-made garments are still at Dunbar, I'll need someone to fetch them. Be a dear and tell Ciar to ready a few riders."

Oliver made a soft noise.

"Oh, hush." Seruf pressed her lips to the boy's nose. "Ciar knows my children are not to be harmed. And you, my dear Oliver," she said as she kissed his brow, "upon your return, you may sample those delightful cookies you were looking at earlier. As many as you'd like. A reward for conquering your silly fear of my Wraiths. It's a fair bargain, yes? Run along now..." Seruf leaned against the doorway as Oliver walked away, her wings puddling about her feet. She was smiling when she turned to me, but her eyes were laced with frost and malice. (I've finally mastered this spelling).

A deep, niggling cold sawed at my bones. And I could not cease my sobbing.

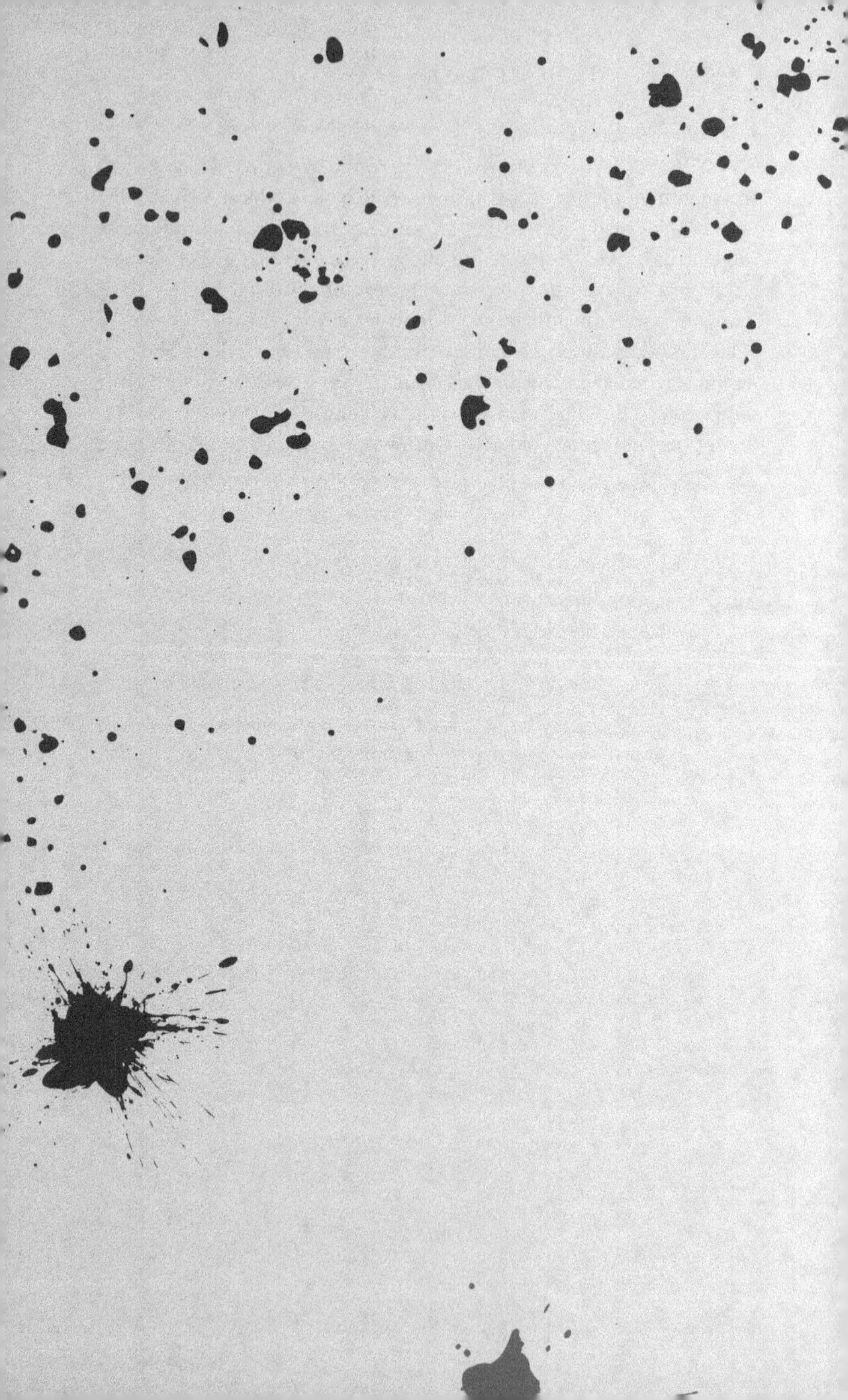

Ramiel

Seruf's home was a gilded cage, but it was a cage nonetheless.

To her, I was naught but an animal—a prized beast with superior lineage—that needed to be beaten into behaving properly.

My first week in Seruf's castle left me bone-weary with exhaustion, aching with numerous slash wounds, and bristling with discontentment. Crying was an "unsavory act," which warranted swift punishment. And as my eyes nearly always brimmed with tears I was not permitted to shed, my face became affixed in an unsightly scowl. I was scolded for this as well.

"Darling, that sour expression is unbecoming. Please remove it from your face." Seruf held a garment against my torso, studying the color against my skin. The gown was entrancing, its rippling texture more akin to liquid than fabric. The rays of colored sunlight cascading through my windows painted the garment a bold yellow, similar to the buttercups that had blanketed the fields around Swindon in the spring. But the gown's color changed when the lighting dulled, more resembling a sky splashed with a sunset's orange ~~hugh~~—hue.

"The color doesn't suit your eyes." Seruf brushed the gown's sleeve against my face, soothing the puckered wounds her wings had inflicted. "Sadly, these are the last of the Celestial fabrics, so we must make do with them. One day, Lasair, we will return to the Celestial

City, and I shall fashion you a gown every bit as brilliant as your eyes."

I'd possessed such a garment once. The tunic Terrick had gifted me was as vibrant as the lilac eyes which peered back at me from the tall mirror Seruf had brought into my room. But I did not tell Seruf this. I preferred Terrick's gift to remain beneath the dirt rather than become sullied by her endlessly roaming fingertips.

"Fret not, darling. This next one will suit you *far* better. The fit will need to be altered, of course. You're quite a bit smaller than its previous owner." Seruf draped the buttercup gown over her shoulder and motioned for two of her children, a girl named Alice and a boy named Eli, to bring the second Celestial garment over. This tunic, even beneath the splashes of tinted sunlight, was nearly as white as Terrick's hair had been.

"Yes, yes...this will wash your complexion out a bit." Seruf caressed my cheek. "But it will allow your eyes to shine. Children," she said, snapping her fingers at Eli and Alice, "dress Lasair and begin making alterations."

"I am perfectly capable of clothing myself." My jaw ached as I ground my teeth around the words.

Eli and Alice ignored me, and my attempt to take the garment from them. They stepped closer and began tugging at the laces of the gown I wore, and their proximity set a rippling itch across my skin. I snarled at them and staggered away, nearly crashing into the mirror.

"Behave, Lasair." Seruf sighed and lashed her wing against my face. "And remove that miserable expression. You are not being tortured—there's no need to act as though you are."

I stilled, moving only to wipe the fresh blood from my cheek, but did not loosen my scowl as Alice and Eli removed my clothing and dressed me in the Celestial tunic.

"Oh dear," Seruf said, "this will need more altering than I thought."

The rippling material looked ~~grizzly~~—*grisly* (I'll never grasp why two such similar sounding words are spelled differently) as it sagged around my body and hung loosely off my limbs.

Alice and Eli exchanged looks of horror and quickly set to work. Alice crouched by my feet, lifting the hem of the tunic to a more appropriate mid-thigh position. Eli stood beside me, folding the sleeves over my hands.

"I suppose I'll fashion you a pair of trousers, as there's no way to lengthen this tunic into a gown." Seruf walked in a slow circle around me, rapping my shoulder whenever I slouched, moved, or had an "unfavorable look," and calling sweetly wrapped commands to the children. "Don't go too short, my dear," she said to Alice. "The shirttails make an endearing skirt, don't you think? And Lasair may yet grow…"

"I have not grown in many years," I said.

Before his death, Terrick had lamented that my days of growing were long behind me. I'd still been a child then, confined above the tannery in Darfield. But I'd been clear-headed that day, enough to remember his comment and the way he'd fretted over my living conditions. I'd given a ~~boyant~~—buoyant response, hoping to lift his spirits: *"I should not wish to grow tall, for I may strike my head on the ceiling as often as you've stricken yours."*

Terrick had laughed—for he had, indeed, battered his head upon our slanted ceiling many times.

Now, as Eli stood behind me, only a wisp shorter than me despite being several years younger, I wished I had grown more.

For his part, Eli wouldn't live long enough to find himself taller than me. Seruf would kill him nary a month later.

"You may yet grow," Seruf said firmly.

My stomach tightened. "I am a child no longer."

Seruf tutted. "Sew the gown for now, Alice dear, do not cut it… Oh, *come now*, children…"

Both Alice and Eli had fled from my side with cries of panic when fiery sleeves encircled my arms.

"How many times must we repeat this pattern, Lasair?" Seruf's wing flogged my cheek.

I'd grown so accustomed to the stinging pain that I hardly flinched.

Seruf, likely realizing her intimidation had lost its ~~effacy~~—efficacy, flicked her wings. "Sometimes I believe you find joy in being tenacious, Lasair. Very well…Come, children." She turned for the door, motioning for Alice and Eli to follow. "We shall take our leave.

You can finish your alterations later, Alice dear. Do not fret; these garments cannot be harmed by her fire. Lasair needs to spend some time alone to consider whether her actions are wise or foolhardy." Seruf paused before she exited the room. "Three days will provide ample time for self-reflection. Wouldn't you agree, Lasair?"

* * *

This, it seemed, was to become Seruf's new tactic: imprisoning me and depriving me of food and drink to force me to relinquish my "stubbornness."

For three days, I ravaged that room, first losing myself to a wild bout of rage as months, perhaps years of pain came bursting forth in a violent rush. By the time it passed, I had screamed myself coarse, and the flames had thoroughly consumed the remaining furnishings.

The two Celestial garments, however, remained unblemished.

I dwelled quietly then in my desolate room of ash, too wearied to move. The nightmares came—memories that left me wrought with grief and fear. Each time I awoke, I found myself swathed in flame.

I was, perhaps, more subdued when Seruf finally released me on the third day, but I was no nearer to controlling the detestable fire.

That day, however, proved to be ~~monumentous~~—momentous.

I'd been walking idly through the castle halls on the second floor as my mind and body warred. My restless muscles ached for movement after such a long confinement, while my mind, shrouded in a haze of fatigue, pleaded for sleep. I did not look at the windows—I so rarely did, for many of them were either shuttered with colored glass or overlooking the human village—until my companion, Alice, screamed.

"Oh no!" She pressed her nose to a clear-glassed window. "Oh no, oh no, *oh no*! We must go. The ma'am will not be pleased if he sees you."

Her sudden babbling behavior left me gaping. "Who—*don't touch me!*" I hissed when she tried to grasp my hand.

She recoiled.

My heart sank as I surveyed my skin, searching for the flame that had surely burnt her. But there was nothing.

Relief made my fingers quiver. "*Never* touch me. Not so long as you value your life."

Alice, wide-eyed and ashen, backed away from me, pausing only when she collided with the wall.

I turned, unable to bear the sight of her frightened face, and found my gaze drawn to the figures outside the window.

A Celestial strode toward the castle, leading a black horse. The Celestial's wings were tucked neatly behind his back—so neatly, I almost didn't notice them until the afternoon daylight cast an ethereal glow upon his feathers. And what magnificent feathers they were. Like freshly fallen snow; a white so dazzling, it hurt to gaze upon them for any length of time.

The Celestial himself was every bit as brilliant as his feathered appendages. He was taller than most men. Broader. His tidily shorn chestnut hair barely brushed the tops of his ears. The look suited him, as long hair would've softened the wonderfully masculine definition of his high cheeks and squared jaw. And his eyes, when he lifted his gaze long enough for me to glimpse them, were bluer than the sky above. Bluer than even Quinn's eyes.

Blue eyes are a silly weakness of mine, I've come to realize.

But I was not *fully* entranced by the Celestial's gaze. Not as I'd been with Quinn's.

The Celestial's eyes were beautiful, but nearly unnatural with their brightness. ~~Wonderous~~—*wondrous*, but also distant, showing little emotion. There was no whimsy or arrogance as there had been in Quinn's eyes upon first glance.

Regardless, while watching this Celestial, who seemed simply too ~~equisite—eqsuite~~ (I detest the spelling of this word) *exquisite* to walk on a land occupied by mere mortals, my stomach did an odd thing. It shifted. Not in the way it would've if I were about to be ill; this was a feeling more akin to riding a horse—or, to be more precise, *falling* from a horse.

"Lasair!" Alice bravely attempted to grasp my hand again.

I startled but never drew my gaze from the Celestial.

The black horse he walked beside was nearly an equal to his magnificence, albeit with a much darker sort of beauty. Although it was not *truly* a horse.

I had not seen a Púca before that day, but I knew of them. 'Twas one of those beasts that had killed Terrick's family, after all. I'd heard tales of their nearly impenetrable scaled flesh, their red eyes, and their curved fangs...all of which the sizeable creature below possessed.

"Lasair! We must go. If the ma'am—" Alice trailed off with a moan.

Seruf's arrival was announced by the sharp rustle of beating wings.

"Ma'am, I—" Alice began.

"*We shall discuss this later.* In the meantime, darling..." Anger skewered Seruf's melodic tone, and her eyes, when she cast them upon me, burned with wrath. "You must return to your room. And *stay there.*"

"Am I to be punished for walking the halls?" I asked.

"*No.* Darling, this is not a punishment. I will return to fetch you before the afternoon is through. And we'll feast tonight—whatever you wish to eat, you shall have in abundance.

Perhaps it was the desperation in her voice that made my skin prickle.

Perhaps it was the looming presence of the Celestial and his Púca that unsettled me.

Regardless, I balked. "You're hiding me away. From him."

A muscle spasmed in Seruf's jaw. "I'm sparing you the monotony of his presence."

"You lie," I whispered. "If that were true, would you not simply caution me against spending time in his company?"

"Your tempestuous scrutiny is a thing to be admired, Lasair. But I'm afraid this is not the time for—" She paused, her red-painted lips thinning.

I returned my gaze to the window, glimpsing the Púca standing before the castle, his reins tied to the hobbling shackles on his forelegs.

The Celestial was gone.

And then I was whisked away.

Seruf flew me to the stairway, a dreary place, as its walls housed paintings rather than windows. No candles lined this murky corridor, but faint wisps of illumination from one of Seruf's wretched elektrik lights meandered to the stair from the floor above.

My stomach shifted, this time very much in the way it did before it prepared to ~~regurgatate~~—*regurgitate* food. And staring at the painting opposite me, which depicted a large and grotesque man consuming the head of a child, did not help to quell the nausea.

I pressed a hand to my mouth and closed my eyes.

From beneath me came the lyrical tone of Seruf's voice.

"Ramiel! Poor sweet thing, did you ride that horrible Púca all the way here?"

I nearly lost control of my ~~rebelous~~—*rebellious* stomach at the sound of his name.

Ramiel. The Conqueror.

Every human knew that name. Most would not dare to speak it. Even Terrick had taken care not to say it needlessly.

And Mama...

She'd spoken of Ramiel only once, in the quiet darkness of our dwelling, her voice little more than a whisper as she recited the tale, one she had learned from her mama, who claimed her own father had originally regaled it. 'Twas a story that outlasted the humans who'd borne witness to the events.

It was the history of an old world, once thriving and teeming with human life. Not a perfect world, for it, too, had seen its share of violence, death, and disease. But life persevered, and humans lived free of Wraiths and Celestials.

Until the Conqueror made this world his home, ~~callislly~~—callously eliminating much of the populace and enslaving those who survived.

Ramiel.

The dreaded Conqueror stood barely a floor beneath me, speaking calmly with Seruf.

"My Púcas are not so terrible," he said, "and it would be in your best interest to learn to ride them. Our wings will continue to weaken while we're trapped here, Seruf."

His voice was unlike any I'd heard before. Quiet, yet powerful. Kind, yet commanding. So deeply masculine, self-assured, yet so very silkily soft. It coated my skin with those pesky bumps that appeared whenever it was cold. Goosebumps, Terrick had called them.

Although I never understood why. Geese did not have bumps on their flesh. (I'd looked once, when I'd been a child. The goose had not appreciated me prodding her feathers.)

"That may be," Seruf responded, "but I should hope we'll not be trapped here much longer."

Ramiel did not answer her. At least, he did not verbalize a reply.

"I'm beginning to think you like it here, Ramiel," Seruf tutted.

"I could say the same for you, Seruf," Ramiel said. "You allow humans to stay in your house."

"*Children.*"

"*Human* children."

Seruf laughed. "I would not judge them against their adult counterparts. Children are unspoiled and untainted by the baseless desires that consume adult humans. It's a pity the Creator deemed they should grow out of their innocence."

"Humans often return to that innocence," Ramiel said, "if they live long enough."

"They return to innocence only when their bodies are broken. Killing them is kinder."

"Perhaps. But the way you do it is cruel."

"They feel no pain when I slaughter them."

"No, they feel it *long* before. Surely you can see the anguish in that girl's eyes?"

I startled, believing he was speaking of me. But my stomach became yet more ~~rebelous~~—rebellious when I realized who he was referring to.

Alice.

She had stood beside me while I'd dawdled by the window. And Seruf had not brought her to the stairwell with me.

Seruf cooed. "Anguish? What anguish? This girl has been spared a life of groveling in the muck with the rest of her species. Haven't you, my sweet?"

I imagined Seruf petting Alice, as was typical for her, and Alice would tremble as all the children did when Seruf touched them.

"I'm sure you did not come all this way to discuss my treatment of children," Seruf prodded after a long moment of silence.

"Indeed, I have not," Ramiel said. "I'm told you've taken more of my fabric…"

"Only a few garments. Gabriel has no need for them anymore."

"And you created a hybrid during our time in Sakar."

Seruf said nothing.

"You led me to believe you were trying to reunite with Ellard." Ramiel's soft voice was barely audible. I sank to my haunches, placing my ear closer to the floor, and strained to hear his next words. "That is the *only* reason I did not punish you for crossing into Sakar."

"I *was* attempting to reunite with him," Seruf said. "Until he tried to kill me…"

"A crime for which he was thoroughly punished," Ramiel interjected. "And you shed not a single tear."

"Why did he deserve my tears? After he betrayed and attempted to *slaughter* me…"

"He shed tears for you when you journeyed here with me. And I'm sure his decision to confront you weighed heavily upon his shoulders. You were *bonded*." Disgust flavored Ramiel's voice. "You surely felt his distress, his *torment*, when I took his Essence. Any other Celestial would have been brought to their knees by their bonded's pain. And you showed no remorse. No sorrow. Nor did you try to stop me."

"Most Celestials do not attempt to *kill* their bonded as Ellard did with me," Seruf spat.

"Most Celestials," Ramiel said, "do not tear apart their Essence to share their powers with *humans*. Perhaps that weakened your bond. I've told you many times now, Seruf, I disagree with the practice of creating hybrids."

"I am aware."

"And yet you've defied me. *Twice*. Tell me, Seruf, what drove you to Sakar for a child when you have an abundance of children here in Uchen?"

"I *took* the child from Uchen." Seruf's voice was grating. "And I only defied you once. The child is the one I pulled from Detha."

Silence swaddled the hall for several agonizingly long heartbeats.

"You told me that child had perished," Ramiel finally said in a light, amicable tone.

"I believed she had. But she *lives*, Ramiel. And—"

"Enough."

"—her power—"

"*Enough*! I've no wish to hear how you mutilated that child. Seruf, you—"

An awful, guttural shriek arose from outside, unlike any I'd heard a human or beast make.

"My Púca grows restless." Ramiel loosed a deep sigh. "I will take my leave. As your hybrid was created long ago, I'll not take her from you. But I *insist* upon seeing her. Where is she?"

"I'm not certain that's wise. She's quite skittish."

"Then make her calm."

"I am trying. But you know how dreadfully sluggish humans are at acclimating to new surroundings. She needs more time."

Ramiel was silent for so long, I began to fear he was scouring the halls in search of me.

I pressed myself against the wall, hoping, perhaps vainly, that I could hide in the shadows.

But then Ramiel responded. "Very well. You may have until my next visit. But, Seruf," his next words were nearly lost amidst the wailing of his Púca, "do *not* discard this child when you grow discontented. She's not a mere human you plucked from your village. *You* created her and bound her to you. Treat her well."

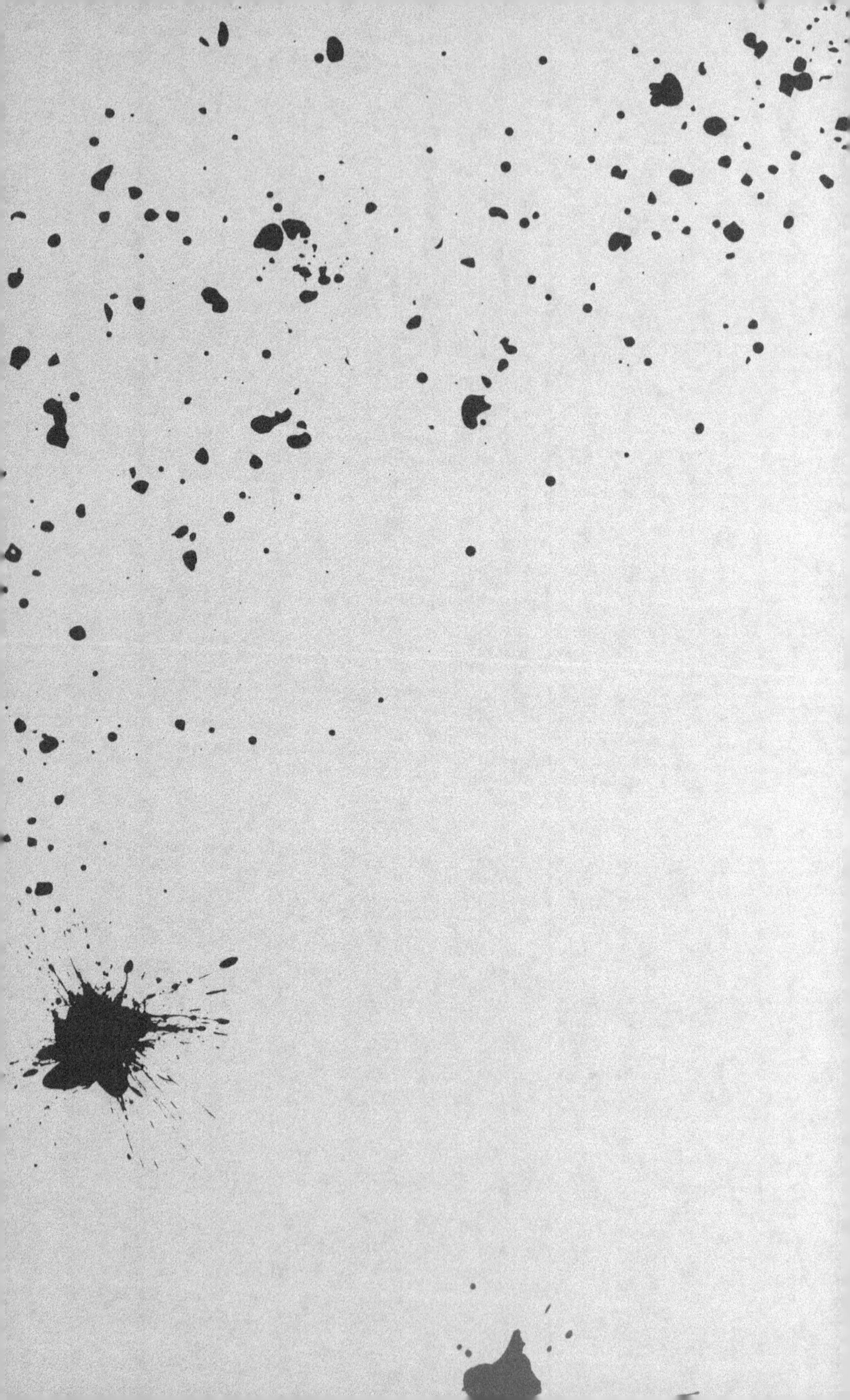

Raven

In the days following Ramiel's departure, I haunted the halls of Seruf's castle, traversing restlessly from room to room. Alice, who'd been commanded to stay at my side, was likely tempted to throttle me, but I simply could not be still, not while discontentment gnawed ceaselessly at my insides.

Walking eased the pain but did not satiate my unhappiness. I'd began to loathe this castle and its endless labyrinth of rooms. The spaces were becoming impossible to differentiate as they were all needlessly large, wastefully extravagant, and meticulously polished.

Until I rediscovered the library.

Standing in that cavernous room, surrounded by the tall columns of leatherbound parchment, gave me a few moments of tranquility. Because the sight, the pungent musk of leather, and the feel of crisp parchment beneath my fingers all reminded me of Terrick. They reminded me of *home*.

And it was that day, as I perused the library, that I first glimpsed the Púca stallion.

'Twas the cry that alerted me to his presence—Púcas made odd vocalizations, nothing like the whinnies and whickers of their equine counterparts. These cries were more akin to the yowls of an unhappy feline.

Alice trembled upon hearing the noise. I brightened and flew to the window.

The imposing black stallion, tinted green by the colored glass, gave me quite a spectacle to feast my eyes upon. As the Wraiths clung to the chains corded around the stallion's head, struggling to restrain him, the Púca danced his way across the rolling grass fields encircling this side of the castle.

"Seruf houses a Púca?" I asked Alice.

"The ma'am has four."

"Four? Why have I not seen them before?"

"They're confined to the stables much of the time, but they're exercised thrice daily, often through the village." She blanched when the Púca loosed another howl. "They frighten me."

Perhaps they should have frightened me as well. But I'd always felt a kinship with animals, and my time in Seruf's home had left me pining for an animal companion such as I'd once had in Swindon.

I whirled from the window and strode across the room.

"Lasair!" Alice dashed after me. "Where are you going?"

"To see them."

She halted. "Th-the Púcas?"

"Well, I've no desire to see the Wraiths."

"I...*They frighten me*, Lasair!"

"You do not have to see them." I stepped into the corridor, leaving her in the library.

"Please, Lasair! The ma'am will not be happy!" she warned.

I did not heed it.

It took several moments of wandering the endless corridors before I found the door which led me outside. And several longer moments of aimlessly wandering the grounds, lamenting that the ~~lumanescent~~ luminescent sun did so little to dispel the oncoming winter chill, before I found the stables nestled in the shade of the mountains that guarded Seruf's home.

The Púcas were housed in a far finer building than their equine counterparts. The structure was made of glittering stone. Its floors were kept in such pristine condition, I had to dig into a crevice to find evidence of dirt. A raftered ceiling stretched overhead, and broad-silled windows blanketed the walls, allowing dappled rays of sunlight to seep through. Stalls lined the aisle on both sides. Not the narrow standing stalls I was accustomed to seeing, but large, airy boxes. Most of them sat empty.

Seruf's four Púcas—the stallion, who'd been returned to his box, and three mares—occupied the stalls at the farthest end of the building. Each wore a twisted chain halter. More chains twined around their noses and looped through tie rings on the wall. The line was so ~~taught~~—taut, the Púcas could scarcely turn their heads to look out their windows. One of the mares also wore chained hobbles on her forelegs.

These were large, strapping beasts with long, elegant legs and powerful rumps. They were built to cover great distances at speed and designed to travel endlessly over all manner of terrain.

Yet there they stood, unable to move about their stalls. Prisoners in a gilded cage.

Much like myself.

Upon my entrance to the stable, the hobbled mare grew enraged. I hoped she would accept my presence and settle, but as I ambled the aisle, the mare's ire festered. She emitted an outraged shriek and writhed against her bindings, pulling the chains so tightly about her face, she bled. Then she tore a slab of wood from the wall, as though intending to impale me.

It took five Wraiths to calm her. Two of them were bitten. Although the Púca's venom did not kill them, the rigid and immobile Wraiths had to be carried from the stables.

I don't know if they recovered, nor do I care.

I had (and still have) little sympathy for any Wraith. But my heart was heavy with sorrow for the Púca mare. She fought so valiantly to be free of her bindings, her red eyes ever fixed on the open stable door. But she was ensnared with more chains and beaten until she quieted.

It was not her fault she'd been made the way she was.

If I'd been braver, perhaps I would have helped her rid herself of the chains.

But I only watched, wary of her flailing teeth, as she was securely restrained once more. And then I was dragged back to the castle, also securely restrained, with one Wraith holding my arm and another clutching my left ear.

"Unhand me!" I yelled.

"The stables are no place for you." The female Wraith twisted my ear, making me yelp in pain.

I silently beseeched my flame to come forth.

It did not.

"That mare is in foal. From *Ramiel's* stallion," the male Wraith seethed. "You almost lost her the babe."

"If anyone were to make her lose the babe, it would be you," I growled. "Beating her in such a—" I cried as the female Wraith pulled my ear so harshly, I feared she would wrench it from my head.

"She would've tore that babe from her belly if she'd gotten free," the female Wraith said. "And she was calm until you walked before her, smelling of blood and...*human*."

A chill shook me to my very core. *"She would've tore that babe from her belly."*

I'd seen such an act before. In Detha.

'Twas not an uncommon occurrence for a woman to resort to self-mutilation to rid herself of a babe. It was, after all, better not to have been born at all than to be born in a place such as Detha. But the act was a violent, bloody one that oft damned the mother as swiftly as it stole the babe.

The Wraiths, however, *rejoiced* at such events.

I'd been so young when I dwelled at Detha, and Mama had sheltered me from much of the town's darkness. But there were sights she could not protect me from, and some moments one never forgets, such as seeing a Wraith gleefully devour the bloody remnants of a woman and her half-formed child.

* * *

"Púcas?" Seruf trilled when the Wraiths told her where I'd been. "Darling—now there, Eimear, you may release her ear." Seruf snapped her fingers beneath the female Wraith's nose. "She's been returned safely...Oh, darling..." Seruf touched my reddened earlobe, murmuring when I flinched. "I'll expect you to take better care next time, Eimear. This very nearly turned into a frightful injury. Lasair is quite small, and she is *my* ~~protojay~~ protégé. You may mark other humans, but she is to remain unblemished."

"Understood, ma'am," Eimear said.

"Yes, only the *ma'am* has the privilege of marking my skin." My bitter remark earned me a sharp wing lash to the back of the neck—far more painful than what Eimear had done to my ear.

"Now, darling." Seruf smoothed her fingers over the welt she'd left upon my neck. "Why did you seek out the Púcas? They're *dreadful* creatures. I only keep them because Ramiel insists I'll one day need them."

"I don't think they're dreadful," I said. "They're beautiful."

Seruf laughed harshly. "Are you sure you do not require spekticles, darling? I would not call the Púcas beautiful. Regular horses, as dimwitted as they may be, are far more pleasing to the eye. Shall I find you a horse? A palomino mare with a golden coat and snowy mane...Yes, that would suit you nicely."

Perhaps Seruf had been correct in her earlier assessment of me, that I found some measure of joy in being obstinate. For as much as I adored horses, I would not have accepted any she offered. Instead, I said, "I'd like to work with the Púcas."

Seruf's eye twitched, as was typical when her irritation threatened to shatter her pleasant ~~fasade~~ (this is spelled with a c, is it not? Facade?). "They're not pets, darling. The Púcas are difficult to control."

"Then I'd like to learn how to control them."

"Why?"

Because I felt kinship with them. I understood what it was like to be a dangerous creature in a world that feared and abused what it didn't understand.

But I could not say such things. Seruf would dismiss the thoughts as folly—and likely punish me for having such notions. So, I told a half-truth. "Humans have always despised and distrusted Púcas. And as humans are rarely correct in their judgement, I don't believe the Púcas to be as despicable as I was told."

Seruf did, after all, relish the degradation of humans.

"Yes." She smiled. "Humans are quite doltish, are they not? But

I'm afraid they were correct in this case. The Púcas are beasts to be despised and distrusted. But"—she tapped her fingers to her lips—"since they remain on my property, and you are susceptible to their venom, it may be beneficial for you to learn how to restrain them. Irial." She turned to the male Wraith. "Which of my Púcas is the most docile?"

"None of them, ma'am."

Seruf narrowed her eyes and raised her chin—the expression Terrick would've called *haughty*. "I'll rephrase, then: Which of my Púcas is easiest for you to control?"

"Normally, it would be Wynn, ma'am," Irial amended. "But she's become unmanageable since she was bred. So I'd recommend the stallion. He's larger than the mares, yes, but has a fear of the whip. So long as there's one nearby, he'll mind himself."

"Very well." The annoyance melted from Seruf's face, like ice dissolving from a flower. A beautiful but wickedly thorned flower. "Teach Lasair to work with the stallion. I would like her to know how to quickly muzzle and confine him. And how to kill a Púca, should all other options fail. Although, the deadly blow should be in demonstration *only*. Please refrain from killing Ramiel's stallion. I've no wish to further fuel his ire."

* * *

I called the stallion Raven, for his scaled skin was as black as a raven's wings.

A wonderfully creative title, yes? Especially as all Púcas were swaddled in black scales.

The stallion already had a name, I was sure, although he was never called by it. The Wraiths referred to him as "the stallion," and Seruf called all the Púcas "beasts," or sometimes "curs." I thought, perhaps, he'd like to have a name.

Although every time I uttered "Raven," he affixed me with a ~~feendish~~—fiendish stare. Perhaps he found his new name as repulsive as I found mine, but I had not the heart to call him a cruel a word as "beast."

Raven was impossibly large. Even when I stood on my toes, I

could not reach the top of his withers. And he was not a tame creature. Merely leading him from his stall was a treacherous task. I wore metal bands on my arms and legs, the areas most easily ensnared by a Púca's fangs, and he remained in his chain halter, with a second set of chains wrapped around his muzzle. And I was ever armed with a long, metal-tipped whip.

I walked on his right side, the Wraith Irial on his left. We would stroll a singular lap around the grounds—an exercise all the Púcas received thrice daily to keep their muscles from ~~atrofeeing~~ atrofying (I've heard this word used, and I've always liked the sound of it, but I've never seen it written).

Raven fumed and fussed endlessly throughout the walk. His hooves were rarely on the ground as he leapt for the heavens, fighting to be free of his restraints.

Irial thrashed him twice on the flank, drawing blood. Raven returned his hooves to the earth with a pitiful warble and shied away from the whip, leaning his shoulder into me.

"Strike him," Irial called.

Raven turned, his red eye looming on the whip, which sat idly in my hand.

"If you don't strike him, he'll bite you," Irial said. "And it's no less than you deserve, you rotten wench."

I lifted the whip, although I did not intend to use it.

Raven stilled. Beneath the chains, his lips curled and quivered.

"Strike him!" Irial raised his own whip.

"There's no need—"

Zoosh-snap.

Once again, Irial's weapon flogged Raven's haunches. The stallion bellowed and lifted his hindquarters in a mighty buck. Blood welled from the fresh whiplash and ran in crimson rivulets down his leg.

My fist tightened around the chain. "He did *nothing* to deserve such a reprimand."

Irial spat at the stallion's feet. "Never wait for a Púca to *do* something. It's right well too late by then."

* * *

Raven was never docile. Even though I treated him with kindness, his dislike for me did not wane.

I took him on at least one outing per day. Two, if I could evade Seruf long enough. After several weeks, Irial stopped accompanying me, declaring that I was skilled enough to navigate the walks on my own.

Truthfully, I believe he'd grown tired of listening to me prattle in Raven's ear. Raven, for his part, tolerated my presence, but his red eyes were ever wary, his muscles remained ~~taught~~—taut, and his ears were always focused on distant things only he could hear. Even when I spoke to him, he did not turn his ears toward me.

Winter thawed. Spring bloomed. Summer's heat baked the earth. Nearly a year had passed since I'd first set foot in Seruf's land, and Raven still had not softened toward me.

Perhaps I should have feared him, this stallion who would have doubtless preferred to kill me rather than spend any length of time in my company. I, however, had become fiercely attached to him. He had proved to be a better companion than any other I'd found in Seruf's home.

Seruf did naught but reprimand me for my petulance and lament that I would never learn to control the flame. "I fear you do not want to control it," she'd begun to say each time it emerged. "You seem to take far too much joy from fighting it."

No matter how I argued that I detested the flame and I longed to control it but simply could not bring it to heel, Seruf continued to insist I was resisting her teaching. So I ceased arguing, although she never ceased scolding me.

I was always accompanied by one of the children Seruf kept in her home, but they held no liking for me. Most were fearful of my power and unwilling to stand too close to me, lest they feel the sting of its embrace. And I had no desire to converse with the Wraiths. So I turned to Raven for companionship.

I was certain he despised me, but his hatred bore me no pain, for he despised all two-legged creatures equally.

I was walking Raven beneath a cloudless sky on a warm morning that smelled of moisture. Although the skies did not look it, there was ~~turblence~~—turbulence in the air. I at first thought Raven was agitated by the weather, for he had morphed into a sky-bound crea-ture, unable to keep his hooves on the ground.

"It's to be a bad storm, then, yes? I suppose it's to be expected; summer rarely relinquishes its hold without a fuss," I murmured to him, keeping his head turned so he could not find a straight line in which to strike a gallop. The angle also kept his a cursed eye on the whip—the only defense I had against his teeth.

~~Salivia~~—saliva dripped from Raven's chain-bound mouth. His tail snapped against his haunches, striking so hard, I worried he'd draw blood.

"I wish you'd not do that," I said. "Does it not hurt?"

He raised his head, emitting his strange vocalization.

I tugged on the chain, digging the metal into his flesh until pain forced him to lower his head. "We're nearly there, Raven. Steady..." Raven's muscles coiled as his right forehoof stabbed the soil. "It would not be in your best interest to give in to silliness now," I said. "If you escape or harm me, I'll not be able to walk you again. And surely you—"

With a roaring cry, Raven rose onto his hind legs, buffeting his head about, desperate to rid himself of the chains. Several links of metal slid through my fingers, but I held fast to the line, even as the chain mangled my palms.

Raven landed and turned, poised to gallop.

"No!" I wrenched the line with all my might and turned his nose back toward me. "You will *not*."

His ears flattened, and his lips curled as much as they were able to beneath the chains.

"Be careful, child."

The voice startled me. Only for a heartbeat, but 'twas enough for Raven to claim an advantage.

He tore the chain from my hands and spun on his haunches.

"No...Raven!" Panic seized my heart as I reached for him. His tail flashed before my face, slicing at my cheeks, and then he was gone.

But he did not go far.

A Celestial stood a mere stone's throw away. Although he already held one Púca, he stretched out his hand and effortlessly grasped Raven's flailing chain, bringing the stallion to a halt.

As Raven roared, a long string of ~~salivia~~—saliva now dangling from his lips, my mouth seemed as dry as the grass after a drought.

Ramiel the Conqueror stood before me, flanked by two Púcas. Raven fought fruitlessly against the chain clasped in Ramiel's right hand, while the pregnant mare, Wynn, worriedly rubbed her lips against the line clutched in his left. "Hello, child." A smile sprawled across his face. "You must be Lasair."

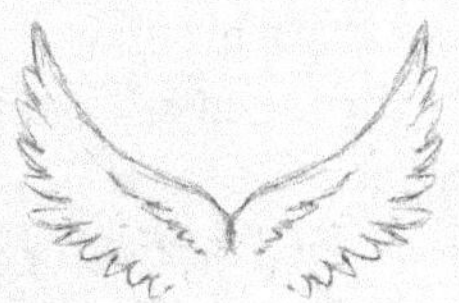

"Does Seruf know you're out here?"

Ramiel's words made my skin prickle. I didn't understand why. They were not demeaning, nor was he speaking out of anger. His smile was quite gentle, and his eyes were warm. He was far more ~~jenial~~ (goodness, this is a word, yes? Geniel...) *genial* than Seruf.

But he spoke to me in an airy tone, akin to a parent berating a ~~belligerant~~—belligerent child. And it made me...

Not angry per say, but irritated.

My belly quivered as I strode toward him. "May I have the stallion back?"

Ramiel's right eyebrow rose, but his warm smile never faded. "It would not be wise. The stallion is agitated and will likely flee again. If I had not caught him—"

"I only lost him because you startled me," I said.

"I apologize for startling you," Ramiel laughed, "but you were losing control over the stallion long before I spoke."

"I was quieting him and only failed to rein him in because *you* frightened me." I turned to the pregnant Wynn, who stood with her head lowered, her engorged belly heaving with her ponderous breaths. "I'll wager bringing that mare out caused his disquiet."

As I spoke, Raven cast an eager eye at Wynn. She loosed a squeal and laid her ears flat upon her head. Raven, no doubt perturbed by her obvious dislike, screamed and rose onto his hindlegs.

"Yes." Ramiel coaxed Raven to bring all four feet to the ground. "I suppose I should have waited until the stud had returned to his stall. Although I did not realize it was *you* who had taken him out."

"I take him out every day." I reached for Raven again, but Ramiel did not hand him to me. After a moment, I closed my fist and drew my arms against my chest, feeling ill at ease. Especially as Ramiel had not withdrawn his gaze from me.

An odd sensation blossomed across my skin. 'Twas not the itch that accompanied the emergence of my fire, nor the unrest that unfurled beneath Seruf's touch. Rather, it was akin to the ~~disconserting~~—*disconcerting* state Quinn had left me in when he'd kissed my hand: a feeling that was neither pleasant nor unpleasant. It merely made one more keenly aware of one's body. For instance, I'd never been so concerned with my posture, so worried whether my hair was still properly plaited, or so distracted wondering if my face was making the expression Seruf occasionally called "sourpuss."

But standing before Ramiel, I fussed, wondering what he saw when he looked at me. A beast, like the Púcas he held, or an unkempt and unruly child?

"You take the stallion out?" Ramiel asked after a tediously long stretch of silence.

"Is that not what I said?"

"Seruf allows this?"

"Clearly, as she's not chiding me for it."

"Child, you are aware these aren't horses, yes?"

"No one would mistake them for horses. And I'm not a child. Not anymore."

Amusement warmed Ramiel's voice. "Indeed, you are not. But you must be careful around the Púcas, little one. A hybrid you may be, but you're not immune to their venom."

At this, Wynn gurgled, and a deep sound of indignation rumbled out of Raven. Ramiel pulled on the chains, stopping only when both beasts recoiled in pain.

"Perhaps they are only violent creatures because they are treated with violence," I said.

"They're violent because their hunger is insatiable," Ramiel said. "They could gorge themselves until they rupture their bellies and would still not be satisfied. It's an unfortunate flaw in their design. These chains keep them from overindulging. The pain distracts them. Imagine being always hungry, little one. It's quite a miserable way to exist."

"That is a ~~calis~~—callous remark." My chest tightened in a hollow spasm. "Many humans are well ~~acquainted~~—acquainted with hunger, especially those living under Celestial reign. 'Tis a misery I've endured as well."

Ramiel inclined his head. "A point well made. And I understand your frustration On the surface, it does seem cruel, using one pain to quiet another. But it *must* be done to keep them contained. So they don't hurt—"

"In my experience, trying to beat an undesirable trait out of a creature only strengthens that trait. And weakens the creature." A hot itch splashed my skin. I turned, placing Ramiel in the blurred fringes of my vision as I breathed deeply, attempting to compose myself, even as unpleasant memories incinerated my mind.

Jaxon and Darragh's beatings, Terrick's tonic, Seruf's lashings... these were all beratements intended to suppress my fire. They had only incensed it and rendered me powerless.

Ramiel stepped sideways, extracting himself from the murkiness of my impaired eyes, and studied me for a moment. His brows drew together, creating a small, dimpled wrinkle between his arched eyebrows. "Seruf found you in Sakar, correct?"

"She found me in Detha first, when I was a babe. But I spent the rest of my life in Sakar."

"And you suffered there," Ramiel murmured. "At the hands of humans."

"No more than I would have suffered at the hands of Wraiths had I remained in Detha."

Raven mewled, growing impatient with standing, and received another harsh admonishment from Ramiel.

"May I please have the stallion back?" I asked. When Ramiel did not move to hand Raven back to me, I sighed. "I am perfectly capable of returning him to his stall. You may carry on with whatever you wish to do with Wynn, although I'd not distress her. She's quite close to foaling."

"I'm well aware. She'll likely drop the babe within the next night or two. All the more reason for her to move about." Ramiel watched me with an inscrutable expression on his face. "Would you care to walk with me? After you've returned the stallion to his stall. We'll not test his resolve any further today."

"I would *not* care to walk with you." Simply standing before Ramiel had unsettled my emotions.

A crease formed in Ramiel's brow. "Humor me," he said. "It will not be a long walk."

It was a command, one so carefully wrapped in soft silks, it was almost easy to disregard.

But those silks concealed thorns.

Unease curdled in my belly as I took Raven from Ramiel's proffered hand and returned the stallion to his stall, apologizing endlessly for the brutality he'd suffered. Raven did not acknowledge my voice, nor did he seem to care for my pity, but I fretted all the same as I rebound him in his chains.

Ramiel still stood on the grassy field when I emerged from the stable. He smiled amicably and raised his hand, beckoning for me to join him.

I did not want to. The brief encounter with him had left me bemused—

No. That is not the word I'm searching for. Befused? Goodness, I don't think that is a word...Befuddled! Yes. The encounter had left me *befuddled*.

I didn't know whether I was angered by his intrusion or excited at the prospect of having someone else to converse with.

I did not know if I found his presence enjoyable or unsettling.

Regardless, I strode toward him, suddenly very aware of how heavily I'd perspired during my walk with Raven.

Ramiel waited until I was beside him before he led Wynn forward. We made an odd sight: an ethereal Celestial walking between a human girl and a pregnant Púca. And I, ever incapable of tactful conversation, asked, "Why are you so invested in that mare's foal?"

Ramiel's wings rustled when he lifted his shoulder. "I want to see what happens when she gives birth."

"I'd imagine it will be the same as any creature giving birth," I said.

"The *act* may look the same, yes. I suppose I should have clarified: I'm interested in what will happen to the *foal*."

I stared at Wynn. Her head was held high, her jaw clenched, and ~~sailiva~~—saliva trickled from between her chain bound lips. "Only the foal? Have you no concern for what will happen to her?"

Ramiel chuckled. "I am sure Wynn will suffer no ill consequences from this pregnancy. She's the strongest mare in my herd. But this will be the first naturally bred Púca born into this world."

"And how does one breed a Púca *un*naturally?"

"My Púcas were not bred nor born." Ramiel paused to scold Wynn when she cast a ravenous eye at me. "I crafted them."

"You *crafted* them?"

"Yes. And I think I succeeded in making them as beautiful and functional as their equine counterparts, wouldn't you say?"

I studied Wynn once more, noting the elegant curve of her face, the radiance of her blood-red eyes, and the way her black-scaled hide rippled in the sunlight. "Yes, they are quite beautiful. But horses offer a wider variety of colors."

"Had I more time, perhaps I would have crafted more colors," Ramiel said.

"And horses do not often attempt to consume their human companions."

"Yes..." Ramiel spoke the word slowly, lingering on the S. "That is where I made my mistake. Horses are too docile, I find, and far too skittish. It is not their fault, as they were created to be prey. I wanted to make the predator, a beast as violent and bloodthirsty as a human male in the heat of battle. I was, perhaps, too enthusiastic with that trait. By the time I realized my error, I had not the power to undo it."

There was a trace of sadness in his voice, as though he truly regretted his oversight.

Beside him, Wynn whined and fixated her eyes upon my face. "Would it not have been kinder to eradicate them when you realized your mistake?" I asked.

"Perhaps. But the Púcas are far too useful to simply obliterate."

"And you want to see if breeding them lessens the undesirable trait?"

"That is precisely my reasoning." Ramiel's broad smile was nearly ~~lumanescent~~—luminescent. "I wish to see whether the foal will be as violent as its parents or more docile. Whether it will be driven to madness by the hunger or be better able to control it. In short, I'm looking to see if the Púcas have a future on this earth."

Wynn tossed her head, her teeth gnawing at the inside of her mouth. Red spittle seeped from her lips.

"It seems cruel," I said.

"I'll not deny that. But it is not so very different from when humans were first created. They were pitiless creatures, worse than any other that walked the earth, prone to fits of jealousy and rage while never understanding what they were envious or wrathful about. And they were oft too obstinate to change, even when they were shown the error of their ways. Many of those early faults have been bred out of them. Many humans now have a modicum of self-control and intelligence. They would not exist as they are today had they not endured the struggles the Púcas now bear."

"A large populace of humans are now enslaved and abused by your kin," I noted. "You take pride in how you *bred* them, and yet you allow them to be mistreated?"

Ramiel's answering chuckle was not as warm as his previous ones had been. Nor was it cold. Rather, it was distant, as though my concerns were notions he'd once found amusing but had since grown bored with. "Well, traits like stubbornness were not *entirely* bred out of the human species. You are evidence of that. Tell me, little one, have you always been prone to willfulness? Or has your recent unhappiness created your surliness?"

"I am as I am," I said. "And I've not had a recent increase in unhappiness."

"So you enjoy living here?"

"...No," I admitted after a long drought of silence in which I'd considered the agonizing and lonely months I'd spent trapped in Seruf's home. "No, I am no happier here than I was in Sakar."

"I suspected as much," Ramiel said. "Seruf is...Well, I commend her devotion. Truly. But she can be difficult to stomach at times." He paused, pressing a hand to Wynn's side when she made a noise different from the others: a long, strained huff.

For a moment, we stood quietly, both observing Wynn as she shuffled, panted, and struck her hooves on the ground.

"She seems uncomfortable," I said.

"Yes." Ramiel ground the chains into Wynn's face when she twined her neck and clicked her fangs at him. "It's likely she'll foal this evening." He smoothed his hand over her heaving belly. "I have a proposition for you, little one."

"For...me?"

He inclined his head. "Once she drops this babe, and I've had time to assess it, I will be returning to Dunbar. When I leave, would you like to join me?"

He turned, fastening his radiant eyes upon me.

There are moments in one's life that remain vivid, no matter how many years pass. Many times, they are the traumas we suffer. Other times, it's the quiet moments that did not seem ~~monumen-tous~~—momentous at the time but later prove ~~pivitol~~—pivotal: moments that create a line between two portions of one's life.

I had a portion with mama, and a portion without.

A portion with Terrick, and a portion without.

Each time the line was drawn, I'd changed. And I always found myself looking achingly back over the line, wishing I could cross it again and return to my previous life. But it was insurmountable: the widest chasm surrounded by the tallest mountains. Once it formed, there was no returning to the other side.

The other lines of my life had been created violently, in great tremors that split and tore at the ground like the mighty quaking earths—

No, that is not the correct term.

Earth quaking. The mighty earth quakings depicted in Terrick's books.

But the earth did not quake when this, the largest and darkest chasm of my life, was forged. The shift was so smooth, I scarcely noticed it.

"Dunbar," I said, "can't be anymore dreary than Seruf's home."

"Is that a yes?"

For a moment, fear clutched me in its icy grasp, preventing me from saying the word I wished to utter. But then it thawed, unable to thrive beneath Ramiel's warm gaze.

"Yes," I said. "Yes, I will go with you."

Departure

Upon arriving into the world, the newborn Púca filly stood on shaking legs and searched for her mother's teat, as all foals do. But she did not suckle for milk. Instead, the filly used her teeth, seeking blood.

Wynn was enraged—'tis quite a sensitive area to be bitten, after all—and attempted to kill her babe.

I arrived at the stables that afternoon to find Wynn hobbled in blood-soaked bedding, still screaming in pain. The filly stood alone in a separate stall, bleating for her mother. Birthing fluid still glistened on her scaly coat.

"Best not wander in here today, little one," Ramiel said, leaning against the filly's stall, watching as she turned her teeth to her own shoulder and suckled the blood that welled from the wound.

"She's mad," I gasped.

"Perhaps." Disappointment darkened Ramiel's face. "But she's not yet fed. She may settle after her hunger is sated—Ah, excellent, Senan! Bring it here. Let's see how she fares."

A Wraith had dragged a goat into the stables.

The wee animal cried, his eyes wild with fear as he stared upon the thrashing, bellowing Púcas. He was little more than a babe himself; his horns were not yet fully grown.

"This is *cruel*," I said as the Wraith gathered the bleating goat and cast him over the stall door.

"It is no crueler than anything else in life. The filly needs to eat." Ramiel laid his hand upon my shoulder when the filly plunged her teeth into the goat's throat. "Best return to the castle, little one. I will fetch you later."

* * *

To say Seruf was unhappy with my decision to leave her home would be akin to calling a winter storm a mild breeze. She was not unhappy, she was *wrathful*.

If the words had come from my mouth, I would have been soundly punished for saying such a thing. But 'twas Ramiel who informed her of the news.

He joined Seruf and me for supper the following evening, giving me a broad smile as he took the seat beside mine and helped himself to a large slice of cherry pie.

"I will be departing in the morning, Seruf," he said between bites, careful to wipe the crumbs from his lips before he spoke. "I'll take the foal. She seems sturdy enough to travel. Wynn and the others will remain here."

"If you insist." Seruf's cheerful tone contrasted with the tension on her shoulders.

"Is the filly well?" I asked Ramiel.

"She is hearty and healthy," he said.

"But is she *well*? Or is she still driven mad with hunger?"

Seruf pinched my shoulder. "Darling, you care far too much for those varmints. Ramiel answered your question. Kindly cease pestering him."

"She's not pestering me, Seruf. And I'll ask you not to speak for me." Ramiel lowered his head to speak directly into my ear. "She has, unfortunately, inherited the insatiable appetite. But I remain optimistic that she will learn to curb her hunger."

The silken ~~tamber~~—timbre of his voice and the way his breath fluttered against my ear...Well, at the time, I had no words to describe how I felt. I could not understand why I shivered, despite the warm flush rushing over my skin. Nor could I make sense of the way my belly contorted...the very same sensation that occurred when I missed a step while traversing a staircase.

With another alluring smile, Ramiel returned to his pie. "Have you anything particular you wish to bring, little one?" he asked after he'd taken another bite.

The tension in Seruf's shoulders increased tenfold. Perhaps it was her rigid posture, her wings slowly rising from their usual relaxed pool on the floor, that had my own back tightening. Or perhaps my position between two irate Celestials had set me ill at ease. Either way, the little food I'd managed to consume prior to Ramiel's arrival turned to rot in my belly.

"I'm sorry." Seruf's voice was little more than a whisper, but it had lost all its sweetness. "I must have misheard that question, Ramiel."

"The question was not for you." Ramiel looked to me again. "My home is well stocked, little one, but you may want to bring your clothing. I will not have anything readily available in your size—"

"Ramiel..."

"If there is anything else you'd like to keep, I'd suggest you set it aside tonight. We'll be leaving at first light."

I startled when Seruf's fingers wrapped around my arm. "Lasair has all she needs here."

Ramiel was silent a moment, nearly two, while he finished consuming the pie. When he spoke again, he did so in a casual tone that suggested he was conversing about something commonplace, such as whether the clouds were indicating a bout of afternoon rain. "Lasair is leaving with me tomorrow."

"She most certainly is *not*." Seruf wrenched my arm closer, nearly pulling me from my chair. "You will not take her from me."

"I am not—" Ramiel began.

At the same time, I said, "I chose to go."

"Lasair, darling, I am not cross with you," Seruf said in her falsely soothing voice. "The fault lies with me. I should have known he would coerce you."

"He did not *coerce* me. I was made an offer, and I agreed to it."

"You do not know what you've agreed to!" Her unyielding grip stole the sensation from my fingers. I writhed, struggling to wrest my arm free.

"Seruf...you're hurting the girl," Ramiel said.

Seruf hissed, and her wings rose farther, stretching above her head. But she released me, and I gasped as a prickling rush of feeling returned to my fingertips.

"Lasair, go set your things aside." Ramiel raised his own wing, using its feathery tip to usher me away from Seruf. "This argument between Seruf and I is rooted in deep wounds, and there's no need for you to witness it."

A part of me, a darkly curious side, wished to stay.

But the unease in my belly bid me to flee.

Ramiel lounged in his chair, smiling lazily at me as I departed. In contrast, Seruf was already half standing, looking poised for an altercation.

The screaming began only after I'd returned to my room. Seruf's screaming, to be precise. I heard nary a sound from Ramiel, nor could I discern what Seruf was saying, but the anger punctuating her words was nearly palpable.

She continued her malicious tirade well into the night, quieting only for a few moments at a time—perhaps giving Ramiel a chance to respond—before resuming with renewed vigor. I did not sleep that eve—how could I, with such a ruckus happening beneath me? I sat in the corner of my room where I often felt safest, tucked in the narrow space between two stone walls, and listened.

At first light, Ramiel arrived to collect me as he'd promised. Despite his equally sleepless night, he looked, as always, refined. His clothes were ~~impecicably~~ impeccably clean and his eyes bright. The only evidence of his tussle with Seruf were the long featherless streaks in his wings.

It was a small measure of comfort to know I was not the only one who bore the physical brunt of Seruf's temper.

"You'll be riding with me today, little one." Ramiel collected my clothing into a leather satchel. "The Púcas are not safe for a human to ride. Is this all you'd like to bring? Nothing else?"

"That is all I own. Everything that has been spared the kiss of my fire, that is." Charred items of furniture were still scattered about the room—victims of my fire's rage.

Ramiel surveyed the ramshackled form of a once elegant chair, which had been wrapped in gold and blue silk before my flame had stripped away its garnish. "Have you any control over this ability?" he asked.

It shamed me to shake my head. Even after a nearly year under the brutal ~~tutelatge~~—*tutelage* of the Firestarter, I still had not gained mastery over the power that plagued me.

Ramiel showed no disappointment in my omission. "It isn't your fault, little one. If Seruf had not disobeyed me—" He paused. "Well, it's no matter. You'll master it someday."

"I think not." I traced a hand over the wall, where my fire had blackened the stone.

"Don't lose hope," Ramiel said. "All living things are capable of improvement. That ability will not rule you forever."

* * *

Ramiel's Púca mare was far larger and more ill-spirited than those housed in Seruf's stables.

"I kept her with the livestock in the human village. She's used to roaming and hunting for her meals," Ramiel told me as we departed Seruf's dwelling and found the mare outside the entrance, saddled and impatiently awaiting our arrival. The Wraith holding her bridle struggled to keep her still.

"And were the humans exempt from The Offering?" I asked. "Given that this mare destroyed their herds?"

"The harvest was bountiful this summer," Ramiel said dismissively. "The humans who lost their livestock Offered crops instead. Now—"

His Púca swung her head, fighting the chains ensnaring her muzzle.

"Tighten that chain, Clodagh!" Ramiel ordered the Wraith.

The Wraith grunted and wound the chains tighter until they made barbaric indentations in the mare's flesh.

The mare's red eyes held naught but malcontent as she watched

Ramiel and me approach. Clodagh tightened the chains ever more, until the mare could hardly breathe with the barbaric metal pressing into her nostrils. She wheezed as Ramiel lifted me into the saddle.

"It's only for a moment, little one," Ramiel chuckled, no doubt sensing the cross words I wished to say. "I wanted to make sure you mounted safely. Aoife is unused to humans."

When he leapt into the saddle behind me, he ordered Clodagh to release the mare from her bindings. Once freed, Aoife whisked her head about, her fangs poised as she strained to reach me.

Ramiel lashed her with his wing and then draped the feathered appendages about my thighs, shielding me. The mare screamed in indignation but faced forward once more.

She did not, however, settle, even hours into our trek. She moved at a restless gallop, staying well ahead of Clodagh, mounted on one of Seruf's Púca mares, who was tasked with bringing the foal to Ramiel's home.

Periodically, Aoife would come to an abrupt halt and attempt to turn her teeth into me. Ramiel, his wings still swathing my legs, sharply reprimanded her each time. And each time, the mare would shriek in outrage before resuming her uneasy gallop. Although she did not sweat as horses did, white foam frothed around her lips.

I, however, had begun to sweat quite profusely. Ramiel was far too close, his chest pressed against my back and his plush wings cocooning much of my body. And I could not say, in truth, that I was uneasy with the proximity. Not entirely, at least.

His touch did not strike fear into my heart, as the touch of humans often did. Nor did it inspire the unrest that accompanied Seruf's caresses. It was neither pleasant nor unpleasant, to be wrapped in his embrace, merely...*perplexing*.

Ramiel's hand curled about my waist when the mare caught sight of a lame fox. She lunged into a rollicking sprint. The fox barked in alarm and attempted to escape but could not move his broken body fast enough to avoid her teeth.

I uttered several crude words—Terrick would have been quite cross with me had he heard the word "feck" tumble so freely from my lips—as I covered my face with my hands.

Ramiel chuckled. "This treat is well deserved. Aoife's patience has been tested thoroughly today. Do not fret so, little one. The creature was not likely to survive long, as injured as he was."

But I *did* fret, for I pitied the animal. 'Twas a wretched fate, to die frightened, in the mouth of a predator.

"You pity the fox for dying, the Púcas for living, and the humans for existing," Ramiel mused. "Is there any creature you don't feel sympathy for?"

I turned my gaze to the wings draped across my lap. In the dappled sunlight, the feathers seemed to have turned a pale blue, like the soft underside of a bluejay. "The Celestials," I said.

A quiver pulsated over Ramiel's feathers, but his voice held no irritation when he asked, "You find us undeserving of your pity?"

"Not undeserving. But pity seems wasted on your kind. You want for nothing. You suffer no illness or injury. There is no pain in your lives."

"How wrong you are, little one." Ramiel pressed his hand to the crown of my head, giving my hair an affectionate pet. "How wrong you are."

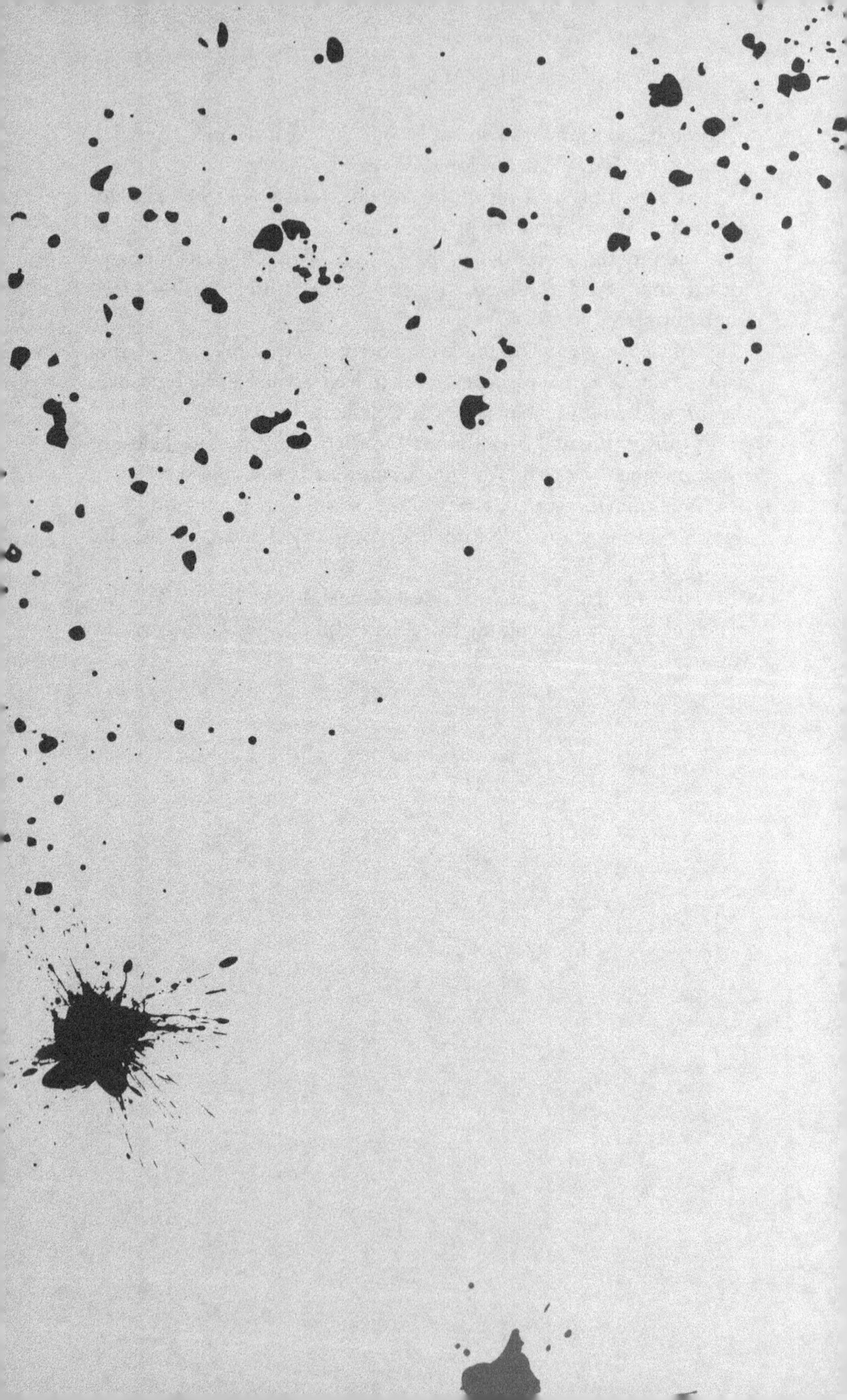

Barbarians

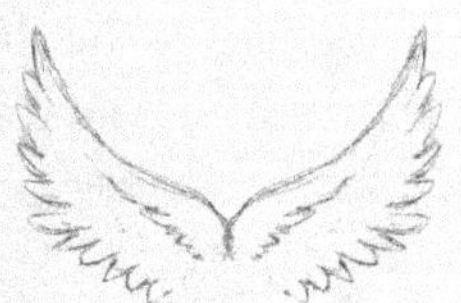

My exercise in ~~uncluddering~~—uncluttering my mind has thus far helped calm me, despite the trials and tragedies I've recollected. Perhaps reliving the hard moments in one's life is akin to lancing a boil: a painful procedure that offers great relief as it purges the fevered blood from one's body. These next memories, however, will require several lancings, and they may still prove folly, as this infection has festered deep inside me.

Perhaps a few years ago, I would have refused to describe these next events. But, in my experience, ignoring a wrathful sore never eased its ache.

And so, I will write (I've finally remembered this word is spelled with a "w") these memories as much as I am able. If only to seek relief from the pain I have carried since I left Norhall with Ramiel all those long years ago.

But I beg of the one reading this—if my ramblings are being read—please do not judge me too harshly.

* * *

It started sweetly. After all, even the most ~~posinious~~—poisonous berry will taste sweet before the toxins take affect.

Ramiel's dwelling was not bathed in splendor as Seruf's had

69

been. His towering stone castle boasted muted shades of creamy whites and slate grays. Firelight illuminated the plainly decorated halls and the humbly furnished rooms. His floors were composed of smooth rock and wore no decorative carpeting, as Seruf's had, nor were his windows shuttered with colored glass.

To someone as extravagant as Seruf, this dwelling might have looked drab, but I found comfort in the simplicity of it. It seemed more human than Seruf's home had. And it was quiet; Ramiel lived a distance from the nearest human village, and only a few trusted Wraiths were permitted to enter his home.

The scenery outside was one of lush trees, still green-leafed when I arrived but beginning to turn yellow and red in preparation for the autumnal shed. And there were Ramiel's Púcas: a herd of nearly fifty, contained in high-fenced enclosures on the east end of his castle. Although the beasts still did not have the room to roam as they likely would have preferred, they were not bound and chained. They could move freely within the confines of their paddock, able to smell the fresh air and see the sky. During inclimate weather, they needed only to seek shelter beneath the expansive pairapet (I believe this is a word. Parapit. Parapet?) of the castle.

"These are all mares," Ramiel told me when we toured the grounds. "They coexist better than I'd anticipated when I turned them out together. As unpredictable as the Púcas are with other beasts, they're surprisingly amiable with each other. So long as I don't allow my studs to cohabit with my mares."

And Ramiel, knowing my adoration of the beasts, gave me a room overlooking their enclosure. I spent many days sitting at my three oval windows, watching the Púcas below. And many nights with my windows propped open, despite the chill, so I could hear their croons and calls. The sounds helped to keep the nightmares at bay.

But they could not vanquish them entirely.

There were still nights I awoke screaming, my skin swaddled in flame, the scent of pine filling my nostrils as the wooden objects in the room burned.

The first time this happened, only three days after my arrival,

Ramiel sent his Wraiths to replace all the wooden items in my room with garish, amber-colored fixtures.

I grimaced when the Wraiths delivered the first item of furniture: a high-backed chair with rigid arm rests and a wide, squared seat. The shape of the chair was not so terrible, even if it did look harsh and uncomfortable. 'Twas the color which had my face pinching into a haughty expression, for the chair was composed of a glistening material that resembled the drainage of an angry wound.

Pus.

The chair was the color of *pus*.

Ramiel chuckled and brushed his wing against my back in a gentle pat, akin to the way a rider would soothe an agitated horse. "I know...these are ill-suited for a female's room. Sadly, I do not have many furnishings left from the Celestial City, so you'll need to make do with mine."

"Yours?" I stepped toward the chair the Wraiths had deposited by the window. It seemed unfitting that an ethereal creature such as Ramiel would own such vile furnishing.

He smiled. "I've always been fond of this chair. I find it's a good place to sit when I'm in a ponderous mood. Do not be deceived by its appearance, little one; it's far more comfortable than it looks."

As I placed my hand upon the surface of the chair, which was cool and smooth, like a river stone that had been weathered by rushing waters, Ramiel shifted closer to me.

Unease gripped my belly when his warm breath tickled the back of my neck. "Are you not worried I'll destroy it?" I asked.

"This is Celestial metal," he said. "Your flame will not damage it. I'm sending my bedclothes as well; they are also impervious to a flame. You'll not destroy anything, little one. Not here." He touched my shoulder before he exited the room—a gentle caress that had my back tightening in a shudder.

* * *

Ramiel kept his distance while the flames were at their height (immortal he may have been, but he was not immune to feeling the sting of fire). But he knew when the nightmares tormented me, for he would visit my room in the morning and leave small gifts. Sometimes, it was a bowl of goat's milk mixed with a bit of honey—a concoction that reminded me, achingly, of Terrick. Other times, he would leave me food: bits of a delectably rich treat he called *chocolate*, or an array of cheeses, which had a wider variety of textures and taste than I'd ever thought possible. Some were soft and sweet, like the cheese Quinn had once stolen for me. Some were firm and tart, and some tasted faintly of smoke. I sampled each one, although I enjoyed the pliable, sweet cheeses the most.

Ramiel would say nothing when he left the food. But sometimes he would indulge in an act of affection before he departed, such as laying a hand upon my shoulder or stroking my hair.

Outside of these occasional morning visits, I rarely saw him. There were days that passed with nary a glimpse of him; he often traveled away from his home, leaving me in the care of his Wraiths, who seemed determined to ignore my very existence. But I found comfort in the isolation.

The nightmares faded, but the fire's restless appetite did not cease. I was ever aware of it churning within me, poised, awaiting an opportunity to seize control. Those opportunities became ever fewer. In those first weeks at Ramiel's home, I accomplished something that had evaded me since my childhood: I relaxed.

I was akin to a horse, finally allowed to roam free after years of being tethered and beaten.

But freedom did not last forever; not when the animal was too valuable to let go.

"Will you accompany me on a walk?" Ramiel asked one afternoon.

I was outside, seated on a downed log surrounded by a canopy of trees. There was a damp chill in the air, winter's bitterness beginning to take hold. But the cold was not unpleasant. Rather, it was crisp and rejuvenating.

I'd been enjoying the peace, listening to the animals scurry about the woods, so Ramiel's disruption was not entirely welcome.

Although, strangely, I did not wish for him to leave.

"I've had my walk for the day," I said.

His mouth curled. "Yes, I've heard you spend quite a bit of your days out-of-doors, an activity I'm glad to see you indulge in. The winters here are often unpleasant. You'd best spend the time outside while you can. But I would like to show you something before it becomes too late in the day."

He stretched a hand toward me.

Perhaps the peaceful wood had left me in far too tranquil a mood to summon my usual petulance, for I only asked, "Will we go far?"

"Only just beyond the trees."

I took his hand, basking in the way his warmth cuckooned— cuccooned (this is a difficult word to spell. Is it cocooned?) my nearly frozen fingers.

"You should wear gloves when you venture outside, little one." Ramiel helped me to my feet and clasped my other hand, rubbing his fingers over my skin.

Being so near to him, scenting the faint hint of cedar wood that always seemed to accompany him, induced the oddest sensations, as though my heart was galloping in a panic even though I did not feel frightened.

Ramiel gave my fingers a gentle, affectionate squeeze, then released me.

I had an urge to reach for him. To reclaim his hands and continue savoring his warmth.

Instead, I crossed my arms over my chest, my skin prickling with confusion and mortification.

"I heard you visited the Púca foal yesterday." Ramiel began walking, motioning for me to follow.

"I did. It seems you have only succeeded in worsening her misery." I fell into step beside him, still shaken, even as my disapproval of his treatment of the Púca filly tempered my nerves.

The filly was being housed indoors, away from the rest of the herd. I pitied the wee beast, orphaned and isolated as she was. So I had gone to visit her, intending to ~~acquint~~—acquaint her with the sound of my voice. But my presence drove the filly to batter herself against the walls of her stall, desperate to free herself and satiate her hunger.

"On the contrary," Ramiel said, "the filly is doing quite well."

"Quite well?" I repeated in disbelief. "She did not seem so to me."

"Well, you are human," Ramiel chuckled. "The scent of your blood would have been tantalizing."

"It drove her to madness."

"But she calmed herself quickly and was contentedly napping not five minutes after your departure. She already possesses more restraint than my other Púcas. In time, she will not be driven to such desperation by the scent of human blood."

"And will you keep her confined until she gains that mastery?"

"No. I am not so cruel. The filly's stabling is only temporary, to give her time to grow. Eventually, she'll be transferred to a private paddock."

"You'll not allow her to join your herd?"

"Not for some time. I cannot be sure how my herd will react to her presence."

"Will they attack her?" I asked, aghast at the thought of the wee filly being savaged by the adult Púcas.

"I should hope not. But Púcas are unpredictable, so she must be capable of protecting herself before I release her. She will be fine, little one," he added, as though sensing my troubled thoughts. And then he inclined his head, a captivating smile unfurling over his lips. "We've arrived. I told you it was not a far walk."

We'd emerged from the trees and found ourselves atop a jagged, steeply sloped hill. Before us lay a village.

A *human* village.

Anger flooded my chest, creating a rippling itch across my skin. "This was what you wished me to see? I have *no* desire to watch humans in torment!"

"Do you not recognize this place?" Ramiel asked.

"'Tis a human village ruled by Celestials. No different than the one at Norhall." Beneath my flesh, the fire burned, restless and ravenous after many days of lying dormant.

"Look closer, little one," Ramiel said calmly. "I think you'll find it's not the same as Norhall."

My palms itched. I rubbed them together and stepped toward the edge of the hill, more to distract myself from the fire roaring through my blood than to humor Ramiel. But once there, with the somber town stretched across the clear sections of my vision, I could not stop my gaze from wandering.

Pale, sickly, and unkempt humans slogged through the muddy streets, weaving through their threadbare wood and straw dwellings. They did not converse, play, or laugh as the humans of Swindon and Detha had done. These humans, thin and weak as they were, toiled in silence beneath the Wraiths' watchful eyes. Many wore frayed scraps of fabric—if they were fortunate enough to have clothing. Some went without, their bare, ravaged backs hunched against the oncoming chill. The dead also crowded the sodden streets. Humans in towns such as these oft perished while working and were left to fester where they fell.

Like Mama.

I fought the urge to close my eyes, to shield myself from the horror, as I spoke to Ramiel. "It's larger than Norhall, perhaps. But it is no—" The words turned to ash on my tongue when my wandering eyes found a large stone house at the edge of the village.

It was a house I knew well.

The last time I stared upon its ~~fasade~~—facade, I'd been a recently orphaned child.

"Varn's home," I whispered.

"Yes. He lives there still...Don't fret, little one. I'll not force you to meet him," Ramiel laughed. "I don't much like dealing with him myself. And we'll not go into town if you do not wish to. But I thought, perhaps, you might have an interest in seeing your childhood home."

And now I recognized it.

My eyes traced the paths Mama and I had once walked, lingering for a long while on the quagmire street where our dwelling sat. The slanted building looked so small, and not only because I stood a great distance away from it. Compared to the dwellings I'd seen in Sakar, my old home seemed pitiable. Far too frail, with its poorly constructed walls and tattered roof, and utterly inadequate to house a mother and her babe.

By contrast, the tomato field, which stretched behind Mama's dwelling and spanned the length of the street, was far finer than any

I'd ever seen in Sakar. Lush, deep green vines sprouted from the rich soil, and each vine bore shining red tomatoes. A man tended the field with his two young boys. The eldest was the same age I'd been when Mama died.

"It was your eyes that entranced Seruf." Ramiel spoke softly, as though trying not to invade my thoughts. "She saw you from this very hilltop and was utterly besotted. You looked more Celestial than human, she'd said, and deserved more than to live in the scrum. I don't condone what she did, but I can't deny you benefited from it—"

"Benefitted?" I turned to him. "In what way have I *benefitted* from what was done to me?"

"You're here," Ramiel said, "speaking to me. When you could've been left to die amongst the filth."

"Humans are many things. But they are not the filthy creatures you and Seruf believe them to be."

"Are they not? Look to your childhood home again, little one. But do so with a critical eye."

I turned again to the tomato field.

The man handed his youngest son a tomato, and the boy held it in his outstretched hands, inspecting its color, shape, and firmness. After a moment, the boy smiled and carefully placed it into the wicker basket at his father's feet. The man stroked the boy's hair, bent to kiss his brow, and handed him another tomato.

My chest ached with memory and with sadness. The man was so very thin, and the cough—the very same one which had taken Mama from me—already had him in its grasp.

Would he die before his sons? The way Mama had perished before me?

Or would he linger into the cold of winter, ailing and weak and unable to collect The Offering? Would the Wraiths accept him if he Offered himself? Or would they dismiss his feeble body and take his sons instead?

The fire pressed beneath my skin as I retreated from the hill's edge.

"Watch closely, little one," Ramiel said.

A red-faced woman marched into the tomato field, a plank of

rotted wood draped over her shoulder. She shouted something to the man, although I was too far away to discern her words.

He shook his head, wrapped his arms around The Offering basket and turned away, calling for his boys to follow.

She yelled once more and struck his head with the wooden plank.

At first, he seemed stunned. He swayed, touching a hand to the blood now streaming down his face.

Her second strike downed him.

As the woman knelt to gather his overturned Offering basket, his children crouched beside his prone body. The thin, panicked wails of the youngest boy reached my ears, turning my stomach to rot.

The woman stood, gathered the full basket against her hip, and strode out of the field.

The woman, I thought, was gripped with madness.

But she was not the only one to partake in savage thievery.

It was nearing sunset. The time for The Offering was nigh, and violence ran amok through the streets of Detha. Humans dashed for their dwellings, and those who made it seemed to find safety. Or, at least, they found a door with which to shield themselves. But the rest, those that had some distance to travel from their fields or herds, were most at risk. Those who had nothing to Offer sought to steal from those who had. Even once an Offering was stolen, the thief had to guard it closely, lest it be taken by someone else. And the Wraiths, usually so eager to flick their whips, did *nothing* to stop this. They watched the spectacle, seemingly entertained by it.

The contents of my stomach felt as though they were frothing into my throat. I had never seen such brutality, even in all the years I'd lived in Detha. Surely Mama had never—

I gasped when my gaze wandered upon the clusters of children tucked in the narrow alleyways between the houses, protected from the mayhem surrounding them.

As I had once been protected from it.

The children were never approached, never struck, never used for bargaining. It seemed sparing them was the only rule the ~~barberous~~ —barbarous adults honored.

"The Offering started as a simple exchange," Ramiel told me. "We gave the humans land, made sure the soil was plentiful, even during the cold months, and asked very little in return: a simple daily offering from their harvests. But humans quickly fall prey to greed. Within a year, they began to withhold their offerings, mistakenly believing that we do not *need* to eat and therefore should not have access to their food. We *do* need to eat, little one." He smiled. "Perhaps not as voraciously as humans, but as long as we are trapped on this earth, we must abide by its laws. And living beings require sustenance. Thus, The Offering became mandatory. When humans still skirted our requests, I appointed my Wraiths as the enforcers of the law. Upon realizing they were outmatched, the humans turned on each other."

As the sun lowered, the Wraiths in Detha began to move, preparing to collect The Offering.

I raised my hands to my face to muffle my appalled sounds.

Flames enveloped my fingers.

I cried and drove my fists into my thighs. "They're frightened," I whispered. "The Wraiths *consume* those who cannot contribute to The Offering."

"I'm well aware."

"But you do not care?"

Ramiel said nothing, his eyes focused on the village and the violent altercation taking place near the center: a woman lay on the ground while a man kicked her face, attempting to pry her arms free of the sack of grain she had clutched to her chest.

"They would not act this way if they were not driven by fear," I said.

"There would have been no need to drive them to fear if they'd simply done what I'd asked," Ramiel countered.

Below us, the man successfully retrieved the sack of grain. He sprinted for his dwelling, while the lifeless, broken body of the woman remained on the street.

"Humans are a fabulous creation," Ramiel said, "but they are flawed. There is still much that needs to be bred out of them. But my father had no interest in perfecting them."

"Your father?"

"You've seen these flaws," Ramiel added. "How quickly did the humans turn on you when they discovered what you could do?"

I said nothing. There was no arguing against a well-made point.

"They are creatures prone to violence. And jealousy. And *greed,*" Ramiel concluded.

I closed my eyes and drove my fists into my thighs again and again. The blows were sharp enough to leave bruises, but I relished the dull ache. It distracted me from the anguish in my heart. "Not all of them." I thought of Terrick, who'd willingly thrown himself into misery to keep me safe. "Some humans are selfless and kind."

"There are always exceptions, yes. But as a whole, they are a species not particularly inclined to kindness."

"You speak as though I am not one of them," I said. "I was born human, and human I remain, even while cursed with Seruf's gift. Their flaws are also my flaws."

"Perhaps." Ramiel swiped a lock of hair from my shoulder.

"Don't touch me!" I recoiled. "The fire—"

"Has receded, little one." Ramiel reached forward again and tucked the lock of hair behind my ear.

I opened my eyes and found him staring at me, his blue gaze filled with affection. "I think you could be something far greater," he murmured.

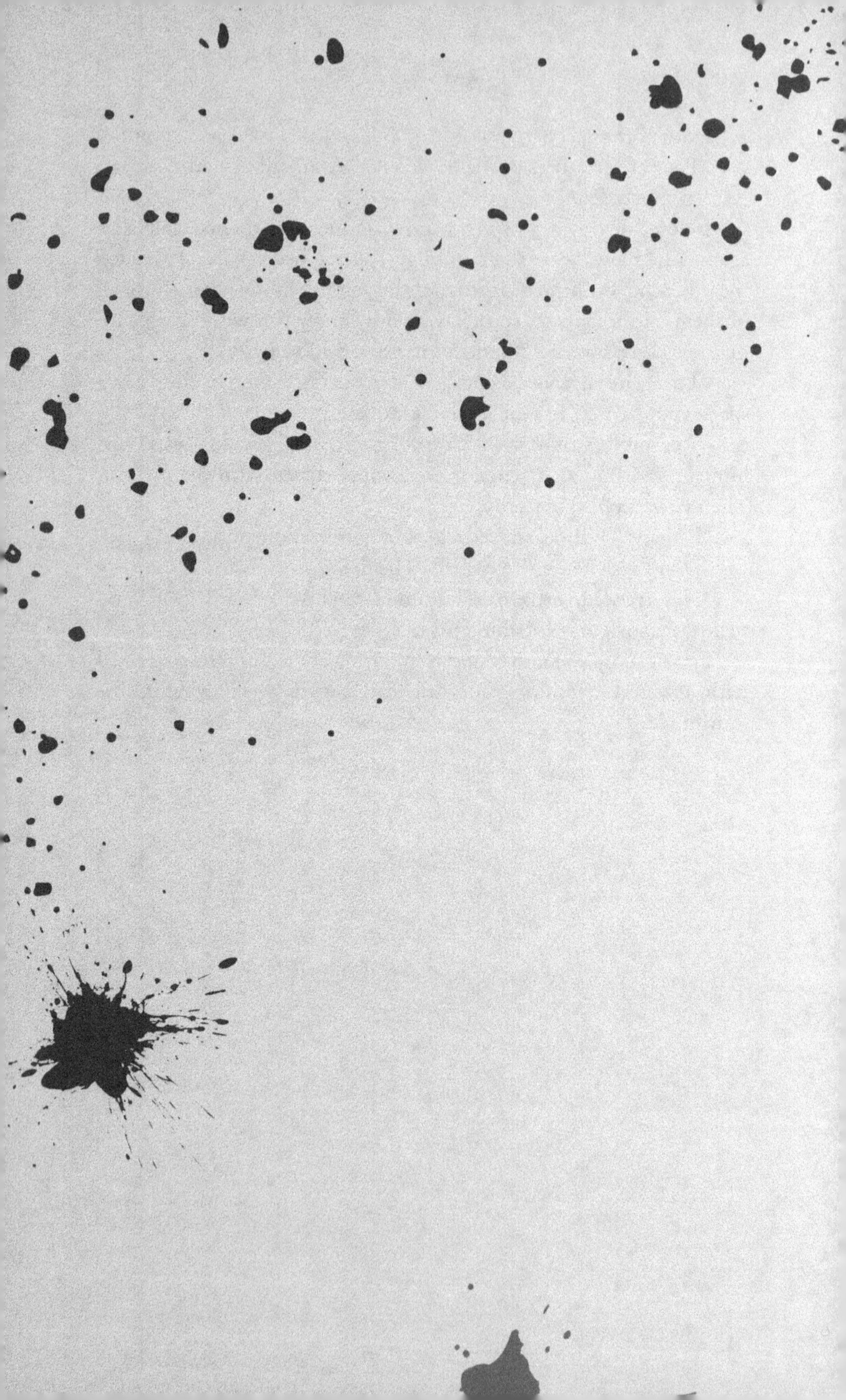

Teeth

I was determined to disprove Ramiel's opinion of humans. I believed, firmly, that the events of that day had been an outlier, likely one provoked by some ruthless command a Wraith had given.

So I returned to Detha the following evening. And the evening after. And every evening for two weeks. Day after day, the sunset brought violence and bloodshed. Sometimes, only a scant handful of humans turned to thieving; sometimes, half the village partook in the vicious raids.

I knew I was judging them harshly and unfairly—after all, failure to make The Offering was a death sentence. And for many, their demise would leave their children behind to fester and perish. But the beastly manner in which they thieved soured my heart. They showed little to no remorse as they killed their neighbors. Some even seemed to *relish* it.

Perhaps seeing the humans this way, acting less civilized than animals, shattered the illusion I'd once had of my childhood home. Those memories had not been pleasant, but I'd labored under the delusion that the humans residing in Detha were good-natured and kind. Now I saw otherwise.

And upon considering it further, I realized the ~~baberousness~~— barbarousness had been present in the Detha of my childhood.

No one had helped me when Mama perished.

No one assisted the families who could not make The Offering.

No one tended the sick or weak.

I'd believed their indifference was caused by fear of the Wraiths. Now I understood that most (perhaps not all, but many) humans were naturally indifferent. They had no inclination toward kindness.

Even the humans of Sakar, free from Celestial rule, resorted to violence at the first opportunity. And I'd borne the brunt of their rage.

My dislike of people had been rooted well before I'd met Ramiel. But those roots deepened as I studied the people of Detha and grew into something worse than hatred.

Disgust.

* * *

As the weather turned colder, and the nights grew longer, I became increasingly confined indoors.

My life had fallen into a quiet lull. Days passed in a lazy, unre-markable haze, often blending with each other. Indeed, the only cause I had to track the days was to count how many had passed since my fire last loosed itself.

Two days.

Three days.

Five days.

The longest reprieve lasted nine full days.

At first, the peaceful solitude left me contented. But loneliness soon darkened my heart. I found myself prone to long periods of stillness where I reminisced about the past and ached to return to the happy days of my youth.

Brooding, Terrick would have called it. I was *brooding*.

My sadness also made me long for companionship. As Wraiths do not provide scintillating conversation, and I was isolated from other humans, I instead sought Ramiel's company.

He was a wealth of knowledge and seemed eager to share his experiences with me. Each question I asked, no matter how simple or complex, received a well-constructed answer.

"Why have your kin forsaken and barred you from returning to your home?" I asked one evening when he'd found me sitting at my window and bid me to walk with him, thus sparing me another night of brooding.

"Because we are in disagreement," he answered. "I envision a different future for our home than many of my brethren do. Perhaps I should not have been so forceful in voicing my opinion. Alas, what is done is done. And no disagreement lasts forever."

"Do you dislike Seruf? It seems you two are often at odds with each other," I queried on another occasion as we shared an indulgent morning meal.

"No," Ramiel said gently. "I have a great adoration for Seruf, but she has become agitated and reckless of late. And I am primarily to blame. Celestials were not meant to reside long on this earth. Time has begun to wear on her."

"How is it that you possess material that does not tear or burn?" This question came because I'd grown quite attached to the white tunic Seruf had given me—a garment far too fine for everyday wear but which I rarely found myself without. It had not diminished in its brilliance, despite the hardships it had endured since transferring to my ownership.

"Ah, yes." Ramiel ran his fingers along the sleeve of my tunic. "Weavers from the City made our clothing, spooling the fabric from the dust of a dying star. It cannot be damaged by any earthen object or element. The colors, sadly, have dulled since we brought them here. You do not see it," he added when I began to protest, "because you did not see the radiance of these garments when they were made."

Sometimes, we'd talk as we traversed the halls, watching the inclimate weather rage outside the windows. Sometimes, we'd tuck ourselves away in what Ramiel called a "sitting room," a space designed for lounging before the fire and indulging in conversation. Sometimes we would speak over our meals.

As the weeks passed, we moved our conversations to the wing of the castle Ramiel called his own.

It was composed of three cavernous rooms: a study, a personal sitting room, and his bedchamber. As Ramiel only used the study to meet with his Wraiths, he left it sparsely decorated with only an expansive writing desk and a few mismatched chairs.

His personal sitting room, however, contrasted sharply with his rigidly tidy appearance. Odd paintings draped the walls—odder, even, than the garish drawings Seruf had possessed. Some of Ramiel's artworks were splashed with color, some were not. Most were made of a strange composition of humans and foreign objects, and nearly all had large columns of text scattered about. Of course, at the time, I could not read the text. But I found myself fascinated by the clean, uniform lines of the letters, which seemed almost magikcal, too flawless to have been created by a human hand.

"They're posters," Ramiel told me, after I'd spent quite a long while inspecting a painting which featured a man and woman standing cheek to cheek, surrounded by blocks of words.

"Are posters different from drawings?" I asked.

"Not entirely, no. Although, many of these are not drawings. They're photographs—images taken of real people."

"Is that not what all paintings are?"

"No, little one." Ramiel smiled. "These were not created with charcoal or brush."

"But there is no other way to capture a person's likeness. Is there?"

"There are other ways. Unfortunately, those methods are not available here. Not anymore." Ramiel stood so close, his arm brushed mine when he reached to trace one of the words. "Can you read what that says, little one?"

"No."

"Perhaps that is just as well." He laid his palm against the art in a moment of quiet reverence. "We salvaged some remnants of the old human world, but not all."

"I don't—" I began.

But Ramiel smiled and ushered me into a long, lush chair, one clearly designed for two people to rest, as he fit comfortably beside me. "Now then, little one, what dessert shall we sample this evening?" His leg lightly pressed against mine as he spoke. "I'm quite fond of the lemon cake..."

Later, I learned that each piece of art had a fictional story

~~enscribed~~—inscribed onto it. Every evening after that day, Ramiel would draw me into his sitting room, gesture to a painting, and regale me with the tale that accompanied it. Most were either horrific stories of murder and depravity or heart-wrenching tragedies, which I found odd, considering the cheeriness of the artwork.

"Humans are often cheered by tales of others' misfortunes," Ramiel said.

"Why do you keep the artwork if their stories are so ~~macbre~~—macabre?"

"They fascinate me." Ramiel touched a strand of my hair, his eyes speculative as he twined it around his finger. "As humans do. I do not dislike humanity, little one. They are a species capable of much creativity and intelligence. They'd be capable of so much more if my father had taken the time to perfect them."

* * *

Although all the paintings in Ramiel's sitting room were intriguing, I became particularly entranced by one that featured a man cradling a woman in his arms. I couldn't say why, although I suppose it had something to do with the vulnerability of the woman's slack pose, as though she were unconscious (I have finally mastered the spelling of this word!). There was no fear in her gaze as she stared at the man who held her, only trust and affection. As if she knew he would care for her.

And the man gazed at her with an expression of pure adoration.

What must it be like to be that woman? I wondered.

I thought of the times I'd been faint. The times I'd wandered through the woods, starving, frightened, and hunted. Or the long days I'd spent chained in the room at Lamex, forced to experience hours of heartbreak and pain at the hands of a man who took far too much glee in inflicting such torture.

What would it have been like to have the devotion of a man such as the one in the painting? A large, imposing figure who could carry me away from the torment I'd suffered. A man who would stare at me as though I were a precious being, one he would fight to protect.

What would it be like, I mused, *to be loved?*

* * *

On a foggy, late-winter evening, Ramiel ushered me into his sitting room, as had become our routine, and regaled me with a story of two ill-fated lovers. Unable to sway their warring families, the lovers, in a moment of witless ill-timing, took their own lives.

This tale did not sadden me as it was likely intended to. Perhaps I had become so dissociated from my own kin, I no longer felt sorrow at tales of their suffering. Or perhaps I was preoccupied, as I so often was, by the deep ~~tamber~~ timbre of Ramiel's voice.

He turned to me after he concluded his tale. "You find this amusing?" he asked. For I had, indeed, loosed a dismissive noise at the conclusion of his tragedy.

"Not amusing," I said, "but silly. Had the boy not been so quick to end his own life, he would have seen his love reawakened."

"Humans are, by nature, impatient creatures."

"But he only needed to wait *moments...*"

"That," Ramiel chuckled, "is what defines a tragedy: how those moments separate happiness from sorrow. And how humans"—he extended his hand, trailing his fingers along my arm—"are often not willing to wait for their happiness."

"It is quite—" My words were swept away in a gasp when Ramiel bent his head and pressed his mouth to my cheek.

My skin was suddenly awash with prickling heat, as though my fire had emerged. But when I drew back from him, frantically searching for the flame, I found naught but my own flesh.

"I'm sorry," Ramiel chuckled. "Did I frighten you?"

Yes, I prepared to say. But I loathed to admit that such an ~~innocuous~~ innocuous act had frightened me. So I murmured an unsteady, "You surprised me."

"Is that all?" A smile fluttered across his face. "So, you would not protest if I did it again?"

He leant toward me. I did not move, nor breathe, as he pressed another lingering kiss to my cheek. I knew he felt the tremor gripping my spine, but he did not comment on it. He stared at me, his eyes as intense as those of the man in the painting, and cupped his hand around my chin. "Have you ever been kissed, little one?" he asked.

My heart gave a sudden painful lurch as a memory of Quinn touching his lips to my knuckles filled my mind.

But to Ramiel, I simply said, "No."

His thumb caressed the corner of my mouth. "A pity. Although perhaps your inexperience is for the better." Ramiel shifted, pressing his thigh more firmly to mine. The warmth of his flesh, even through the layers of clothing, was startling. "For if you had been kissed," he murmured, "it would have been by a human boy, who are, at best, bumbling buffoons. And you, little one, deserve better."

He angled his head and touched his mouth to mine.

I stilled, confused by the slippery sensation of his lips stroking mine. 'Twas not at all unpleasant—there was no denying Ramiel was skilled in the art of kissing—but it was new and strange. Each glide of his lips induced more of the burning sensation within me. His hands roamed slowly over my sides, kneading and caressing in soft patterns that left my belly quivering and my mind befuddled as I tried to sort my uncharted emotions.

Ramiel's wings unfurled from behind his back and twined around me. They were as soft as the downy fur of a young rabbit as they brushed my neck and cheeks, while his hand flexed around my chin.

And all at once, my ~~tumoltuous~~—tumultuous emotions settled on something familiar: curiosity.

If his touches could make me experience these wildly conflicting sensations, could mine do the same for him?

I grasped the front of his shirt, tracing the shape of his chest through the fabric. That did not draw a reaction from him, but stroking his wings garnered a soft sigh.

On that breath, he pulled away.

I craned my head up, seeking him.

This time when he kissed me, the contact was not merely two pairs of lips touching. His tongue pressed into my mouth, an invasion so foreign and startling, I reacted purely out of instinct.

Ramiel drew back with a hiss when my teeth clamped onto his tongue.

"Little one, I admire your spirit. But there are times you use teeth"—he tapped a finger to the tip of his tongue—"and times you don't."

I raised my chin, hoping he was not able to see the heat flushing across my cheeks. "It felt strange."

His laughter was deep and warm. "You hardly gave it a chance. It'll be a pleasurable act for both of us. Trust me." He brushed the top of his wing against the side of my throat. "Would you care to try again? I'll go more slowly this time."

I should have said no.

But I was so captivated by him, and by the peculiar emotions gripping me, that I found myself nodding.

* * *

I shall not further detail my relationship with Ramiel. These memories are as conflicted as the emotions I felt during my first kiss.

But I need to make something quite clear: Ramiel never harmed me. Nor did he force me. He simply took advantage of a version of myself that was too young and unwise to grasp what was happening. I was a child, having lived only eighteen years on this earth (or seventeen, or nineteen, depending on when I was born). This is why I find these memories so difficult to write. Because I see now what I couldn't then.

After that day, during which Ramiel schooled me on many carnal activities, I was thoroughly consumed by him. A dangerous thing, to be sure. For my heart was lost, and my mind was alight with feelings of love, and I was bent entirely to his will.

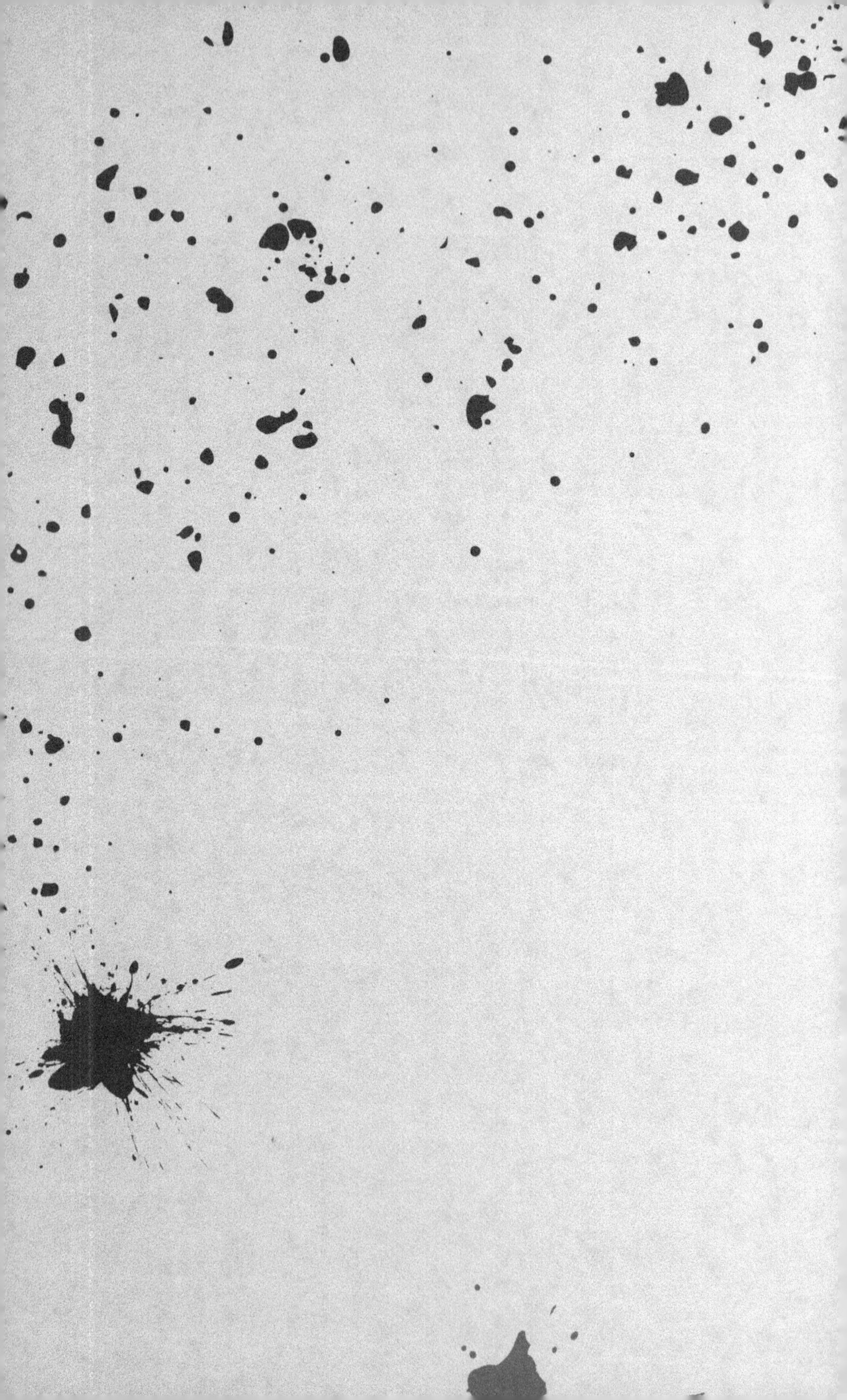

Icarus

Winter thawed. Spring blossomed. I was steeped in contentment, but Ramiel grew restless.

We slept in separate quarters as my fire was most likely to loose itself while I slumbered. But most mornings found him collecting me from my chambers well before daybreak. It was *far* too early to be awake; the birds did not even rise at such an unsavory hour. But Ramiel was always awash with enthusiasm and energy as he brought me to his bedchamber.

I need not divulge what happened once we arrived there.

After our...well, *physical pursuits* ended, I would lie abed for a while longer, sluggish and reluctant to begin the day. Ramiel, however, would immediately spring to his feet and dress himself—a fascinating thing to watch, as he wore three layers of clothing, all tailored to accommodate his wings. The first layer was a plain white tunic, which he fastened by threading buttons along the front. Afterward, he would slip into a flimsy cloth vest before he slid his arms into the outer tunic, which looked stiff and only fastened in the middle, leaving the lower flaps dangling about his thighs and a portion of his vested chest exposed.

He insisted these rigid garments were "proper."

I thought it was silly to don so many useless layers of clothing, although they did make him look rather majestic.

"I was hoping you might do me a favor." Ramiel turned to me one spring morning as he buttoned his outer tunic and bent to kiss the top of my head.

"Of course," I said without hesitation.

Ramiel's smile widened. "My brother, Raphael, has been on earth for some time, dwelling in the city of Niall. I've been trying to deliver a message to him—one of peace," he added when I frowned. "I'd like to come to an agreement with him. It's past time for us to return home. But Raphael bids his hybrids to kill any Wraith I send to Sakar, and after the *dreadful* business with Ellard"—his brow furrowed—"I cannot risk breaching Sakar's borders again. But my brother will not protest *your* arrival."

I must have made a sound of distress, for Ramiel smoothed a hand over my hair. "He would not harm you, little one."

I did not know if it was his touch that made my stomach unsteady (his touch always incited my insides to do strange things) or if it was the thought of returning to Sakar. "It is not your brother I fear," I said.

Ramiel's eyebrow arched. "So, what do you fear? The humans?"

When I remained silent, he laughed. "Little one," he said, drawing me in for a kiss, "it is *they* who should fear *you*."

"They *do* fear me," I said. "And that fear leads them to savagery. I've suffered at their hands before. I've no wish to do so again."

"Nor will you have to. If they *dare* to threaten you, remember this..." He cupped my chin and raised my head, forcing my eyes to meet his. "It takes naught but a few seconds to light a human's flesh ablaze."

* * *

A week before I was set to depart, Ramiel and I traveled to a seaside city named Oakwell, where he'd bid the humans to fashion me a vessel to traverse the waters with.

Oakwell was a place every bit as unpleasant to behold as Norhall and Detha. Humans toiled beneath the lash of Wraiths' whips and festered in their own filth, but some small mercies had been granted to these inhabitants that their kin inland had been denied. Tall, proud trees wrapped about the town, providing protection from the harsher elements. The human dwellings, although still inadequately sized, were composed of sturdy wood. And many of the humans did not tend or gather food for an Offering.

"Terran often wanders," Ramiel had told me as we entered the city, "and we are not so unreasonable that we would force humans to prepare food for a Celestial who rarely occupies the lands."

"Terran?" I'd asked, for it was a name I had not heard him utter before.

Ramiel chuckled warmly. "Worry not, little one," he said, even though I had expressed no worry. "Terran has no liking for social interaction and will likely seek solace elsewhere for the duration of our stay, lest I force an introduction with you. Now." He pointed to the trees on the south edge of the city. "The entrance to the sea is just beyond those woods. Many of Oakwell's humans spend their days there, building and maintaining my vessels. Much of Uchen is separated by the sea," he added when I'd begun to ask why he had the need for more than one vessel, "and traveling across its waters is becoming a rather...*cumbersome* affair. I would prefer my brethren to have access to vessels should they wish to use them. *Your* vessel," he said as he stroked his fingers along the curve of my neck, "is waiting for you."

I was, admittedly, flooded with disappointment upon seeing the vessel for the first time. It was pitiably small next to the towering structures it floated alongside. Indeed, it was barely large enough to hold the cloth sail that encompassed much of the deck. But whereas Ramiel's vessels were built to accommodate a Celestial's strength, mine was crafted for a human's.

Ramiel spent several days schooling me how to maintain the vessel, navigate the waters, check the direction of the wind, and when to lower the sail and use the oars to steer myself clear of the rocks.

I departed on a sun-soaked morning. The passage from Oakwell to Sakar took mere hours, although it seemed much longer as the endless bobbing atop the rollicking waters left me violently ill. By the time I reached land, I was in too weak a state to row properly. I struck one rock. Then another. A third, and then a fourth, before the vessel grinded (is this a word? Grinded? Ground?) to a halt. And

I was so grateful to see solid ground that I fell upon exiting and landed, face-down, in the surf.

I lifted myself from the water and became ill once more when the blood surging from my battered nose splashed over my tongue. And I still had to pull the vessel more firmly onto shore, lest the tide sweep it back to sea. A task that was *maddeningly* difficult for my ailing body, especially as I had to navigate not only the rocks but the dozens of other ships which lined the beach. Their owners were nearby, but none offered to aid me as I battled the waters. Most were too absorbed in their own comings and goings to notice my arrival. Even when I came fully ashore, removed all my belongings from my vessel, and walked toward their town, they did not spare me a glance.

The only time I garnered a stare was when I passed a robust and weathered woman who sat atop a hulking rock, weaving a net. In using my darker tunic to stem the bleeding from my nose, I'd allowed her to glimpse the white tunic I wore underneath.

Ramiel had bid me to wear the garment, as it would remain intact if my fire loosed itself, but warned that its radiance would draw suspicion, so I concealed it beneath a large brown tunic. I'd brought several additional tunics, trousers, and another set of boots with me, storing them in my satchel, along with my provisions and the letter Ramiel had asked me to deliver to his brother.

The woman paused when my garment sparkled in the late afternoon sun, but she did not comment, nor did she remark on my haste to conceal it. She merely huffed, "Are ye from Laewaes, then? Thought ye'd have a wee bit of fun on the sea, eh? Serves ye right. Ye young waifs never learn—don't want to take the time to get yer sea legs under ye or understand how to pilot a ship. Mark my words." She waved a gnarled hand in my face. "The sea is unkind to all folk. Especially to those who don't respect it."

And then she resumed her weaving, silently dismissing me.

She reminded me of Beda, the unpleasant cheese merchant who despised children.

Had I not been so ill, I might have said something to her. But it took all the energy I possessed to quiet my stomach as I began the trek up the cliffs into the city.

The day had dawned warm but was beginning to cool as the

afternoon stretched on. And the wind atop the cliffs was bitter as it buffeted me on my still unsteady legs. The air smelled of salt and fish. Even the people ~~stunk~~—~~stank~~ (which is the correct word to use here? Stank?). They stank of the sea.

Perhaps I had grown used to living amongst the Celestials, who did not carry smells as humans do. Regardless, I was quite glad I'd purged the contents of my stomach while on the vessel. Had I not, I would have expelled them onto the shoes of passerby.

This was a small town—smaller even than Swindon. And the houses were...*unusual*. There were no rows of tall buildings, only clusters of long, short structures so covered in green moss and seagrass, they looked more akin to hills than dwellings.

But humans certainly dwelled there. Although Muirin was small, it was disproportionately crowded and entirely unfriendly.

"Have ye no eyes in your blasted head?" a man barked at me when I trod on his young son.

In truth, I had not seen his son. The two had been walking hand in hand alongside me. While the man was large enough to cast a shadow on the edges of my limited vision, his son was not. So, when I'd moved to the side to avoid an oncoming horse-drawn cart, I'd stepped on the boy's foot.

The boy had immediately begun wailing—an infuriating overreaction, as I had not stepped on him hard enough to cause pain.

"Apologies," I said. "I was distracted..."

The man gathered his crying son into his arms. "Don't walk about if you can't mind your feet." He deliberately knocked his shoulder into mine as he walked away.

A deep itch blossomed across my skin as the fire swelled in my veins. I drew my arms around myself, pleading for the flame to calm, even as a part of me was seized with a disturbingly dark desire to watch the boorish man and his overly dramatic urchin burn.

* * *

On the edge of Muirin, away from the worst of the crowds, I purchased an aging stallion from an equally decrepit farmer. The man did not question my need for the horse, nor did he seem to notice that Ramiel's silver pieces were smoother than the coins humans used. His hands were so roughened with years of work and weather exposure, he likely could not feel the difference between polished silver and coarse.

"Where you be heading?" The man pocketed the silver pieces and led a long-limbed chestnut stallion from his moss-coated stable.

"Niall," I said.

"Ach. Young thing like you, no wonder it's the city you're cravin'. Niall is a long ways away, though. If you be wantin' my advice, not that anyone does, you'd be better crossin' into Swindon or Kilerth." The man lifted a saddle onto the stallion's back, rubbing absently at the jagged tear in the pommel. "Not as grand as Niall, to be sure, but if it's an escape you're looking for, you'll find it in any of those cities. And you'll be needin' only a few days travel. Niall will be takin' you a few weeks."

Swindon. I felt an ache of longing upon hearing its name spoken in the man's gravelly voice.

But rage also sparked within me.

"I wish to see Niall," I repeated, rubbing my wrists together to alleviate the itch dappling my flesh. "Would you tell me the way?"

"Ach, well, I suppose you're intent on seein' the white castle, eh? It's a beauty, alright," the man said. "Or so I've heard. Never cared much to be going there myself. It's easy enough to find. You go south...likely'll pass either Swindon or Kilerth, in case you change your mind. And you keep traveling inland until ye find yourself in the woods. Turn east, cross the river, and you'll find yourself in Niall. And this fella..." He patted the stallion's neck. "He may not be as fast as he useta be, but he'll be gettin' you there safely."

The stallion had a scraggy coat and mud painted on his legs and belly. He wasn't as fine to look at as Ramiel's Púcas, but his brown eyes were warm and kind. I stroked his muzzle tentatively, afraid he would feel the heat raging beneath my skin.

The stallion nuzzled my palm and nipped his lips around my fingers.

The rage inside me lessened, and the itch eased. How could I feel anger when this large, gentle creature showed me open affection?

The stallion stood still while I mounted him, his ears attuned to my movements and voice. I needed only to click my tongue to ask him to move forward.

"You be careful traveling a distance alone, lass," the farmer called when I bid him a farewell.

My stomach tightened at the word "lass." The first time I'd been called that name in well over a year.

My unease deepened further when the farmer continued, "There was talk, 'bout a year ago now, mayhap more, that Seruf hid a hybrid in Sakar. No one rightly knows if it's still here or not, but best keep your eyes open. I'd hate to see a pretty lass like you crossing paths with a Firestarter."

* * *

I named the stallion Icarus, after the story Ramiel had told of the human who wanted to fly so he could better admire the sun's enthralling beauty. A Celestial helped him to build wings but cautioned against flying too close to the sun's heat. The human Icarus had not heeded the warning. He melted his wings and perished in the sea.

I was determined the equine Icarus would not meet a similar fate.

Thankfully, my flame did not hunger for horse flesh as it did for humans. Regardless, I made sure Icarus was tied a great distance from me while I slept.

Each day, we set out at dawn, usually at a walk to give Icarus's old joints a moment to loosen, and we traveled until the moon rose. Icarus was sure-footed, easy to handle, and made for a ~~wonderous~~— wondrous travel companion. He adored having his ears massaged after I removed his bridle and thoroughly enjoyed his twice-daily grooming sessions, during which I wiped dirt and sweat from his fluffy coat with a bit of cloth.

The days passed with a quiet, peaceful ~~candance~~—cadence.

I could have avoided the town and continued my trek in solitude. But when I saw the mass of dwellings and heard the babble of civilization, I was inexplicably drawn to it, as an insect would be riveted by a dancing flame.

It was Swindon. I needed only to see the first row of houses and the familiar curve of the stone streets to recognize my childhood home.

I wish I could lie and say I only had a desire to revisit fond memories. To gaze upon the shops Terrick and I had once frequented, wander the streets I'd roamed as a child, and see Terrick's home and reminisce on my golden memories with him.

And I did, truly, wish to do all those things.

There was a part of me, however, that rode into Swindon with a darker intent. A part of me that wished to inflict pain upon the people who had once shunned me.

I tried to temper that malicious side of myself. For several moments, I rode quietly through the town, observing, not seeking to harm anyone, even though my flame broiled beneath my itching flesh.

Until I passed the inn.

The Black Bull Inn was precisely as I remembered it: perched at the corner of a sweeping intersection, the windswept sign waving jovially over the faded black door.

Then, as if fate itself were cursing me, the burly inn keeper, Lorcan, threw open the door and stepped outside. His booming voice hummed a soft tune as he swung a wicker basket in his right hand. It was mid-morning. No doubt Lorcan had his supplies laid out in preparation for the evening meal and was heading into the market to fetch any missing items.

Icarus must have felt my hesitation, my *fury*, for he halted. His tongue rolled over his bit, reminding me to loosen my grasp on his reins. I did so, but I did not relax.

Lorcan stopped and absently stroked Icarus's nose. And then, in his normally cheery manner, he raised his head to offer me a greeting.

I had a mere second to absorb his appearance: his dark hair was duller, his face bore more age lines, and he seemed both taller and broader than he'd been when he was the friendly innkeeper and I was *cailín álainn*.

It took him a moment to recognize me. I had changed more drastically than he, but my abnormally colored eyes remained the same.

"You!" Lorcan's basket slid from his hand. It struck the street and rolled, the handle brushing against Icarus's hind ankle. Although

Icarus was not the sort to spook easily, the tension radiating from the two humans around him had frayed his nerves.

He bucked.

Lorcan snatched my leg and pulled me from the saddle.

I fell, crying out when my head collided sharply with the stones.

Icarus ran, desperate to escape the oncoming destruction.

Lorcan stood over me, breathing raggedly, his weathered face blotching with angry red patches. He called me a name I did not understand at the time, but I would later come to understand its meaning and despise him all the more: "vicious cunt."

My vision swam. The fire rushed through my veins, ravenous and raging.

Another man emerged from the inn—a boy, little older than me.

"Bradley, fetch me a sword. Or a knife. *Quickly*!" Lorcan shouted.

I laughed as cold, heartless words twirled over my tongue. "It matters not how swiftly he runs. A weapon will not save you."

On that morning, as I sat streets away from my treasured childhood home, I found I had no will to battle the flame, nor did I feel pity for those who would be devoured by its wrath.

I rose to my feet and exhaled slowly, releasing the tension in my belly and the tenuous hold I'd maintained over the fire. The flames roared in triumph as they engulfed my body. For me, the sensation was akin to being wrapped in a warm embrace. But for those around me, a caress from my flame would bring their demise.

As the fire swaddled Lorcan, he attempted to flee back to the safety of his inn, where I'd once stood in his kitchen and watched him sprinkle berries in my porridge.

Those memories enraged me the most: recollections of the innocence of childhood, forever tainted. Betrayal from a man who'd once treated me as though I were his own daughter and now harbored such hatred toward me.

They had done this. The humans. For ~~ostrasizing~~—ostracizing me and treating me with violent hostility. For never seeing me as I had been: a frightened child who'd sought naught but comfort and understanding.

Fire enveloped my heart as I grasped Lorcan's tunic. He bellowed when fabric and flesh melted, but I felt no sorrow for him.

"Look at me," I said.

Lorcan remained facing away, struggling to be free.

"*Look at me!*"

He turned, his eyes wild with pain and fear as the fire continued to ~~injest~~—ingest his flesh.

"I never wanted to hurt anyone," I said. "Why couldn't any of you have seen that? Why couldn't you have *attempted* to understand my pain?"

Lorcan writhed. The sweet stench of his burning flesh filled my nostrils.

"You lashed out at me in fear. Struck me in anger. Scorned me. Ridiculed me. *I was suffering*!" I screamed. "And no one cared. Not even you..." The words burst out of me as a sob. "I loved you once. *Trusted* you. And you turned your back on me when you discovered I was different. The Celestials are right. Humans are despicable creatures."

Lorcan's face dissolved into disfigurement. His mangled body was unrecognizable from the man who'd once grasped my hand and brought me to meet his prized bull.

He would not be long for this world.

I walked away and left him to die alone.

The residents of Swindon flooded the streets, drawn by Lorcan's wails. Familiar shouts soon reverberated around the town: humans calling me a Firestarter. Seruf's hybrid. A *monster*.

They scattered about, drawing weapons, preparing to fight.

My flame reacted accordingly, stretching outward from my skin, giving me as wide a wingspan as any Celestial had ever possessed.

Archers fired their arrows but seemed unable to aim through the smoke and flame.

I sauntered unhindered through the streets of Swindon, my fire arcing toward the heavens. Although I did not actively seek to kill another human, many found themselves unable to escape the fire's fury.

As I traveled, I gazed upon the places that held the fondest memories: the shoemaker's shop, where I'd purchased my first pair of boots; the seamstress, where I'd so anxiously awaited my first tunic, a *blue* one. I'd hardly been able to keep myself still while I was measured for the garment.

Those buildings crumbled.

Then I entered the bustling market, where Terrick and I had ventured every morning and where I'd claimed my first victims, Darcie and Grady.

Memories of that day swirled about my brain as the fire swirled about my flesh. The market booths, and the wares they carried, were reduced to ash.

The only place I could not bear to revisit was the street where Terrick and I had dwelled above his bookshop. I would not, *could* not, watch Terrick's home being destroyed.

But, as the rest of Swindon burned, I knew his prized bookshop would not be spared.

The flames only receded from my skin when I left the ruined town and entered the forest. Behind me, Swindon was fully ablaze. Long columns of smoke billowed upward, casting a dim pallor over the landscape. The squalls of the dying filled the air, frightening several woodland animals.

Ramiel had been right. I had naught to fear from humans.

The predator, after all, did not fear its prey.

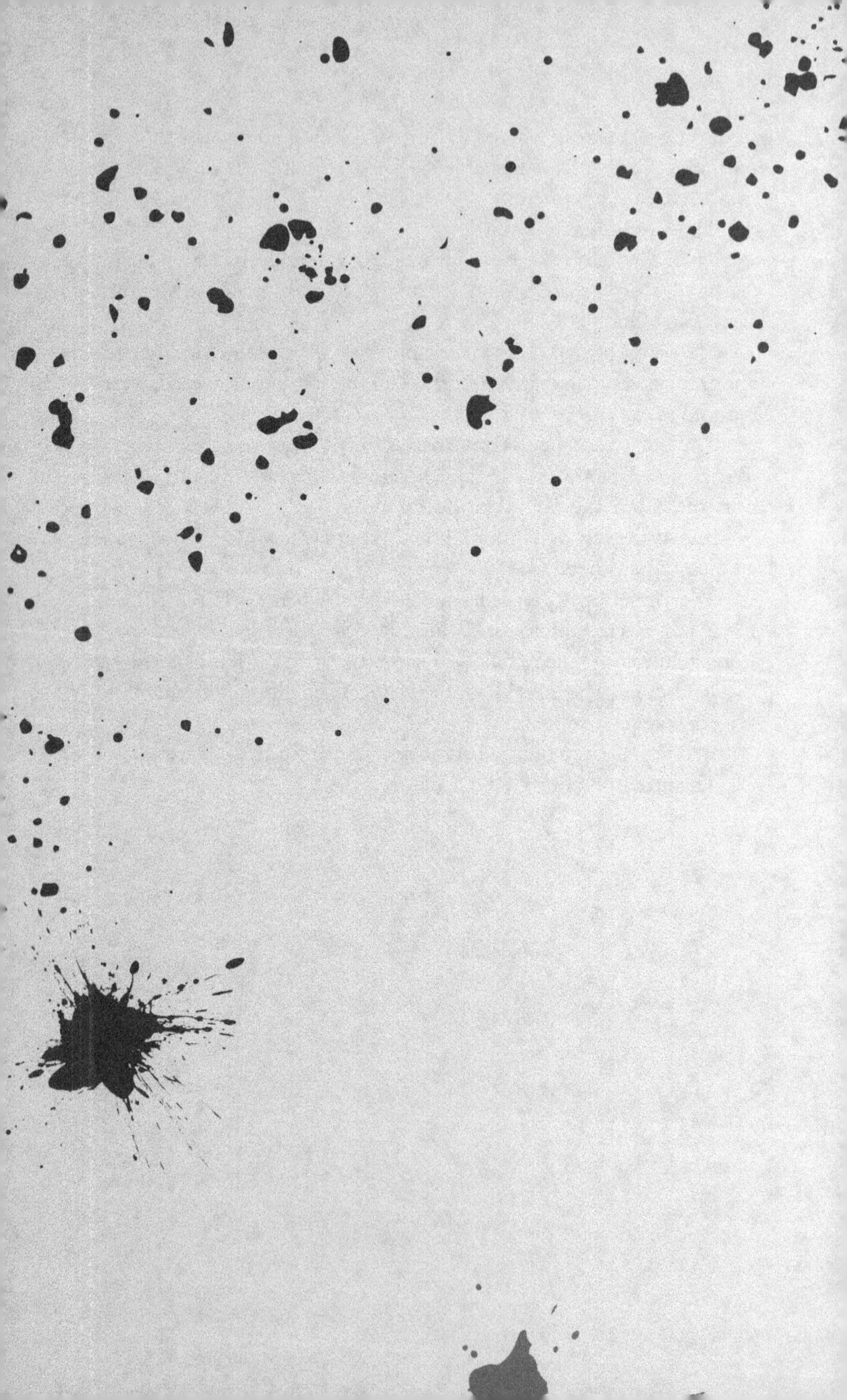

Predator

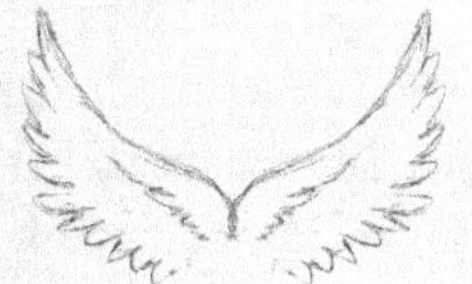

Monster.

I've been called this many times throughout my life, but this is one of those pesky words that has multiple meanings.

Monsters are great, inhuman beasts, like those featured in Terrick's fiction books and Ramiel's artworks. But they are also wicked, depraved, and cruel humans.

But what *made* a human wicked, depraved, or cruel? What threshold must they have crossed?

Were they considered cruel when they acknowledged but ignored the suffering of a neighbor? When a human submitted to their base, animalistic instincts, were they regarded as depraved? What of those driven to violence by fear or grief? Or those who'd see a loved one in danger but choose to flee and save themselves?

Were all who killed, no matter the reason for their action, befitting of the title *monster*?

Was I truly a monster? Or were they?

Perhaps the answer is as complex and confusing as the word itself.

Perhaps we are all monsters.

* * *

I don't know how long I huddled in the forest in the aftermath of Swindon's destruction. An hour, perhaps two. I held no remorse for what I had done. Or perhaps I did and my emotions were simply too ~~tumoltuous~~—tumultuous for me to grasp. I certainly mourned, but my thoughts were filled only with the Swindon of my childhood; the jovial place I'd once called home. The warm, cherished memories of a bygone life.

Memories that now lay scattered in the ashes behind me.

I shed many tears that day, for the life I'd lost and the innocence that had been taken from me far too soon. For the hurt I'd caused and for the lack of sorrow I felt at the demise of the town and its people.

My tears were only soothed when Icarus's warm muzzle pressed against my hip, searching for the berries and leaves I often kept in the fold of my tunic. But my outer garment had long since disintegrated, along with Icarus's treats.

Still, he searched for them, nudging me insistently. And upon seeing my mount covered in soot and ash but otherwise unharmed, I was overcome with giddy relief. I flung my arms around his neck, pressing my tear-stained face to his mane. Icarus did not recoil. He'd witnessed the full capacity of my power, and he regarded me no differently than he had before. I was, to him, still the human who carried the delightful snacks in the fold of her tunic.

Animals were willing to forgive. Humans weren't.

"Thank you, my friend," I whispered.

He had helped me greatly, and in more ways than one. In fleeing the fire, Icarus had kept Ramiel's letter safe.

My satchel remained securely fastened to the pommel of the saddle, its contents undisturbed and unburnt. I rummaged through it, retrieving a fresh tunic and set of trousers. As I slid another brown tunic over my white one and prepared to remount Icarus, the sound reached my ears: a seemingly tangible wave of ~~forlorne~~—forlorn cries and agonized keening.

I should have left Swindon to its suffering, but I was wary of doing so. Always before, when I'd fled from the destruction of a town, I'd been hunted. And I refused to repeat that malicious pattern. They would hunt me no longer.

I mounted Icarus and returned to the city.

The air was rank with the stench of decay and smoldering flesh. It unsettled my stomach, although I dared not cover my nose to lessen the smell's impact, lest the motion be seen as a weakness.

Plumes of smoke still surged from the ruined buildings. The streets were nearly impassible beneath the jagged hills of smoldering wood and bone. Icarus tensed as we came upon the rubble, but he was a faithful, steadfast stallion. Although he snorted and tossed his head in agitation, he strode through the streets, his hooves crunching over the skeletons of this once thriving town.

Swindon was no more.

People still lived, but they were little more than shadows of their former selves. Most bore burns. All were coated with ashes of the dead and seemed dazed and disoriented as they meandered through the debris.

At one time, I might have pitied them.

But humans had never pitied me, even when I'd been every bit as confused and frightened as those who now traversed Swindon's ruins.

Why should I extend them a courtesy they'd always denied me?

Upon noticing me, some survivors began to scream and hurl accusations. The shrill sounds caused my ears to ache.

"Enough!" My voice sounded far deeper than normal—the voice of an angry adult rather than a frightened child.

The townspeople stopped, perhaps too weak to continue fussing or too frightened to disobey a command.

"I have never..." I began, pausing to comfort Icarus when he was spooked by the collapse of a ~~delapidated~~ dilapidated building. Once he steadied, I began again, "I have *never* wished to hurt humans. I've repeated this statement countless times, but you seem incapable of understanding. So, I shall repeat it only once more, and hope you heed my word. I do not wish to harm you. But I will *not* allow you to harm me. Not anymore."

Dozens of glassy, frightened eyes stared at me. In the distance, someone retched; others begged for water. Those who were sprawled along the streets, blistered, mutilated, and tentatively clinging to life, pleaded for an end to their suffering.

"I know word spreads quickly in this land," I spoke over the torment. "Gossip, I suppose, is a part of the human condition. But if you share the news of what happened here today, share this message as well. My name is Lasair. I *am* Seruf's ~~protojay~~ protégé. And I need to travel across Sakar. If I am left to journey in peace, I shall not harm another human. If I am attacked—"

I faltered when movement caught my eye.

A woman lay on the ground, not a body length away from where Icarus and I stood. She was badly disfigured; the mucusy remnants of her blistered flesh had sealed her eyes closed and flattened the hooked curve of her nose. But I still recognized her.

Carragh. The once kindly bread maker who'd fancied Terrick.

She stretched a mottled, trembling arm toward me, as though recognizing my voice.

I looked away. "If I am attacked again," I shouted, "Swindon will not be the only town I destroy."

* * *

Was my request so difficult?

I thought it simple: Let me alone, and I'll let you alone. But evidentially, 'twas a concept beyond the humans' comprehension.

Twice, I was attacked.

The first was courtesy of five men who cornered me near the river. All had survived the ~~massacar~~ massacre at Swindon but had seen my fire consume their loved ones. A part of me sympathized with them. I was well ~~acquainted~~ acquainted with the hopeless grief in their eyes. So, I *tried* to be sensible.

"I'm sorry for the pain I have caused. Truly." As the mounted men surrounded me, I dismounted from Icarus. "But if you do not leave here, I will—"

The knife whistled as it traveled through the air and embedded itself into my leg, piercing my flesh and puncturing my bone. But confoundingly, I felt no pain.

I became ever more befuddled when my fire emerged. I had not sensed it fighting the confines of my flesh as I always had before. Instead, it arrived swiftly and rose to heights greater than

I'd ever seen, swallowing not just the men and their horses but any vegetation and wildlife dwelling nearby. Thankfully, some creatures fled to the safety of the river's rushing waters, including dear Icarus.

Then, as quickly as it had flared, the fire dissipated.

It was an oddity I quickly dismissed. I had, after all, been stunned by the knife puncturing my left thigh, a wound that only began to ache after my flame left me.

When I was attacked again less than a day later, by a much larger group of men and women, my fire acted as normal.

I did not try to reason with this group, for they approached me at a full gallop, their weapons drawn, intent on spearing me at speed. I dismounted, chased Icarus away—a pattern he'd grown accustomed to—and beseeched my fire to emerge. It did so slowly this time, once again coating my body in a prickling itch as it burst through my flesh. It was not as large nor as violent as it had been the day before, but it made easy work of my would-be attackers.

The horses, thankfully, had more sense than the humans aboard their backs. They threw their riders and scattered, evading my flame. I was relieved at that, for although I felt little remorse for the humans I killed, my heart ached for the animals.

And the horses proved useful. Because after the humans died...

It both shames and horrifies me to write this now. I'd almost considered omitting it, but memories such as these have long burdened my heart and mind, and I'd like to be rid of them.

That afternoon, beneath an increasingly cloudy sky, I scavenged for the bodies that remained intact, of which there were three: two women and a man. They would not be easily identifiable with their grotesquely mottled flesh, but they did not need to be. The mere sight of them would be enough.

It took a great effort to lift those bodies onto the backs of three skittish horses, especially as the festering wound on my thigh made me unstable. But I was fueled by anger, hatred, hurt, and a determination to send my message.

Once the three ~~maymed~~ (this is a tricky word, considering how short it is) maimed corpses were secured to the saddles, I sent the horses away, bidding them to take their masters home.

* * *

I did not know if my message had been received and finally understood or if I'd encountered a prolonged bout of good fortune, but the rest of my trek was completed in relative peace.

The spring days turned ever warmer. I normally did not begrudge the sun its heat, but I was hesitant to shed my outer garment and reveal the white tunic, so I sweltered beneath my layers of clothing.

Although I stayed near the river and was easily able to keep the wound on my thigh clean and dressed, I could do nothing for the pain. It became nauseating, especially as I spent long hours in the saddle, using my legs to signal Icarus and keep him steady.

And my fire grew ever more temperamental.

One morning, a tongue of flame appeared above the wound as I cleaned it. It lasted only a heartbeat, vanishing before I could douse it with water, but it left me shaken for the rest of the day. On another occasion, thin tendrils of fire curled protectively around my thigh. The flames were so slight, they were hardly discernible in the afternoon sun, and I rode some distance before the aroma of burning fabric and leather alerted me to their presence.

'Twas the wound, I believed firmly, that had set my power on edge. I did not want to consider the other possibility: that I'd made a grave error in allowing my power to run unbridled at Swindon. After all, one could not rein in a stampeding stallion once the bridle was removed.

As the days passed, I longed for the journey to end. I'd begun to imagine myself returning to Ramiel's side after successfully delivering his letter. He would smile upon seeing me disembark from my vessel and sweep me into a loving embrace. Perhaps Raphael would provide a response that would leave Ramiel so ~~boyed~~—buoyed, I'd be rewarded with a kiss. Or perhaps Ramiel would be so appreciative of what I had done for him, he would kiss me regardless.

Those imaginings deepened my resolve to continue onward, even as they also left me aching to turn back.

I was sure my fire would be more at ease once I returned to Ramiel. *I* would be more at ease. But until my missive had been delivered, I would endure my power's restlessness. I had no other choice—I would *not* disappoint Ramiel, not when he was relying on me to do such an important task.

When I finally glimpsed my destination against the pale dawn of my fourth week in Sakar, I could not stop myself from making a noise of ~~exhileration~~—exhilaration, which startled the normally stoic Icarus.

I bent to stroke his neck, an apology for the fright, and startled myself when I noticed the flame wrapped around my middle fingers. Once again, it disappeared before it could harm Icarus or damage my reins, but its fleeting presence deepened the yearning to return home.

I trembled as I cantered Icarus up to the broad, rock-faced wall erected around Niall's city.

"Halt!" a male voice shouted from atop the wall.

I drew Icarus to a stop and angled my head back, trying to discern the speaker. But the wall was too high, and the early morning too full of fog, for me to see properly around the shadowed edges of my vision.

"Who are you?" the voice called, gentler this time. A conversation rather than a command.

My skin still prickled. Not with the advent of my fire but with the unsettling sensation one gets when one enters a place that is entirely foreign to them and becomes stricken with the notion that they've visited it before, perhaps in a forgotten childhood memory.

A tremor gripped my spine. "I am a traveler."

"From where?" The voice pressed.

"Muirin."

"You're a long way from the coast. What brings you this far inland?"

This I could not answer truthfully, but I fabricated a lie easily enough. "I'm told the castle at Niall is a resplendent sight to behold. And I wish to see if its splendors were truthfully reported."

"Indeed? And who told you this?"

I allowed my eyes to scale the height of the wall, but I still could not see through the fog coating the top. "A friend."

'Twas not a lie; the decrepit farmer had been friendly enough when he offered his advice. And a friend had also spoken of Niall on the night I fled Darfield.

"An old friend?" the voice pressed. "Or a current one?"

Irritation pricked my stomach. "I don't see how this is relevant, but it was an old friend."

"Truly? Well, that's a pity."

"How is it a pity…" I trailed off, stunned, as a figure leapt from atop the wall. The man plummeted to a low-hanging sconce and grasped onto it, halting his descent. There he swung, his feet waggling playfully in the air before he released his hold and gracefully dropped the last short distance to the ground.

He turned to me then with a self-satisfied smile as he brushed his walnut-brown hair out of his remarkably blue eyes.

My heart seized, and I loosed an unsteady breath to alleviate the tightness in my chest.

"A pity," Quinn said, "because I was hoping to be a *current* friend."

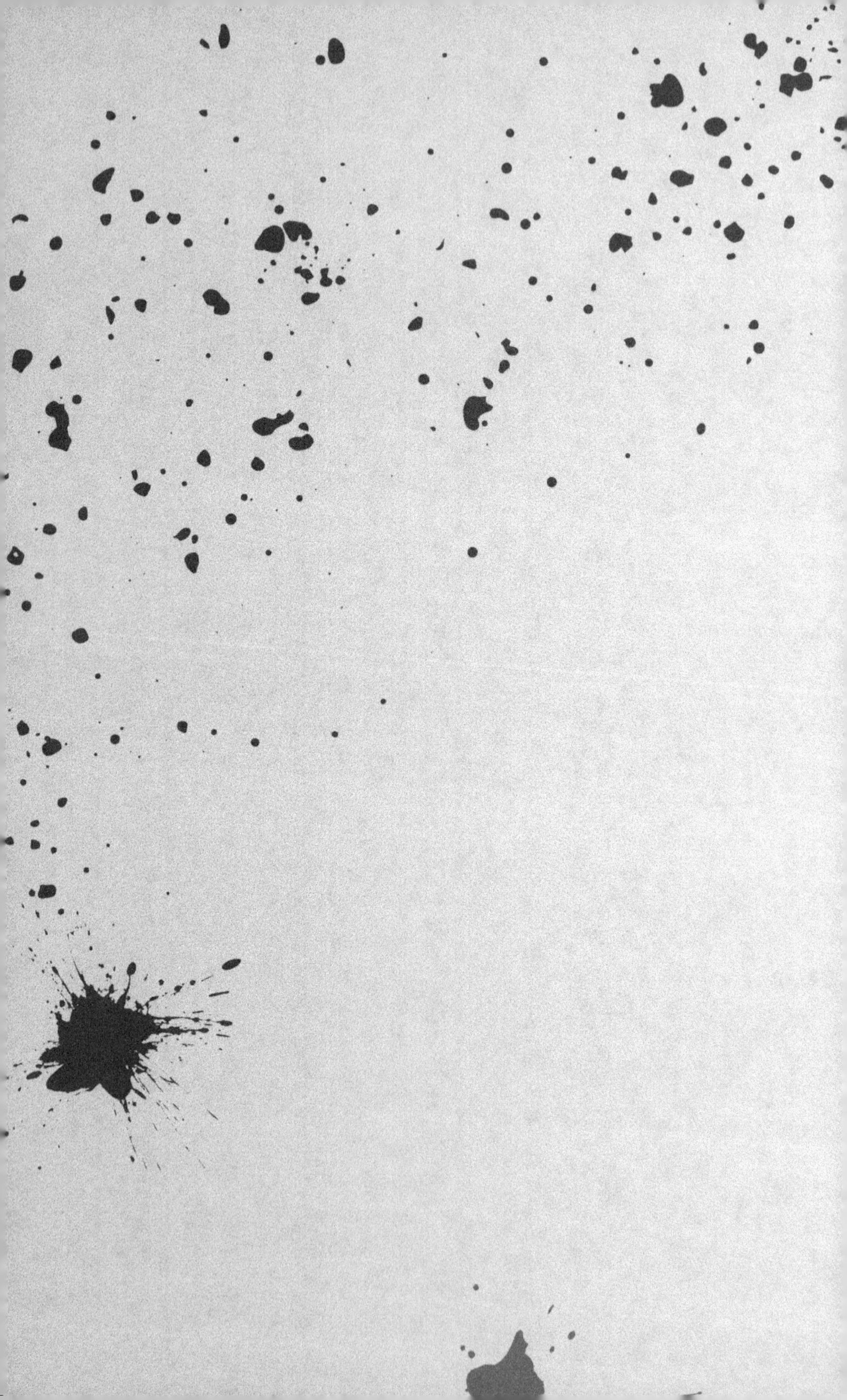

Quinn

The past year and a half had been *very* kind to Quinn.

Thick bands of muscle swathed his previously lean body. With his tunic sleeves rolled to his elbows, I glimpsed the flex of those muscles as he lifted a hand to his head, idly combing his walnut hair. His face had lost much of its round, boyish charm. Instead, the lines of his jaw and cheeks were hard, softened only by the coat of dark whiskers that encircled them.

His appearance left me utterly flabbergasted. (This is a word, yes? I heard it once and liked how its sound captured the sensation of being too stunned to form a coherent thought.)

And time, it seemed, had not dampened Quinn's delight in disobeying orders. Not two heartbeats after he landed, a din of admonishments followed him.

"Quinn! You bloody reckless bastard," a man cried.

"Stand aside!" a woman commanded.

Quinn looked over his shoulder, waved to the people atop the wall, and sidled around Icarus to stand at my right side.

"What are you—" I began.

"Shhh," he hissed. "Roise has an arrow aimed at you."

Anger seized my belly. The *audacity* of humans. They would shoot a stranger who had not threatened violence?

"We know what happened at Swindon," Quinn said. "And I

cannot claim you are an innocent traveler when you ride to our gates wielding fire." His gaze fell to my hand, where a pale wisp of flame flickered above my knuckles, thankfully a safe distance from Icarus's mane.

Once again, I had not felt the emergence of my power, and its sudden, almost ~~innoccuous~~ innocuous appearance alarmed me. But I said nothing.

The flame vanished as quickly as it had appeared.

"Have you come to destroy Niall, Lass?" Quinn cupped his hands behind his head, creating a ~~fasade~~ facade of lazy relaxation.

"If I were planning such a thing, I would hardly confess it to you," I said.

"*If* you were planning such a thing, I would have thought you'd wait until you were *inside* the city before you loosed your power. But I cannot guess at your plan, nor can I speculate on how your mind works. I'm only a *former* friend, after all." His blue eyes shone all the brighter when he smiled.

"And if I am here to burn Niall?" I asked.

"I suppose I would step aside and allow Roise to shoot you." He yawned.

My eyes wandered along the height of the wall. "I hardly think you're adequately shielding me."

"It was adequate enough to keep them from seeing the flame. Otherwise, Roise would have loosed the arrow already." He frowned. "Your face when you saw that flame...You seemed surprised. Have you still no control over your power?"

"I have no need to control it. I care not who it kills." A ~~taught~~ taut pain gripped my jaw as my teeth ground together. "Not anymore."

"Quinn, you are not here to woo passerby!" Roise's impatient bark tumbled from the fog-shrouded wall.

Quinn bounced on the balls of his feet and waved dismissively at his comrades.

"Idiotic boy," a man growled. "This is why I *loathe* being stationed with youngins. They have no sense."

"It would be a great pity if you were to burn me, Lass. As you can see, I have important responsibilities now." Quinn thrust his chest outward.

"I can see you are still *shirking* those responsibilities."

"It is my job to question travelers. The reasoning is admittedly petty: Niall's merchants detest competition from lesser cities. So, I am to ask any person seeking admittance into the city if they are a merchant seller. If they are, I am to then ask what wares they wish to display. *Petty*, as I said. But with these fresh sightings of the Firestarter, I have also been instructed to contain, by whatever means necessary, any who seem to be a match to her likeness. So, Lass, I beg you to forgive me, but I must ask...*What wares are you planning to sell in our city?*" He spoke his last question in a booming shout.

Icarus startled. His jarring movements sent pain to grip my wounded thigh. I swallowed my whimper as I gathered the reins into my trembling hands, steadying him. "What is wro—"

"It's another bloody merchant," came Roise's voice. "That's the fifth one this week. Fecking cads."

"Are we certain it's *only* a merchant?" queried another woman. "Quinn! What color are her eyes?"

"Blue," Quinn reported. And then, in a whisper only I could hear, he added, "It's a *partial* lie. Lilac has blue in it."

"Ach, the boy's suited to handle this one," Roise grumbled.

A strange, warm emotion unfurled inside my chest.

Quinn had helped me. *Again.*

I didn't know *why* he continued to aid me, and I wasn't entirely sure I could trust him, but my heart swelled with gratitude all the same.

"Thank you," I said.

Quinn gave me a self-satisfied smile. "Now." He lowered his arms and rested his hands upon his hips. "I've given us some moments to speak. And I'd like you to tell me, *truthfully*, why you have come to Niall. I know you have no true wish to see the castle," he added when I opened my mouth to repeat my earlier statement. "You're a bloody terrible liar, Lass."

"I am *not*."

He raised a brow.

"Lying has saved me before," I insisted.

"I *sincerely* doubt it. Likely, someone took pity on you and allowed you to believe your lie had succeeded. I would do the same if circumstances were different. But I cannot allow you into the city until you give me a truthful answer."

A truthful answer.

Ramiel had bid me not to tell any human—even old (or current) friends—about his letter. And perhaps I could have fabricated another half-truth, one that would pass even Quinn's shrewd scrutiny, but I was hesitant to lie to him.

He had, after all, saved me, even though he *knew* of the atrocities I'd committed at Swindon. He deserved my truth.

"This cannot be common knowledge, you understand?" I began.

Quinn pressed a finger to his lips and traced a small X.

It was a strange gesture, and I must have made an unkind face in reaction, if his gleeful laugh was any indication.

"It means the words are barred from leaving my lips," he told me. "Your secret stays with me, Lass."

I stared at the lips he'd so kindly drawn attention to, marveling at their lush curves. "I am here to deliver a message to Raphael," I said after I silently chided myself for my wayward thoughts. "Nothing more."

Quinn choked on an incredulous laugh. "A *message?*"

"Is that not what I said?"

"I'm assuming it was not a *human* who gave you this message?"

"No. It was not."

"Right..." He spoke the word slowly, as though savoring it. "Is this message a hostile one? Should I be attempting to take it from you?"

"I-I do not know. I haven't seen its contents."

His eyebrows drew together. "You have extraordinary self-restraint. I would not have been able to carry a message across Sakar without reading it."

"Fortunately, I am not as prone to prying as you. Even if I were, it would do me little good. I can't read."

Quinn looked puzzled by my confession, as though he believed me to be jesting but could not find the lie in my eyes. When I raised my chin, daring him to question me, he shrugged and said, "I can read it for you."

"Absolutely not. The note is meant for Raphael." Ramiel had been quite adamant about this.

"Who is, unfortunately, not here and hasn't been for some time."

A peculiar sensation swept over me, as though my belly had been shackled to Icarus's hooves. "I was told this was his home."

"So were we. But he's not been seen here since I arrived six months ago."

"Does no one know where he is?"

Quinn smiled ruefully. "Celestials don't deign to inform humans of their comings and goings." He watched me as he said this, perhaps waiting for a rebuttal.

I said nothing.

"Very well, Lass," he said, tapping his hand against his thigh, "you can enter the city and wait for Raphael's return. I will help you find accommodations, but know that I cannot aid you if you loose your flame within these walls. You *will* be killed, and your attack will be folly. Niall won't burn as easily as Swindon."

"All things made of flesh and bone are easily burned. Niall's size will not protect its humans from a ravenous flame." I attempted to say these words with the same bitterly indifferent tone Ramiel had always adopted when speaking of humans.

I failed.

Quinn's smile grew, as though he found humor in my poorly delivered threat.

"I do not wish to enter the city." My next words were plenty ~~brusk~~-brusque (which is the correct spelling?) as they were tinged with mortification.

"You could hand your letter to me." Quinn's eyes glimmered with mischief. "And be on your way."

"As I've already said, the information in this letter is not meant for you."

"I would turn it over to my commander to hold until Raphael's return."

"*After* you read it, I'm sure."

"Of course."

I'd forgotten how infectious his smile was. For although his remarks often left me with a desire to scream in frustration, I always found myself smiling back at him.

"Perhaps your commander has information you are not privy to," I said, "and is aware of when Raphael intends to return."

"Doubtful." Quinn lifted his shoulder. "He's often lamented at the fickleness of Celestials."

"That doesn't mean he's unaware of Raphael's whereabouts. Perhaps if you were to tell him of my letter..."

"Or I could simply *give him* your letter so he will not have cause to question how you came to possess a message from The Conqueror."

"Will he not question the same of you if you hand him the letter?"

"Certainly, but he knows me. And I can spin a lie more believably than you, Lass." Quinn stepped closer to me.

I pulled on the reins, drawing Icarus back.

"If you do not trust me to deliver your letter," Quinn said with a wink, "you can still await Raphael's return without dwelling in the city. There are shelters in the woods. I can tell my commander you wish to harvest the land and are asking to be recognized so you are not detained if you approach the gates again."

A barrage of feelings waged war within me.

I was warmed by his considerations but suspicious of his reasons for helping me.

I was overjoyed to see him, even though his reappearance made me ache for things I'd always wanted but had long since given up hope of obtaining.

"Why are you helping me?" I managed to say. "Again? After what I did at Swindon and Darfield...surely assisting me puts you in danger of punishment."

Quinn's widening smile dimpled his left cheek. "I wish to keep you nearby."

"No doubt hoping to steal the letter, yes? Or perhaps you think it safer to kill me in my sleep?"

He clicked his tongue. "Your thorns have sharpened since we last met, but you need not build them so high, Lass. At least, not with me. I do not have such elaborate plans. I only want to be better ~~aquainted~~ —acquainted with you. Each time we met before, one of us was fleeing from something. We now have a moment to stand still and simply know each other. I want to take advantage of it." He moved closer, grasping Icarus's bridle to keep him still when I tried to back him away.

"You're daft," I said. "Utterly brainless. To stand so close to me when you know—"

"Ah, this is why I enjoy your company!" He chuckled and squeezed my thigh. "You keep me humble."

"There isn't a humble bone in your body."

"Perhaps not. But I believe you will carve one for me." His smile grew ever more dazzling. "I still like your spark, Lass." This was said in a low, gruff whisper. A sound that left my skin covered in those prickling goose bumps.

Quinn drew away, sliding his hand from my thigh.

And I *mourned* the loss of his touch.

I was so thoroughly distracted by these unwelcome desires, it took me a moment to realize he'd healed my wound.

* * *

Deep in the woods of Niall sat a stooped wooden building. This, Quinn said when he guided me to the hut, would provide me shelter and solitude while I awaited Raphael's arrival. It was small, barely taller than Quinn and little more than a windowless room. The inside smelled of the earth after a hard day of rain, and it was furnished with only a single straw mattress. It was a structure intended to provide shelter to those hunting in Niall's woods, not a long-term dwelling.

But shaded by towering trees, which were beginning to grow their summer leaves, the hut became a peaceful home.

Days passed in a lazy trickle.

Quinn visited me nearly every afternoon, although he could not steal away for long. He brought samplings of food from his preferred merchants, flasks of his favorite ale (which tasted akin to horse urine that had been left to fester in the summer sun), and he regaled me with tales of the vapid lives of Niall's residents.

Occasionally, he would pry, asking of my life at Darfield before Terrick's death or questioning what had become of me after I'd left with Seruf. I never answered, still wary of his intentions and sure he would report any useable information to his commander.

But he oft replied to his own inquiries. When a question about Terrick went unanswered, Quinn responded with a story of his own mother, whom he had not seen since he was turned into a hybrid.

"She used to *beat* me," he said as he leaned against the tree opposite me, idly plucking leaves off a fallen twig. "Five elder brothers, and she laid not a hand on one of them. It was always me who suffered her wrath."

"I can't imagine why," I said. It was easy to envision Quinn as the miscreant amongst his siblings who drove his poor mother to madness.

Quinn's lips curled. "Lass, I don't know what you're imagining, but I was a delightfully well-behaved child."

"I'm sure your mother begged to differ."

"She was a mad old cad." This was said with a wash of affection. "But she cried when Raphael took me." He paused, watching a leaf flutter to the ground. "I was seven years of age, and I was *forbidden* from returning home. I've not seen her or my brothers since."

Sorrow filled me. I knew all too well the pain of being separated from a mother, and it saddened me that Quinn had also suffered such a fate.

But Quinn shook his head, laughed, and pointed his now-bare twig at me. "Do you remember when you became a hybrid, Lass? It was a bloody painful experience, wasn't it?"

I did not answer. But Quinn was far too happy to relay his misery.

His visitations, brief as they were, had become an addiction.

I'd always had an inexplicable liking for this blue-eyed boy who I'd known only in passing. But seeing him each day, conversing with him, watching him delight in our playful bickering, and noting how careful he was with me, respecting my desire for distance and secrecy while never letting me delve into lonely melancholy...

It felt as though I was falling into a pit. One that had beckoned me to leap into its depths by offering ~~wonderous~~—wondrous, exhilarating emotions. The bottom of this pit held naught but pain and misery, despite its fanciful promises, but each time Quinn smiled or spoke or teased, I plummeted ever further.

When he wasn't there, I fought to banish him from my mind and despaired whenever I gazed into the trees, waiting to hear his horse's hooves.

In his absence, my days were blissfully boring affairs.

I awoke each morning, often nauseated and shaken by the gruesome images that still plagued my dreams. Bathing in the cold waters of the nearby pond chased the dregs of sleepiness and the spindles of unease away, although I dared not drink from the pool. It made me ill, as stagnant water was wont to do. So Icarus and I made a twice daily trek through the woods to the babbling stream, which offered fresher water.

At night, Icarus and I rested together outside my hut, listening to the chirping of insects and animals. I feasted on the food Quinn had left me, Icarus filled his belly with grass and leaves, and we both ended our days contented and with full bellies.

I preferred to sleep outside, with the breeze skimming my cheeks, safely away from anything that might burn if my fire raged. It never did, even when my nightmares left me weeping and aching with sorrow. Instead, the flame had begun to emerge when I was contented. The outbursts were mercifully brief, the fire rarely strong enough to wield damage, but their frequency left me unnerved.

The incident at Swindon seemed to have changed something within me.

But I put the worries out of my head as best I could, certain Ramiel would have the answers. If, I often thought glumly, I ever returned to him.

It was my eighth day in the woods when my fire made another frustratingly brief and sudden appearance. I'd been eating the berries I'd plucked from one of the shrubs surrounding my hut. Elder berries, Terrick had once called these. They had been his favorite.

The flame lingered only a heartbeat but turned the fruit in my hand to a ~~vichid—vishid~~-viscid (I should learn to avoid using words I have difficulty spelling simply because I like the way they sound) liquid that clung stubbornly to my skin. I attempted to remove it by wiping my quivering hands on the leaves, but the tenacious liquid remained. I'd begun to trek to the lake when I was halted by the sound of hoofbeats.

Icarus, standing on the other side of the hut, raised his head and pricked his ears.

I froze, the stickiness on my hands forgotten, as Quinn's brown and white mare burst through the trees at a brisk trot. Quinn sat astride her back, smiling down at me.

The tension in my belly melted into excitement. "Has Raphael returned home?" I asked, as I always did upon Quinn's arrival.

Quinn drew his horse to a halt and frowned mockingly. "Lass, you continue to wound me by speaking of another man in my presence. Do you realize the damage such a slight could do to a boy's ego?"

"Your ego is large enough to be impervious to damage."

"You offend me again. And here I always think you'll be happy to see a friendly face…"

"Perhaps if the face wasn't yours."

Quinn's deep laugh was harsh and breathy, almost grating to the ears. But it caused a violent stirring in my heart, as though the organ had turned itself upside down.

I *enjoyed* throwing ~~barberous~~—barbarous words at him because he delighted in them, and I delighted in watching his glee.

It was outlandish. That this boy I knew so little about held such sway over my emotions.

"I'm sorry to say that Raphael has not returned, Lass." Quinn dismounted and stroked his mare's muzzle. "So you'll have to deal with my wretched face today. For the *entirety* of today. I am off duty! And I thought, perhaps, you'd like to ride with me. I'm assuming you have not found the waterfall yet?"

"I have not."

"Excellent! We will go today."

"Did I say I wished to see the waterfall?"

"No." Once again, his broad smile revealed the dimple in his cheek. "But given how miserable you often are, I believe you *need* to see the waterfall."

The sight of that dimple left my belly tightening against a warm rush of perplexing emotions. Perhaps because it was so boyish and endearing, a contrast to his otherwise harsh and angular face.

"I am *not* miserable," I said.

He snorted, a sound akin to the one Icarus made when he sniffed for food.

"I am not," I insisted. For I truly wasn't, although I've been told (by many people) that my face rests in a sour expression that most mistake for contrariness.

"So you say." Quinn plucked a leaf from the ground and dropped it on top of my head. "But you *rarely* allow yourself to smile."

"Sakar has given me little reason to smile." I brushed his leaf away.

"We shall remedy that." He clapped his hands against his thighs. "Saddle your horse, Lass! I will have you *shining* with glee by day's end, mark my words. By the way...have I told you how I love your tunic?" he added, motioning to the white garment I never concealed in his presence. "You are *radiant* in it."

He had, of course, said this before. Many times. Each time, I heated beneath his praise—but not in a way that signaled my fire. This was a deep, pleasurable warmth the likes of which I had never felt before, even during my days with Ramiel.

I was utterly besotted with this blue-eyed boy.

And it frightened me.

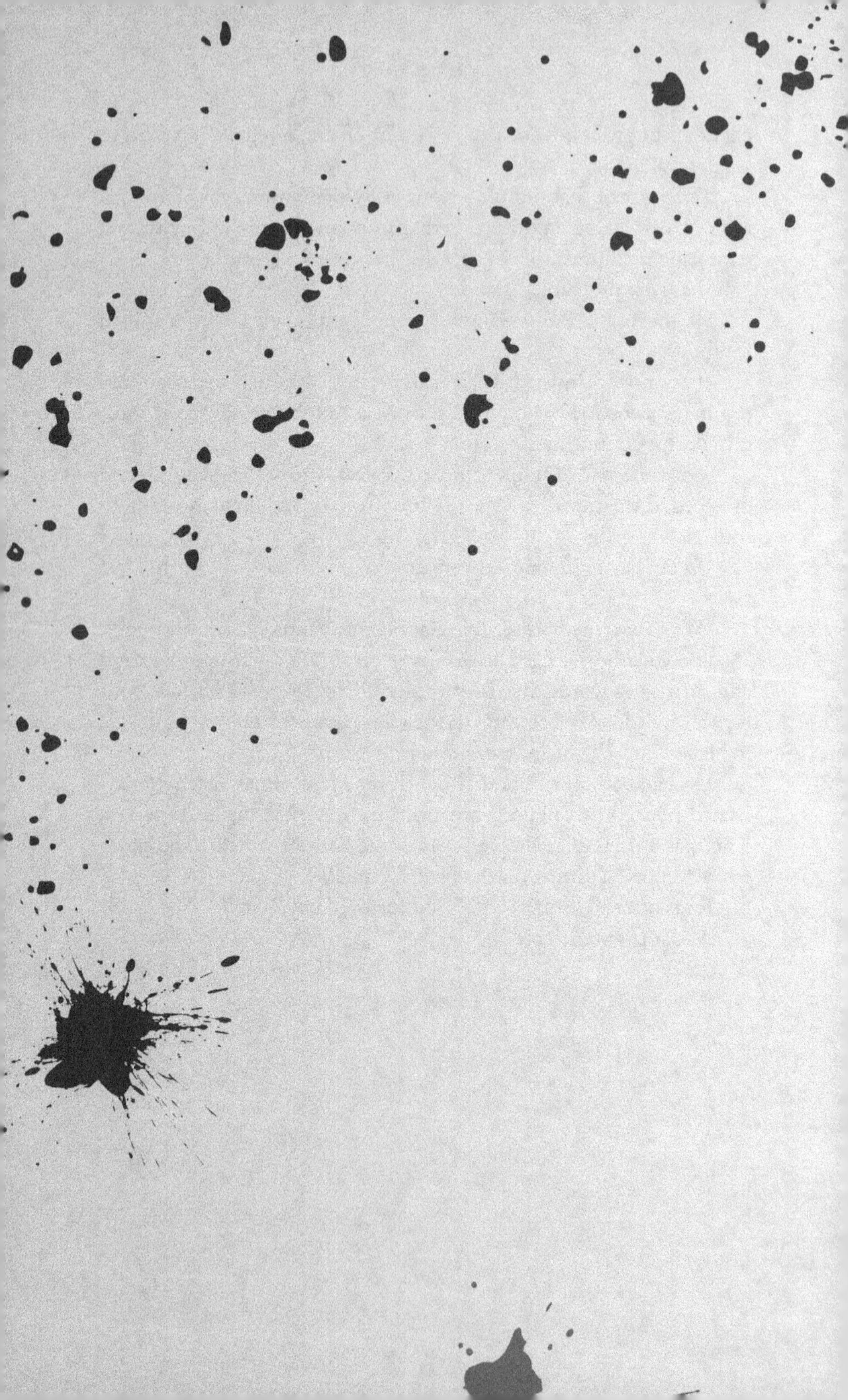

Waterfall

As we mounted our horses and traveled through the woods, we made idle conversation.

Quinn asked me where I'd dwelled the past year and a half. A question I did not answer, so he told me he'd resided for several months at Bullmar, a city near the ill-fated Vaporia, where he'd seen me leave with Seruf. Until he'd grown restless and, in an irresponsible manner so representative of Quinn, he fled Bullmar, abandoning his duties and seeking refuge at Niall.

"Still in the fecking army," he bemoaned. "The curse of being a bloody Healer. But Niall has a more ~~lustrus~~—lustrous atmosphere and taverns that allow me to play on occasion."

"So you've returned to the harp, then?" I asked.

"Sadly, no. There is not a pub in Niall that has a harp. But I've grown fond of the lute." He turned, propping one hand on his mare's backside for balance as she walked in front of Icarus and me, and gave me a puckish smile. "I've also been told I have the *best* voice in the city."

"Doubtful," I said.

"People oft *sing* my praises."

"They're likely wailing from the assault to their ears."

"I knew you would think me a liar. So, I shall demonstrate.

Consider yourself lucky, Lass. The girls of Niall *beg* to have me serenade them." He cleared his throat, threw his head back, and bellowed,

> *"There once was a lass who laughed for me*
> *As a diversion so I could be free."*

"That," I winced, "is *horrid.*"

'Twas not me making a sardonic jest; his grating, warbling tenor was *dreadful.*

And he seemed aware of his shortcomings as a vocalist, for he waggled his eyebrows. "You don't enjoy my singing?"

"I'd rather have my ears speared with a sword."

"You simply haven't heard the best part of the song." He cast both his hands into the air, screaming to the heavens.

> *"Her laugh was akin to a goat's yell,*
> *But in love with her I still fell.*
> *Her eyes like thistle, her blood like fire,*
> *Ensnared, my heart could not deny her."*

My lungs, it seemed, had forgotten their purpose. But as I opened my mouth, unsure of whether I would scold Quinn for likening me to a goat or bluster in mortification over the declaration I was certain was false, even as my heart yearned for it to be true, his mare startled. She leapt into the thickets, panicking when her forelegs became ensnared in the vines. Quinn laughed as he clung to her back.

"It seems your horse agrees with my assessment of your singing," I said.

"Indeed. It's my misfortune that I'm out here with two very difficult-to-please ladies." He righted himself in the saddle, patted the mare's neck, and glanced at me again. "You are quite correct, though. I *am* an appalling singer."

Several moments later, as we continued through the woods,

Quinn began thumping his hands against the pommel of his saddle, creating a gentle, agreeable rhythm. An appalling singer he might've been, but his hands were still capable of crafting sensational music, even without his harp.

It was not a hard trek to the waterfall. The trees and underbrush were thick, but the ground was level and firm. We could've quickened our pace, but Quinn seemed content with the walk, likely because he spent half the journey facing the wrong way in the saddle.

"At some point, you'll be stricken by a low-hanging limb," I berated when he turned and tossed a pinecone at me.

"I'm trusting you to tell me if you see something obscuring my path," he said.

"I will not."

"Then I shall be rendered unconscious. And you will need to tend to me."

"I won't do that either." But I would. And he knew it as well as I.

He plucked a leaf from a branch and blew it in my face. When I hastily raised my hand to catch it, he doubled over, seized by uncontrollable laughter.

The sun had reached its highest point by the time we arrived at the waterfall—which was hardly a spectacle, considering we stood atop it. From here, we saw naught but a narrow rivulet that twined and twisted around weather-worn rocks before tumbling off the edge of the cliff. Its waters raged so loudly, Quinn and I had to shout to hear each other.

"We must go down." Quinn dismounted and loosened his mare's cinch.

"Go down?" I asked.

"There's a path. It's easy to navigate, and the horses will be fine here. Come on." He tugged my leg when I was slow to dismount.

Instinctively, I recoiled from his touch. Not because I found it unpleasant. Rather the opposite; the warmth of his hand seeping through the fabric of my trousers was a comfort, one I would've loathed to see ravaged by my flame.

Quinn immediately withdrew his hand. "Apologies," he murmured as he turned back to his mare.

I dismounted, shame and discomfiture squeezing my chest, and loosened Icarus's cinch. After ascertaining the letter was safely concealed within my satchel—as Quinn was quick-fingered and had a penchant for sneakiness—I joined him at the waterfall's crest.

The roaring water was deafening as it plummeted the length of the cliff and into the pool below. So when Quinn asked me an outrageous question, I thought the noise had caused me to mishear.

"Excuse me?" I asked.

He smiled and lowered his head, placing his mouth closer to my ear, then repeated the question. "Are you still unable to swim?"

"S-swim?" A cold, nervous sweat dampened my back as I stared at the frothing waters. "I thought you said there was a path?"

"Oh, there is," he said. "But the shortcut is far more exhilarating."

"And the shortcut would be...?"

Quinn's smile broadened as he pointed to the pool below. "We jump."

"Absolutely not," I said. "The fall would crush us!"

"If that were true," Quinn chuckled, "nearly every youngster in Niall would be long dead. 'Tis a common game, Lass, to dive off this cliff."

It seemed impossible that one could survive plunging such a dizzying distance into unkind waters. "It's a barbaric game." I tucked my hands behind my back, praying the fire would not make an appearance. "Tempting death by leaping from a cliff."

"We prefer the word '*fun*,'" Quinn said. "The pool is deep, and the distance is not enough to harm a person."

"It will harm me. *I cannot swim!*"

"Yes, but *I* can. I asked if you could only to gauge if you would need my assistance. You needn't worry, Lass. I would not let you drown."

I watched as the hissing river rushed by us. Its waters seemed *angry* as they gathered momentum to take the fall.

Angry or perhaps *enlivened*.

"The leap is thrilling." Quinn kept his mouth close to my ear when he spoke so I could hear him, but he refrained from touching me. "It's the reason so many, young and old alike, travel here. And it's why I've brought you. Tell me, Lass, when was the last time you allowed yourself to feel joy? To partake in a silly action simply because it's exciting?"

I folded my arms over my chest but said nothing. In truth, I couldn't remember the last time I had experienced joy as he'd described. Surely my time in Swindon with Terrick had provided numerous such moments. But on that day, mere weeks after I'd destroyed my childhood home, those golden memories seemed little more than a dream.

Quinn stretched a hand toward me. "Will you take the leap with me, Lass?"

I stared at his hand, tempted, but did not take it. "And what if I do not find joy in this plummet? What if I become so frightened, my power looses itself upon you?"

Quinn's laughter boomed, but he tried to suppress it with a cough upon seeing my agitation.

"You think this funny?" I seethed. "When you *know* I can't control—"

"You didn't think that excuse through, did you, Lass? We're dropping into *water*," he said. "I doubt even your flame can survive such a submersion."

Heat crawled along my skin—not from the emergence of my power, merely an uncomfortable sense of embarrassment. Quinn, of course, was correct. That pool was likely the only place he would truly be safe from me.

But I was, and still am, prideful. So rather than admit my oversight, I grasped his hand and dragged him to the edge of the cliff.

His soft laugh warmed my insides. But upon looking down, a cold sensation invaded my belly, and the stone beneath me seemed suddenly unsteady.

"I'd advise you *not* to look below your feet if you're averse to heights," Quinn said.

The dizziness eased when I raised my gaze to the blue-skied horizon. But now my stomach rippled as though I'd ~~injested~~—ingested a large quantity of winged insects.

Fluttery, I believe this sensation is called.

Quinn was far too close. Not touching me, aside from where I'd grasped his hand, but I sensed the waves of warmth radiating from his body and scented the earthen aroma which clung to his skin. And I longed, *hungered*, to feel him.

His hair, which looked as though it would be softer than rabbit's fur, beseeched me to comb my fingers through the strands. The snatches of tanned skinned swathing his neck demanded my caress. But 'twas the plump curve of his lips which called to me the loudest. I wondered, feverishly, how they would feel pressed against my mouth.

All at once, the plummet seemed far less terrifying than remaining atop the cliff.

I flung myself over the edge, pulling Quinn with me. As my body fell, my innards felt as though they'd been left clinging to the cliff face. It was an *appalling* sensation.

And a thrilling one.

The drop took mere seconds, but it created such a stir within me, I had to scream to release the wild emotions churning inside my chest. Beside me, his hand still clasped in mine, Quinn hollered something. But his words were lost as we hurtled into the water.

The cold bit my flesh, even through the fabric of my tunic, and caused me to take an ill-timed gasp. A plume of water rushed into my mouth. I choked, but as I was now fully submerged, it only brought more water into my lungs.

The ~~exhileration~~—exhilaration from the fall contorted into panic.

I'd been in this position once before, thrashing and choking, straining to reach the surface and watching it drift farther away.

Before I'd begun to flail in earnest, two hands fitted themselves beneath my arms, holding me steady. Even in the murky darkness of the pool, Quinn's blue eyes shone with a vibrant ~~hugh~~—hue. He held me close to him as he swam for the surface.

When we emerged, the air did not bring immediate relief. I continued coughing, expelling the water that had entered my lungs —a ~~grizzly~~-grisly sight for Quinn to endure, I was sure. But he said nothing as he drew me to his side and kicked lazily, moving us away from the rushing fall and into calmer waters. His hand moved against my hip in a soft, circular motion. "If you had waited," he laughed when I'd finished ~~regurjitating~~—regurgitating water, "I would have told you to take your last inhale *before* we hit the pool."

I glowered at him, which, as usual, only broadened his smile.

"Are you alright, Lass?" he asked, his voice gentle.

I turned from him—as much as I dared, at least. With my feet dangling helplessly in the water, I was not keen to break his hold. Beside us, the waterfall cascaded down, creating a cool, crisp mist that colored in the dappled sunlight. It was nearly awe-inspiring in its height. I could not see the clifftop. Even as I angled my head, placing the cliffs directly in the center of my damaged vision, I could not discern where the rocks ended and the clouds above began. And the thought that I had leapt from such a height had that fluttery sensation beginning anew within me. My heart swelled with mirth, becoming so full, my body simply couldn't contain it.

I laughed. For the first time in many years.

I'd forgotten what a powerful action laughter was, capable of soothing sorrow, pain, and fear. And seemingly able to reverse time.

As I floated in that pool with Quinn, I became a child again, giddy and carefree.

Perhaps a bit *too* carefree.

When Quinn tightened his hold on me, likely because my exuberance had shifted me out of his grasp, I turned my gaze to him again.

"I see age has not taken away your proclivity for pig squealing, Lass," he said.

I had not the mind to respond, for I was busy observing the beads of water clinging to his eyelashes. He blinked, catching one of the droplets on his cheek, where it rolled through his whiskers and evaporated on the curve of his upper lip.

I kissed him.

And I'm not sure which of us was most surprised by my action.

I made an unseemly noise and drew away almost as quickly as I'd lunged forward.

Quinn stilled, which caused us to sink. Him more so than me. As his head disappeared beneath the surface, he pushed me upward, keeping me above water. When he reappeared, shaking his hair out of his eyes (and thus splattering my face) he did not smile. Instead, he had a stern, concentrated expression that looked unnerving on his normally ~~boyant~~—buoyant face.

Shame flooded me as he clutched my waist and began drawing me backward, swimming for the bank. "Apologies," I sputtered. "That was...well, it was quite rude. I'm afraid some of your hubris may have—"

He closed his mouth over mine, swallowing my words.

"I needed to find shallow waters." His laughter fanned across my lips. "So I could stand and kiss you properly."

My feet still dangled. "I cannot stand here."

He smiled and wrapped his arm around my midsection, gathering me to his chest.

Quinn kissed deeply. Roughly. His whiskers were coarse, and they scratched my chin and cheeks. His teeth sometimes caught on my lips. But the small, sharp stings, combined with the silken caress of his mouth and the lingering strokes of his tongue, induced a fiery ache within me. It *hurt*. So much so, I arched into Quinn, begging him to soothe the pain he'd caused. He tightened his hold, allowing the water to rock our bodies against each other. The friction worsened the heat but also seemed to be the only thing that could douse it.

"*Lass*." Quinn turned his restless lips to my neck. His teeth traced my flesh, gently at first, in a way that made me shudder, and then harshly, biting until I squirmed and gasped.

His laughter sparked something within me: an irritation that he was delighting in my torment, and an overwhelming desire to have him suffer as well. So I turned my teeth to him, biting the soft lobe of his ear.

Quinn's body bowed into mine as a stream of guttural murmurs escaped him.

Those sounds brought my movements to a halt, as they were not so dissimilar to the whimpers of those who had perished in my flame.

Horrid thoughts crawled to the forefront of my mind, ravaging the pleasurable ache and replacing it with genuine agony.

Despite the water cradling our bodies, I imagined my hands,

which were pressed to Quinn's chest, turning to flame. I envisioned him burning, *screaming*.

"Lass..."

My name escaped his lips in a shrill rush. But it wasn't until I was beneath the water, without him, that I realized I'd thrown myself out of his arms.

He dove, finding me just as I began to struggle, and brought me back to the surface. But my panic had not fully dissipated. I fought against his hold, convinced I would burn him.

"Lass...*stop*..." Quinn's pleas filled my ears as he swam, clumsily dragging me through the water. "It shallows more over here. You're alright. I won't allow you to drown."

When my feet connected with the pool floor, he released me. The water was still deep, rising nearly to my chin, but I was able to stand.

It wasn't until moments later, after I'd drawn my trembling hands out of the water and found them free of fire, that I finally calmed.

Quinn stayed an arm's length away. He was silent for a moment, allowing me to compose myself. When he finally spoke, his voice held none of its normal teasing ~~cadance~~ cadence. "Lass, as much as I'd like to consider it a compliment to have a girl dissolve into hysterics while in my arms...I saw the fear in your eyes. What happened? Did I move too quickly?"

"No." I lowered my hands back into the water. "'Twas naught to do with your skill as a kisser—or lack thereof." The jest tasted bitter on my tongue.

Quinn did not laugh. "What happened?" he asked again.

I did not respond.

For another moment, there was silence, broken only by the rushing of the fall behind us and the plopping of water splashing against our stationary bodies.

"Lass," Quinn said in a coarse whisper, "how many times have you been hurt by humans?"

A cold laugh escaped me. "An oddly worded question. Shouldn't you wish to know how many humans *I* have harmed?"

"No. I want to know who harmed *you*."

Mortification cast a hot itch over my skin. To mask my unease, I spoke with a bravado I did not truly feel. "I've slaughtered most humans I've encountered and ~~desimated~~—*decimated* the town where I lived in my youth. It matters not what slights they've committed against me."

"It matters a great deal." Quinn combed his sopping hair away from his eyes. "I know you don't wish to harm people, Lass, and I see the way you look at me sometimes, as though you are waiting for me to betray you. Or perhaps waiting for me to harm you." He paused, stirring the water with his hands. "I know you were hunted after you fled Darfield. I don't know precisely what happened, but I've heard the way people speak of you. The way some gloated about seeing you in chains. Or *beaten*..." His lips thinned. "They think you're a monster because you're different, and it frightens them. But with the way you've been treated...well, we must all seem like savage animals to your eyes."

"Humans are far worse than savage animals," I said.

"Some are, yes. Not all. Although I suppose if you've only been exposed to cruelty, it's easy to think we're all full of malice. I do not blame you, Lass, for the lives you have taken. Nor do I entirely blame them for hunting you. Fear changes people. Fear and grief. So, I'll ask again: How many times were you harmed by humans?"

At this, my mind went not to Jaxon and Darragh, nor to Byron or my many hunters, or to *any* who had physically harmed me. My thoughts turned to Swindon and the people I'd once loved. Their rejection, their *hatred*, had not physically wounded me, but it had created a lash upon my heart that would never heal.

But I could not bring myself to say this. Instead, I paddled my hands through the water, searching for Quinn's. When I found them and clasped my fingers around his, he sighed and gripped me right back, smoothing his thumb over my knuckles. "I don't understand why you treat me with such kindness," I finally admitted.

"I like you, Lass."

"You hardly know me!"

"But I'd *like* to. If you'd allow me to."

"I-I can't. I'll harm you—intentionally or not."

"A risk I'm choosing to take."

The yearning hollowing my chest was so vast, so deep, it stole my breath. "What do you *want* of me?"

Quinn frowned. "Pardon?"

"There must be a reason for your kindness. Do you seek to distract me and gain easy access to the letter?"

"You think I'm deceiving you?"

"Will the letter still be in my satchel when we return?"

"Of course. I'm with you. How could I possibly steal it?"

"You could have sent a friend to lift it while you had me distracted."

"I didn't—I wouldn't. Lass, *stop...*"

I'd released his hands with a disbelieving sound and turned away.

He touched my chin, coaxing me to face him again. "I have no wish to steal from you. But you're correct. I did want something from you today. A smile." His thumb skimmed my cheek. "Which you gave me. And you laughed as well, so I received far more than I'd expected." He moved closer, crouching until he was the same height as me. "You have lived a hard life, Lass. I saw it in your eyes on the very first day we met. Yet you still shine brighter than most—although you turn your thorns upon any who try to bask in your light." His eyes danced with impish glee when I scowled. "Since our first meeting, even as we've spent years apart, you've never been far from my thoughts. And I've always wondered how brightly you would shine if I took away some of your anguish."

He tilted his head toward me, slowly, as though waiting for me to protest. When I didn't, he pressed a lingering kiss to my brow. "If I have any ulterior motive," he murmured, his breath causing my skin to raise into those pesky goosebumps, "it is only a desire to be with you. To make you *happy.*"

"And why would you want that?" I asked. "When I continually insult you?"

He was pressed so closely to me, I felt his laugh. "Your insults hardly have teeth, Lass. And perhaps it is good for my *overly large ego* to be with someone who isn't easily charmed."

"There is little charming about you."

"I'm quite certain there is." He drew away with a smug, self-satisfied expression. "After all, my kiss left you so overwhelmed, you *melted* into the water."

I was unable to tame my boisterous laugh. "That is *not* what happened."

"Perhaps not." He pressed his lips close to my ear. "But—"

"*Oi!*"

Quinn and I both startled when a shout rang from atop the cliff.

"Quinn! I thought that was ye down there," a man called. "And with a lady, eh?"

Joy

Panic and betrayal tugged at opposite ends of my heart. "You bloody liar! You *did* send a friend to lift the letter! After you swore you hadn't," I seethed at Quinn.

"I *didn't*." Quinn's eyes widened, and the color leeched from his cheeks. "Lass, I—"

"I hope yer not down there rutting and sullyin' that water," the thunderous voice called.

"Ach, I'll wager they are. Ye better get yer skivvies back on, Quinn. We're coming down." The second speaker was every bit as blaring and boisterous as the first, although perhaps not as resonant.

I saw naught through the plumes of mist which shrouded the top of the falls. But Quinn's eyes were sharper than mine, for he glanced up and loosed a relieved laugh.

"You sent them here. Didn't you?" I spat.

"*No.* And they're not here to rob the letter, Lass. I *promise.* When I make an oath, I don't take it lightly, and I swore to protect your secrets. No one knows of the letter. Braxton and Belanna"—he tilted his chin toward the waterfall—"are members of the army, but they despise soldiering nearly as much as I do. They're here for the same reasons we are: to escape and have fun."

"Braxton and Belanna?" The names tickled my brain, drawing a long-lost childhood memory forward. Before I could grasp onto that memory, the first of the two newcomers dropped into the water with a booming ~~catterwall~~ ~~caterwal~~ caterwaul.

"Ach!" The newcomer whistled as he emerged from the depths and swam away from the roaring fall. "I'll *never* grow tired of this." He flicked his head back, shaking a wild mane of red hair out of his eyes. He was round-faced and boyish, perhaps a year or so younger than me, and recognition immediately speared me.

Braxton and Belanna.

They were twins who'd lived in Swindon, three dwellings away from Terrick's. During my first year there, they'd been closer than kin, until they'd left abruptly one summer eve. They'd been called to serve in the army, I would discover later, despite their guardian's best efforts to hide them away and keep their powers concealed.

Braxton paddled lazily away from the churning waters which surrounded the fall, an impish smile gripping his face. "Who's yer lady?" he asked Quinn.

I turned away. Quinn, no doubt sensing my tension, moved sideways, using his body to shield me from Braxton's prying eyes.

"Ach, there's no need for that, Quinn. I'll not be stealin' her from ye. But I'll not be creatin' a ruckus if she realizes yer a cocky sod and decides to leave ye for me."

Quinn laughed. "Oh, she's aware of my cockiness and scolds me for it quite frequently."

"Does she, now?" The water made a gentle plop as Braxton swam closer.

Quinn sidled to the left.

"Must be a pretty one, eh?" Braxton clicked his tongue. "If ye feel the need to hide her. Afraid she'll leave ye? *Ye could do better, lassie!*" he called to me.

At that moment, Belanna crashed into the water with an ear-aching yell.

"Oi! Belanna!" Braxton cackled when she surfaced. "Who's Quinn hidin'?"

"Why would I know?" Belanna asked.

"Yer a lady, are ye not?"

"Aye. And yer thinkin' me being a lady means I know every female in Niall, eh?"

"Don't ye?"

"Do ye know every male in Niall?"

"No."

"Then why should I know every female?"

"Because ye gossip more than I." Braxton punctuated his words with a cheery titter.

"Hardly."

Quinn remained uncharacteristically silent during this exchange. I chanced a look over my shoulder and found him standing stiffly, his arms outstretched above the water, using every part of his towering body to conceal me.

My heart gave a strange, too-hard pulse. I touched Quinn's back, intending to thank him for protecting me, but he startled at my touch. And I paused, marveling at the lines of muscle rolling beneath his wet tunic.

Quinn looked back at me, mischief dancing in his eyes.

We both flinched at Belanna's next words.

"Yer cavortin' with the Firestarter, Quinn?" she tutted. "*Naughty.*"

Quinn stiffened. "How could you possibly—"

Braxton's laugh swallowed the rest of his words. "Oi, it *is* the Firestarter, eh? I didn't see that."

"Of course ye didn't. Because ye *never pay attention.*"

"Bah. That's yer duty, Belanna."

"A hawk's nestin' in that maple," Belanna told Quinn. "Just beyond the pool. She's seen the girl's eyes."

"Ah. I saw it through the *frog*," Braxton said. "He's noticed the eyes are different. Canna say rightly how, though...He don't see color, do he? But the rat there in the thicket remarked on her eyes too..."

Belanna and Braxton were not only identical in their looks and sound, but both were also Speakers: hybrids capable of communicating with animals.

"So this is why ye've been ~~gallavantin'~~—gallivantin' off every day. *Without* inviting us," Belanna said to Quinn. "Ye've been allyin' with the Firestarter?"

"She's a childhood friend," Quinn began, "nothing more—"

He paused when I ~~wayded~~—waded out from behind him. There was, after all, no sense in continuing to hide when Braxton and Belanna had eyes in every crevice of the forest.

"Ach, blimey!" Belanna shook her sodden red hair out of her eyes as she laughed. "*Lass?*"

"Who?" Braxton's brow furrowed.

"Lass," Belanna repeated. "Terrick's daughter—do ye not remember Terrick? From Swindon?"

"Oh, aye. It was always me sent to drag ye from that bookshop, wasn't it? I'd not easily forget..." He trailed off with a gasp. "Lass? Our friend? With the goats?"

"*Yes.* Bloody fecking...do ye *ever* pay attention?"

"Only when it's important."

"Why do I not remember ye having those eyes?" Belanna asked me.

"Why do I only remember yer goats?" Braxton queried.

"I am *very* curious about this friendship." Quinn grinned, even as he kept his eyes affixed to me.

"We were babes then," Belanna said.

"Was she prickly and tempestuous?" Quinn waggled his eyebrows at me.

"Oh, aye." Belanna nodded. "Had a right smart mouth with the adults too. Me mam was always *itching* to swat her with a broom."

"Ah. So you don't brandish your thorns purely for my amusement. I'm a bit disappointed, Lass. I always believed I got preferential treatment from you." The dimple in Quinn's cheek deepened as he scooped water into his cupped hands and deposited it over my head.

"I had to grow *more* thorns to keep you away. But you continue to blunder through them." I shuddered when the water trickled down the back of my neck. I was not tall enough to drop water over his head, but I gathered what I could into my hands and thrust my arms up, dousing his face. He sputtered and then doubled over in a rumble of laughter.

An answering chuckle roiled around in my belly, but it dissipated quickly when Belanna swam closer, her shrewd gray eyes studying my face. "Ye destroyed Swindon, eh?" Her voice was calm.

"Yes." There was no sense denying it.

"Burned it right to the ground, did ye? I sent two birds there—they saw nary a building left standin'," Belanna pressed.

"Those buildings were made of wood and straw," I said. "They were easy to burn."

Belanna chuffed. "There a reason ye did it?"

"Yes."

"Care to share?"

"I hardly see the point, as my punishment will be the same regardless. I doubt *very much* your commander will care for the *why* of the situation."

"And who"—she turned her gaze to Quinn, who'd been silently watching our exchange—"said anythin' about takin' ye to our commander?"

"I'm assuming that would be your next course of action upon discovering my identity."

"Ach, that'll be the thing with assumptions: they're usually wrong, eh? Or so says me mam..." She smiled.

Quinn laughed. "My mother used to say the same."

"Oh, aye?"

"Yes. Must be something all folk say when they age."

"Heaven help us if we start spoutin' that nonsense."

"You just did," I told her.

"Ach, but I was quotin' me mam," Belanna said. "There's a difference."

"Is there? Your mother was likely told such a thing from her mother and repeated it to you. Now you've just done the same."

Belanna frowned.

"Don't use logic on her, Lass," Quinn jested. "Her wee brain struggles with such things."

"That's quite enough from ye." Belanna flicked water at Quinn. "Ruddy bastard. Anyway, I've no interest in takin' ye to our commander, Firestarter. It's a right headache to report somethin' like this to one of them dunders."

"They ask too many questions." Braxton swam next to his sister.

"And are oft left *impressed*," Quinn spat the word. "Which is an excuse to set you more responsibility."

"Aye, and get more sets of eyes on ye," Belanna added.

"I can see you're all diligent soldiers," I remarked.

"If they wanted us *diligent,* they shouldn't have forced us into this, should they?" Belanna idly paddled her hands through the water. "'All hybrids are duty bound to serve in the army until they be twenty-one years of age. Afterward, they be free to leave, unless circumstances warrant their return. At which time, they be duty bound to serve until their services are no longer required.' Bollocks."

"I've naught but a year left," Quinn declared.

"Bugger ye," Belanna and Braxton said as one. "We've still four years," Belanna added.

"Such a shame. Worry not, I'll enjoy the freedom enough for the three of us." Quinn laughed at the expression which darkened the twin's faces—one Seruf would have called *sourpuss.*

"Ach, yer a Healer, though." Belanna gave Quinn a mischievous smile. "Mighty valuable, ye are. They'll not want to be givin' ye up so easily. Mark me words, they'll find a cause to call ye back before you've enjoyed a month of freedom."

"Perhaps." Quinn waggled his brows. "But they'll not be able to call me back if they can't find me."

His joviality, and the twins' playful bickering, were infectious, but my answering laugh had become lodged in my throat. I had to swallow thrice to clear the obstruction and free my voice. "Your situations could be far worse," I said. "You could be hybrids cursed with a perilous gift. And you could be hunted for it."

Quinn's smile faded, and his eyes, when he turned them to me, were solemn.

Not for the first time, I pondered what my life would have been like if I'd been taken into the army at a young age as Quinn, Belanna, and Braxton had been. Would I have learned to harness my power, as they'd learned to harness theirs? Or would my fire have continuously evaded any method of restraint?

Perhaps nothing would have changed had I been taken to the army. Perhaps everything would have.

"Right." Belanna struck the water with the flat of her palm, grinning when I startled at the reverberating crack. "I don't know about ye lot, but the trek here worked me up to quite an appetite."

"Aye. And the duck we lifted this mornin' will not be keepin' much longer in this heat. Ye missed that, Quinn." Braxton's eyebrows wiggled. "Took it right out from under Ruairí's greasy nose, we did."

"Ruairí?" Surprise warmed Quinn's laugh. "How did you manage that? The old blaggard has a fast-roaming eye."

"Aye. But if he's got a pretty lady in front of him, his eyes don't roam."

"He's a feckin' shite," Belanna said. "I thought I was gettin' me tits groped. And I couldn't well tell him to bugger off with Braxton takin' his sweet time pickin' what he wanted."

"And ye'll be thankin' me for that when ye taste the duck," Braxton said. "It was his finest cut."

"There's plenty for the four of us." Belanna turned her eyes toward me again.

The swift change in conversation left me thoroughly befuddled. I'd spent too much time in near solitude, or in the company of Celestials, and had become deacclimated (it's silly this is not considered a word; if one can *re*acclimate, why can they not also *de*acclimate?) to the sound and speed of human conversation. "Four of us?" I questioned.

Beneath the water, Quinn's hand nudged mine, no doubt because he'd sensed my tension and confusion. I reached for him, threading my fingers through his and gripping so tightly, it was a wonder he didn't flinch.

"Yes, *four*," Belanna said. "Unless yer ability somehow exempts ye from eatin'?"

"You would invite me to dine with you?" I asked. "After I confessed to destroying our childhood home."

"Luckily for ye, any we loved left Swindon long ago. Had they not, I'd not be in so charitable a mood." Belanna lifted her shoulder. "But ye said ye have yer reasons. Can't say that makes what ye done dandy in my eyes, but Quinn trusts ye. That's enough for me. For now."

"Me as well." Braxton nodded. "Although, if ye burn me sister or me horse, I'll not be very forgivin'. And there'll be not a place ye can hide where I can't find ye."

My fingers must have trembled because Quinn smoothed his

thumb over my knuckles. "If she's to burn anyone," Quinn said, "it'll be *you*, Braxton. You have the fattest hide; we could make a feast out of you."

When Braxton scooped water into his hands and threw it, Quinn ducked, dragging me beneath the surface with him. I gasped and would have ~~injested~~—ingested another large mouthful of water if Quinn hadn't been so quick to press his lips to mine, stealing a brief, sweet kiss before he lifted us out of the water. And I was so flustered by the warm, pleasurable sensation coiling in my stomach that I at first didn't notice Belanna and Braxton had left us. They swam toward the right bank, where our four horses now stood, eating the tall stalks of grass while they awaited our emergence from the pool.

"Belanna called them down," Quinn said when my eyes fixated on Icarus and the satchel strapped to his saddle. "Your letter is safe, Lass. I promise. Come..." He pivoted, grasped my arms, and swam backward toward the bank.

"One of these days, you'll collide with something and regret not facing forward," I berated him.

"A pain I will gladly bear," he murmured. "Because I'd rather be facing you, Lass."

I was helpless against my giddy smile.

* * *

Some memories are so cherished, so steeped in bliss, they oft feel surreal. As though they'd been naught but a dream.

That afternoon had been a dream.

After confirming my letter was, indeed, secure and undisturbed (and enduring several moments of Quinn's silent boasting once I conceded he'd been truthful), I sat near to the water, keeping my feet submerged in the safety of its depths. Quinn, of course, knew my reasoning for doing this, but Braxton and Belanna likely thought it an odd place to sit, as the bankside was mud-slick and speckled with barbed rocks. They said nothing, however, as they set their places beside me and laid their feast out on a saddle blanket.

The food they'd brought was not nearly as extravagant as the meals Ramiel and Seruf had provided, but I found I preferred the plainer taste of human-cooked fare. I consumed every morsel I was given. My stomach was *quite* unhappy with me that eve, especially as I'd also laughed more that day than I had in a long time.

Many of the conversations we shared have long since faded from my memory. Some were riotous stories of childhood antics. Others were starry-eyed ponderings of hopeful futures...ones that would never come to fruition. The words and stories might have dimmed, but the laughter and joy still shine, even after all these years.

I'd awakened that day still harboring an abhorrence toward humans, but I would sleep that night with a softened attitude. Not all people were contemptuous. That had been something Terrick had firmly believed, and a notion I had done my best to cling to, even though every human I'd encountered had proved the opposite. But on that afternoon, Quinn, Braxton, and Belanna would finally imprint Terrick's teachings upon my heart by giving me the one thing every other human had withheld: kindness.

Not all people were contemptuous.

Some were ~~wonderous~~—wondrous.

But this was, unfortunately, a lesson I learned far too late.

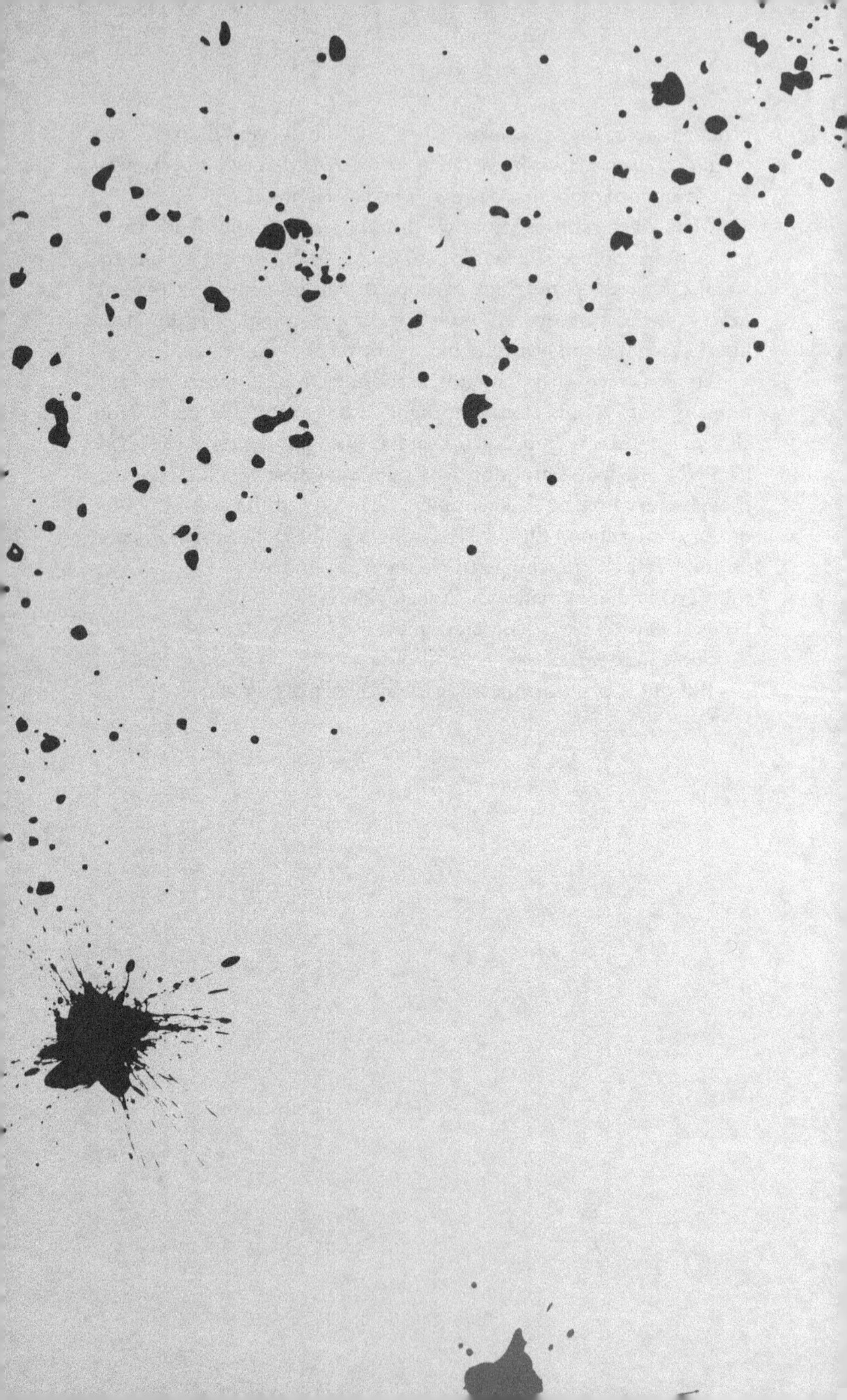

Tragedy

"Lass," Quinn declared when he next visited me two days after our trip to the waterfall, "I have something important to tell you."

"Oh, yes?" I raised my chin to meet Quinn's gaze as he sat atop his brown and white mare. "Has Raphael returned?"

"I would not consider his return *important*," Quinn said. "A tragedy, perhaps. But no, Lass. His home remains vacant." He nudged his mare to where I stood beside Icarus, combing the burs and branches from his mane. Icarus whickered softly and rubbed his nose against the mare's muzzle.

He was nearly as taken with her as I was with her master.

"For you, my lady." Quinn held a long-stemmed rose toward me. "Best be careful grasping it, though. I picked one nearly as thorny as you." He wriggled his thumb to show me the small puncture the thorns had left behind.

When I took the flower from him, its barbs gouged my flesh, but the pain was ~~aswayged~~—assuaged once I caressed the silken petals. It was the lushest, reddest rose I had ever seen. "Thank you," I murmured, startled by the strange, full sensation that rose in my throat, one that normally accompanied the ~~diluge~~–deluge of tears.

But I was not sad.

I steadied my wayward emotions and said, "Was this the important thing you wished to tell me? You found a magnificent rose?"

Quinn's eyes brightened. "The rose is important, yes. But not *nearly* as important as what I have to say next. Because I, dear lady" —he leant back, rummaged through his saddlebag, and withdrew a bundle of leather-bound parchment—"I am going to teach you to read."

And thus, over the next several days, Quinn became my tutor.

We sat in the shade of the trees, basking in the dappled sunlight. He often lay on the ground, reclined on one elbow with the bound parchment open before him. I oft perched against a nearby log, close enough to see the lines he drew on the page but maintaining a distance, in case my flame should decide to loose itself.

"I'm fairly certain those lines do not equate to the spelling of your name," I said one afternoon.

Quinn stared at the letters he'd scribbled on the parchment. He'd recited each individual letter as he wrote them down, and thus began the confusion.

"If you were to say that word as you've written it, your name would be Qu-you-I-an-an," I said.

"That's precisely how it's said. I've just never had the heart to correct your pronunciation." He chortled at my scowl. "Now, Lass, you must remember the Q changes its sound when placed next to the U. Rather than *qu* and *you*, it becomes *qui*."

"You're mocking my inability to read, aren't you?"

"I would *never*."

I frowned. "It makes little sense. Why does a letter change its sound when placed next to another letter?"

"Because those letters form the word. The Q and the U sound like *qui*. There's the first part of my name. The second is simply *in*. You do not need to say the N twice."

"Then why is it written twice?"

"For emphasis. Quinnnnnnnn." He held his breath, humming the last letter of his name until I tossed a bit of dirt in his direction. "The same is true for your name, Lass." He chuckled as he placed his quill back on the parchment.

A sense of foreboding seized me.

L, A, S and S. I recognized the letters he wrote, as Quinn had already schooled me on the alphabet, but I knew not which name they spelled. The one Seruf had bestowed upon me? Lasair, The Firestarter and killer of humans. Or the one Terrick had gifted me? Lass.

I wished to be Lass when I was with Quinn. Not Lasair.

"Would..." I fought to keep the tremor from my voice. "That not be el-ah-ssss?"

"Close," Quinn said. "But the L and the A together make one sound. *La*."

"La-sssss. *Lass*!"

"Yes!"

Perhaps it was the soft, pleased expression that crossed Quinn's face or the sensations of pride and relief swirling within me that sent me sliding from my log and closing the distance between us, pressing my lips to his. 'Twas a mere whisper of a kiss, but it left us both red faced and smiling.

"What about the name 'Terrick?'" I asked Quinn when I returned to my log. "Can you show me how to spell that?"

"Of course." Quinn flipped the parchment onto the other side and began writing.

After several days of study, I was able to read my name, Quinn's, Terrick's, and had also learned the spelling of various towns, such as Darfield and Niall.

Quinn did not write Swindon on his parchment, but I told him of it. I spoke of Terrick's bookstore, the goats I'd kept in the livery barn, the friendships I'd found and lost there, and the night I became branded as a monster.

"You were naught but a child, Lass! To treat a *child* with such malice..." He looked horror stricken at the conclusion of my tale.

I said nothing, and I could not bring myself to meet his worried gaze.

"Humans have certainly left an ill impression on you, haven't they?" he murmured. "Is that why you destroyed Swindon?"

"I'll not discuss Swindon's destruction," I said, appalled at the tears warming my eyes. "Can we continue spelling?"

"Of course. But Lass...you *can* tell me. If ever you wish to unburden yourself of the memory."

"I wish to learn reading."

He taught me other simple words: cat, horse, tree, water, and food. Indeed, he had far more luck instructing me than Terrick ever had. Likely because my childhood impatience had been tempered, and I was no longer dulled by Terrick's tonic. I was now willing and able to absorb the information.

Had I remained in that wood, as I so very much longed to do, I may have learned a wider vokabulary by summer's end.

Time, however, was as cruel as it was indecisive.

The torturous and scarring periods of my life seemed to stretch endlessly, with minutes feeling more like years. But the moments I wanted to stay in forever often passed far too quickly.

The days I spent with Quinn were always doomed to be tragically, *painfully* brief.

* * *

On my third week in the wood, a bitter unease began to eat at my belly.

It worsened each day, when Quinn brought news that Raphael had not returned to Niall, and I didn't understand why. Ramiel had anticipated the task to take weeks or even months, likely knowing his brother was fickle. He would not yet have grown frustrated by my lack of progress.

So why, I wondered, had I become so ill with ~~constornation~~—consternation?

'Twas not shame over the destruction of Swindon. Not *entirely*, at least. In the tranquil, woodland nights, I'd shed my tears for my childhood home, anguished over the lack of remorse I'd had for the demise of its people, and allowed myself to wallow in the disgust, the *loathing*, I felt for myself.

But none of those turmoils caused my restlessness.

Quinn was undoubtedly the source of some of my befuddlement. I was utterly content with him, and I worried Ramiel would be upset by my heart's betrayal. Ramiel had opened his home to me, provided me comfort and security, and entertained my endless curiosities. The only repayment he'd asked was for me to deliver a message to his brother and return to Uchen with a response. And rather than journeying across Sakar to search for Raphael as I should have done, I was dallying in the woods with a human boy.

But the sensation in my belly was...*different*. It's difficult to describe; it was the slithering of remorse, the spinous pain of apprehension, and something *more*. A cold emotion I had no name for. A sense of...wrongness (is this a word?). A sense that something was *amiss*, although I knew not what.

As the wrongness grew more persistent, so did my fire.

Flames enveloped my fingers when I plucked my morning berries. They danced over my skin when I sat by the pond, basking in the sun's warmth. They had not yet loosed themselves upon Quinn, but he'd witnessed the flame's volatility when he'd taken me on a stroll through a nearby daffodil field. The meadow had been ethereal; long, rolling waves of sunshine stretched beneath a cloudless sky. Quinn had plucked a flower for me. I'd held it in my hands, savoring the delicate softness of the yellow petals against my flesh.

My fire consumed it, leaving me holding naught but a sprinkling of ash.

* * *

On my fourth week in the woods, my fire assailed another being of flesh and bone.

The morning had dawned bright and warm, with only a tepid breeze. I'd not slept well in the night, finding the air too hot. But I was not in an ill mood. On the contrary, I'd laughed when Icarus returned to the dwelling coated in a craggy layer of mud.

"Were you jealous of Quinn's mare?" I asked. "You turned yourself into a two-colored horse as well?"

Icarus shook himself, flinging bits of mud onto the trees around him.

"Right, well, I'll not be leaving you in this condition. The mud will make sores beneath your saddle."

Icarus did not protest when I dredged a bucket of water from the lake and washed him. He enjoyed it, standing in the shade of the trees while I fussed over him. It was a soothing task for me as well, to wipe a damp rag over his fur and watch the mud dissolve.

I hummed while I worked, trying to mimic the charming tune Quinn had last played for me by drumming his hands against a downed log. My voice likely sounded dreadful, but Icarus turned his ears to me, so it seemed he did not mind.

I stroked his freshly clean neck, smoothing my hand over his glistering fur.

Fire erupted from my fingertips.

It clung to Icarus, ravenous and violent, as it bubbled over his flesh. He turned away from me with a pained squeal and I watched, horrified, as he bucked and shook his head, attempting to dispel the flame.

The sharp, smoked scent of his burning flesh wafted into my nostrils, rotting my stomach.

"Icarus!" I seized the bucket in my flame-wrapped hands. I had hardly enough time to upend it, dousing Icarus in water, before the wood buckled.

It was not enough.

The roaring fire devoured his shoulder and set its greedy teeth upon his back. I could do nothing else for him; not while the flame remained bonded to my skin.

"The lake! Icarus, you must go to the lake!" I waved my arms, attempting to chase him.

He shied backward, his rolling eyes fixed upon my flame-sheathed hands.

"Icarus!" He became a shadowed image in my tear-blurred eyes. "Go to the lake, Icarus! *Please!*"

"Lass?"

Quinn's voice was hardly discernible over Icarus' wails.

My blood turned bitterly cold, even as the fire still raged.

Quinn never arrived so early in the morning.

But there he was, already dismounted from his shying mare and running to Icarus's side.

I turned away, clutching my stomach. "Quinn," I gasped, "*leave!*"

"Lass...*feck*! Lass, wait here!" Quinn's voice was lanced with pain.

He must have touched the flame and felt its fury.

I pressed my hands to my ears, and a sound erupted from my

throat—one so animalistic, it might've come from a beast. But 'twas a cry I knew well, as I'd heard it leave the lips of hundreds of humans before they perished.

And perhaps it was only fitting that my own body should be stricken by the same agony I had forced them to suffer. For although the flames cascading over my flesh would never harm me, my insides had been lit ablaze and would soon burn, blacken, and fade to ash.

I retched. The few berries I'd managed to consume at daybreak left a bitter flavor on my tongue, and that taste caused me to retch again. The lingering fragrance of cooked flesh made me ill a third time. I was so weakened by my repeated bouts of heaving that I crumpled, my backside landing in my puddle of sick.

"Lass."

I hadn't heard Quinn return, and I had to strain to detect his murmured voice over my harsh breaths.

"Lass...look at me..."

I pressed my brow to my drawn knees, fighting yet another urge to be sick.

"Lass, it's alright. Icarus...he'll scar, but the burns are not so bad."

Lies. I had seen the fire crest over Icarus's back. I'd *heard* him dying. So I refused to believe Quinn's placating words.

"He's alright, Lass. Only shaken." Quinn himself sounded shaken. "Can you look at me, Lass?"

I would not.

He exhaled and, shockingly, moved closer to me. The tips of his boots were visible through the gap between my knees. "It's gone, Lass," he said. "The fire."

I had not felt the flame depart, but when I glanced upon my hands, they were naught but bare skin again.

"Can you walk with me? To the pond?" Quinn asked. "You were ill—and I would hate to see your beautiful tunic soiled."

The white Celestial garment would not soil, but I did not tell him that. I rose to my feet, recoiling when he offered a hand to aid me.

"Apologies," he said. "I'll not touch you, Lass, but please grasp onto me if you feel unsteady."

I did not dare take his hand, although he offered it to me each time I wavered.

I had to pause twice on the way to the pond as my stomach was still unsettled and my knees would not stop quivering. Quinn waited silently beside me each time.

When we reached the pond, I saw Icarus secured to a tree near the bank. His left side was mutilated; raw ripples of blistered flesh covered his hide, and only spatterings of his red coat remained. He turned his head toward me, the whites of his eyes plainly visible, even from a distance.

I looked away.

The pond water, which spent much of its day in direct sunlight, was warm. But I shivered as I ~~wayded~~—waded to my waist and washed the remnants of my sick away.

"Lass?" Quinn walked into the pool and crouched beside me. He did not touch me, but he was close enough for me to feel the heat ~~emenating~~—emanating from his skin. It beckoned me, making me crave the weight and comfort of his arms. But it was folly to yearn for such things. To hope for a future with this boy when my very touch had the power to steal his life.

"Lass..." Quinn began again.

"I'm tired," I interrupted.

"I'm sure you are. You should rest. Perhaps change into dry clothing...Have you any other tunics?"

"This is not a fatigue sleep can cure. I'm tired of...*this*." I chaffed my hands together, digging my nails into my skin. Wishing fervently the fire would *leave me be* but knowing I was forever cursed to remain in its grasp. And then I stood, stumbling through the water as I climbed the sloping bank.

"Lass!" Quinn sprinted to catch me, his frantic movements sloshing water against the backs of my legs. "Lass, *wait*..."

"I must return to Uchen, with or without delivering my missive." I dared not look at him.

"Lass." Quinn moved in front of me, blocking my path. When I attempted to divert around, he blocked me yet again. "*Look at me, Lass.*"

I wouldn't. "You know what I did to Swindon—"

"I know what Swindon did to *you*," he interjected.

"—and you saw how I hurt Icarus," I said. "If I stay here, your fate will be far worse."

"You didn't intend to harm Icarus."

"It doesn't matter! I didn't *intend* to hurt most of the humans I've killed. They died anyway. And those who dared to confront me met far more spectacular deaths."

Again, I tried to circumvent him.

Again, he threw himself in my path.

"Quinn, please!" I cried.

"I want to help you, Lass," he said.

"And what can you do?" I asked. "What wisdom do you possess that Terrick and the Celestials did not?"

"Perhaps it is not a matter of wisdom," Quinn said, "but of finding a different approach. If you were to explain what they tried and how your power works, perhaps I—"

"*I don't know how it works!*" I raised my trembling hands. "It used to be I was in danger of loosing it when I became distraught, as I am now. But now the power is dormant when I am upset and volatile when I am calm."

"Perhaps the power's volatility is not *only* determined by your emotional state. When I learned to heal—" Quinn paused to thwart another of my escape attempts. "I was told that my ability required calm and focus—quite a difficult state to maintain when those I heal are usually in hysterics. No matter how I tried, I could not find the calm I needed to call my power forward. Until I found the harp, and I was so entranced by its beauty, I bartered everything I owned with Hugo, the innkeeper, to be granted one hour each day with it. I was forever changed by that arrangement. Because while I could not sit still for meditation, grew quickly bored with reading, and cared not about my combat training, I could spend an entire day at that harp, learning to play it, without ever becoming restless. It was the calm I'd lacked when trying to use my power. And once I found that focus, I mastered my ability. To heal someone, I need only think of the last song I composed, and my power emerges."

The laugh that escaped me was bitter. "Are you suggesting I might be cured if I learned to play the harp?"

"If you wish to play an instrument, I will gladly teach you, but I am not suggesting it will ease what ails you. I'm merely wondering if your power is governed not by emotions but by your state of mind. Or both. And should that be the case, perhaps I can—"

"No."

I did not shout the word, but I might as well have with the way Quinn recoiled.

For a brief, terrifying second, I thought the fire had emerged again. Upon confirming it had not, I swallowed my tears and fought to steady my voice. "I thank you for offering help, but I can't accept it. You are one of the very few humans to show me kindness and I—I can't risk hurting you, Quinn. And I *would* hurt you eventually. Even if you were careful, and even if your theories prove to be true. Because what you fail to consider is that you needed the focus to *draw your power forward*. I would need it to keep mine at bay. If there is a moment when I am not as focused as I should be, and you are standing too close...Death by fire is a horrific thing, Quinn. I will not risk forcing you to endure it. So, I must return to Uchen."

"Lass..."

"Since Raphael has abandoned his home, it seems I've no choice but to leave the letter with you." I closed my eyes, bidding my mind to refrain from haunting me with images of a disappointed Ramiel. Or worse, a *wrathful* Ramiel. My mind, of course, did not heed my plea. But although those images speared anguish into my heart, the thought of staying and potentially harming Quinn caused me more pain. I *had* to leave. If risking Ramiel's ire was the only way to ensure Quinn's safety, then so be it. "I'd ask you not to read the letter, but I suppose it matters not if you do. As long as you deliver it."

"*Lass!*"

"I will leave I-Icarus with you as well. I know he's old and not as fine as the other horses within Niall, but he's a gentle companion—"

"*Stop*! Lass. *Please.*" Quinn tentatively raised a hand toward my face.

I should have drawn away, but I stilled and allowed him to rest his palm against my cheek. It was a minuscule gesture, so light, it could hardly be called a touch, but it *hurt*. The pain that lanced into my chest was one I was well familiar with: the sting of loss and the slow demise of hope and childhood dreams. Everything I had ever wanted was contained within that touch: love and companionship. A life with a boy who'd swept me off my feet when I was young.

I had, indeed, fallen in love with him that day he collided with me on Darfield's streets. I had not realized it at the time, but Quinn had laid claim to my heart. Perhaps it was silly to fall for the first boy who'd made me laugh, but I had. And in the years that followed, although Quinn and I had precious few moments together, my affection for him only deepened.

I did not realize I'd begun sobbing until Quinn touched his other hand to my face, drying my tears.

"I'm sorry, Lass." His breath whispered over my brow. "For everything you've suffered and everything you're still suffering. I'm *sorry*. You deserve so much more than what this life has given you. I wish I could do something to ease your pain."

"You can't. And I'd not ask you to." It took a tremendous effort to raise my head and face the hurt in his beautiful blue eyes. "I *will* return to Uchen, Quinn, to my home with the Celestials."

"Lass, the Celestials...they care so little for mortals. That's no place for you to live."

"I can't live amongst the humans," I said. "So where else shall I go? If it helps to ease your mind, know that I am well cared for in Uchen."

He did not protest when I left his embrace, nor did he attempt to stop me when I walked back to my dwelling. But he fell into step beside me, his eyes tracking my movements as I found my satchel and rummaged through it, retrieving the letter.

"I'll not take it," he said when I turned to hand it to him.

Frustration sparked within me. "And why not? Being petulant will not coerce me to stay..."

"No, Lass, I will not take it because I do not need to." He inhaled, closing his eyes. "Raphael returned to Niall this morning."

Raphael

As Icarus was in no condition to bear a rider, and I would not ~~ackwess~~—acquiesce to sharing a saddle with Quinn lest my power loose itself, we freed the horses into the woods and walked to the city on foot. And perhaps this was quite fortunate, as a horse would've sensed and detested the barrage of emotions I experienced when the wall's great stone gates opened to admit us.

As soon as we crossed the threshold and entered the city, we were swallowed in a sea of humanity. People lurched to and fro in hurried, heedless steps, oft trodding on their fellow citizens.

A tall, fine-boned woman turned the corner and struck my elbow with the edge of her wicker basket. 'Twas a painful blow, but she did not look at me to inquire if I'd been injured. She was so absorbed in the petty disagreement with the man walking beside her that she paid me no mind.

"Are you alright, Lass?" Quinn asked.

I nodded and checked to confirm the woman's jostling had not disturbed the hooded cloak Quinn had given me. "It would be best if we concealed your eyes, Lass," he'd said when he handed me the garment. Although it was far too warm for such cumbersome outer-wear, I was grateful for the shade of the hood. It concealed my twisted mask of confusion from him.

The woman had left me bristling with revulsion and burning

with envy. As much as I loathed her carelessness, I also *pined* for it. 'Twould have been a dream to wander the streets as she did, with nary a care for who I touched or jostled.

Instead, I strode beside Quinn with my arms bound so tightly around my body, my ribs ached in protest.

Quinn, perhaps seeking to distract me from my troubled thoughts, explained each of the tall, pale-stoned buildings which framed the streets. Most were shops, inns, or dwellings, but there were an array of other businesses as well.

"Lyla," Quinn said, gesturing to a lean building with green paint splattered over the door, "schools the city children on reading and writing. Mayhap you'd like to speak with her? Yes, I know you are not a child," he added with a soft laugh as though I'd scorned his suggestion, when I hadn't said or done anything of the sort. "She's a kind woman," he continued, "and a good tutor. She would be more than willing to help."

I moved away from the building, scrabbling against my persistent tears.

We strode past a market booth which boasted colorful bits of cloth in shades I'd never seen humans produce before: soft reds akin to an azalea flower, greens that resembled moss ponds, and blues brighter than the sky above us.

Quinn paused beside a strip of lilac fabric.

I continued, wary of halting in such a crowded area, and stopped only when I was able to tuck myself into the shadows of a narrow alleyway.

Quinn watched me with a soft, sad expression, until the round-faced cloth seller approached him. "Ayda!" He smiled and waved to the woman. "That color looks *lovely* on you!"

"Always the charmer, eh, Quinn?" Ayda laughed and smoothed a hand over her blue gown. "But you should not be wasting your charm on one such as me. Find yourself a girl your own age."

"Oh, I have," Quinn said lightly. "But she's a stubborn sort who needs a little convincing."

"So she doesn't like ye back, eh?"

"She does. She just won't admit it. And my dear Ayda, I'm

hoping you'll be able to assist me. This tempest of mine loves lilacs, you see. So I was hoping to get a bit of this fine cloth for her..."

"Oh, aye, I can give you as much as you want." Ayda's voice was warm and comforting. "You sure don't like to make things easy on yourself, do you, Quinn?"

"Easy is dull." Another smile danced over Quinn's lips as he angled his head to meet my gaze.

Afterward, we strode through the market side by side once more while Quinn fiddled with his newly purchased lilac cloth. "You know, for *years*, I thought your name was Lilac. A fitting name for a girl with such captivating eyes." He waggled the fabric in my face. "But Lass suits you better. Ah! The Greasy Swan!" Quinn pointed to a squat building with a chipped plaque nailed to the door. "I play the lute there—yes, Lass, that is a swan on the signpost. Looks like a malformed chicken, though, doesn't it?"

I said nothing. I hadn't even looked closely enough at the sign to remark upon the design, but Quinn was determined to carry on the conversation as though I were remarking upon everything he said.

"They do also serve swan there on occasion. You'd have to try it before dismissing it, Lass. It is not my favorite fare, but others are quite fond of it."

Again, I had not dismissed or commented upon the swan meat.

"Old Paddy there," Quinn said with a gesture to a crooked building with a slanted roof, "makes the finest bread in Niall. You'd adore it, Lass, as he bakes the dough with *cheese*."

This notion left me conflicted. Although the bread sounded delectable, my stomach soured as I pondered its taste and texture.

"And...ah, Gowan! Yes, I know it's garish, but it matches your eyes!"

I hardly raised my gaze, intending to dismiss the building in question, but I halted, stunned by the towering stalk of a lavender flower, which spanned the entire ~~fasade~~—facade of the two-story structure.

"It's a painting, Lass." Quinn looked utterly ~~boyed~~—buoyed to see me react to something. "Isn't it stunning?"

It was. But I said nothing.

"He could teach you to recreate the painting, Lass," Quinn added. "He's a skilled educator. Perhaps I'll learn alongside you."

I had a strange sensation in my throat, and my stomach was threatening to rebel, so I dared not speak. I didn't know if I would break into tears upon opening my mouth or if I would become ill. Or, more likely, I would become ill *and* summarily break into tears once my stomach had concluded its purge.

I turned away, narrowly avoiding trodding on several toes in my haste to escape.

Quinn sighed and sprinted to catch up with me.

And even through all my toiling emotions, the proximity to humans, and Quinn's endless attempts to brighten my spirits, my fire remained dormant.

It took an agonizingly long time to navigate the city. I'd begun to wonder if Quinn was leading me in circles to procrastinate when we emerged from a narrow side street, and I saw Niall's castle for the first time.

There are simply no words to describe the splendor of this building. It was awe-inspiring, its beauty rivaled only by the Celestial dwellings of Uchen. The walls reminded me of my white tunic: far too ~~lumanescent~~—luminescent to have been crafted by human hands. Except, unlike my tunic, the glistening white stones did not change color in varying light. Rather, they brightened beneath the sun and dimmed when brushed with shadow. I could only gaze upon the shaded towers; the parts of the castle blanketed in light were painful to behold, akin to staring directly into the sun.

Quinn grew quiet as we approached the castle. So quiet, in fact, that I drew my gaze away from the building to look at him, concerned he was no longer by my side.

Upon seeing he had my attention, Quinn stopped. "May I touch your hair, Lass?" he murmured.

I nodded, even as my belly gave a nervous ripple, and held still, hardly daring to breathe as he approached me. He slowly, tenderly, drew my hood back.

I closed my eyes, lest a passerby glimpse their color.

"I've noticed something, Lass." Quinn moved behind me, his fingers twining through my hair. "The fire travels along your skin, but it does not rise to meet your hair. Therefore, I am hoping this will last. You can open your eyes, Lass. There is no one here to see them."

I did so cautiously and stared in shock at the lock of braided hair resting over my shoulder.

Quinn had threaded the lilac fabric through the strands.

It was sloppily done, as his hands were not well practiced in the art of hair plaiting, but it was beautiful nonetheless.

My eyes ached with unshed tears, and I turned away before he could see the heartbroken longing on my face.

* * *

The inside of the castle was not nearly as splendid as the outside, perhaps because the interior was made for humans rather than Celestials. Tarnished stone covered the floors and walls, and there were no draperies, paintings, or elektricity to brighten the space. The narrow, twisting stairwells Quinn and I navigated were dim and dreary, illuminated sparsely by candlelight. Hybrid soldiers milled about, clad in thick leather and heavily armed. On several occasions, we had to flatten ourselves against the walls to allow clusters of soldiers to pass, as the enclosed spaces weren't wide enough to accommodate large groups. My heart fluttered in my chest each time, worried I'd be recognized or that the fire would make an ill-timed emergence. But it remained dormant, and most soldiers simply tipped their chins in gratitude and continued on their way.

Some, however, grew suspicious of the hooded girl Quinn had brought into their midst.

"I was instructed to bring her to Raphael," Quinn said when one of the soldiers, a bullish man with puckered claw marks on the side of his neck, questioned us.

"Instructed by whom?" the man rebutted.

"A superior."

"Which one?"

"Aoibhinn." Quinn did not blink when he gave the name.

The man scowled. "Who the feck is that?"

"Oh no…is this not common knowledge yet?" Quinn bounced on the balls of his feet. "You were at the morning meeting, yes?"

"Meeting? What are you on about?"

Quinn clicked his tongue. "Raphael called us into the hall at dawn. Evidentially, you missed it. He's brought new recruits from his travels, and you'd best be learning their names because they all rank above your station."

Somehow, his slippery evasions worked. The bullish man, and all others who questioned us, allowed us to pass.

We were soon ushered into Raphael's sitting room, which was not so dissimilar to Ramiel's: spacious and colorfully decorated. But where Ramiel preferred his artworks, Raphael favored his trinkets. Swords, axes, and bows hung from his walls, books filled his shelves, and small figurines, akin to the little Dorothy doll I'd had as a child, danced across his furnishings.

And the furnishings themselves were odd. They resembled velvet-wrapped crates, with their rigid edges and shapes. Even the chair Raphael rested upon was a low, boxy seat that looked far too unyielding to be comfortable. But he sprawled upon it in a lazy, contented manner, with his legs draped over the squared armrests and his wings pooled around him; one feathered appendage rested upon the back of the chair, the other brushed against the ground. His feathers were a snowy white laced with streaks of moss green—a fascinating shade, capable of looking both grimy, as though the white had been soiled, and breathtakingly beautiful, with those vibrant swirls of color glimmering more brightly than any jewele.

Upon our entrance, Raphael ruffled his feathers but did not move otherwise.

His resemblance to Ramiel was plainly evident. Both had chestnut hair, although Raphael favored a longer, more unkempt style. Both were tall and broad, although Ramiel was the narrower of the two—and the finer looking, for Raphael's face, while pleasant, was not as well defined. And his dark eyes were not as remarkable as Ramiel's blue ones.

Raphael looked, for lack of a better term, more *human*.

But he was still an ethereal being, and his presence left Quinn ill at ease. "My lord…" Quinn's voice was thin with uncertainty.

"Please do not call me that," Raphael said dully. "How many times must I repeat myself? I wish to be addressed by my *name*, as you address your fellow kin by their names."

Quinn swallowed. "Apologies, Raphael. I—I know you've only just arrived, and I hate to trouble you…"

"Rest assured, you are not troubling me, my boy. I've been away far too long and have sorely neglected my duties. Now"—Raphael waved his arm in Quinn's direction—"I suppose the food distribution has seen its share of issues since my departure?"

"It has, yes. But I-I've not come to discuss those matters with you. I—We…" He fidgeted, perhaps debating whether to be truthful about our reason for being here or to say something that would waylay me in delivering my letter.

So, I spoke first.

"It is *I* who wishes to speak with you, Raphael," I said. "Quinn was only my guide through the city."

Raphael raised his head, eyeing me speculatively. "You are not a member of my army."

"No."

He exhaled. "Then I suppose things are worse than I feared. Very well, girl. What is it you wish to tell me?"

"Your brother has asked me to deliver a message."

"You'll have to be more specific; I have many brothers."

"Your brother Ramiel."

At this, Raphael's illusion of laziness crumbled. "Ramiel?" His wings stiffened and arched upward. "I have received no recent reports of Ramiel crossing into Sakar."

"He remains in Uchen," I said. "I—I am a child of Uchen. He wanted to avoid unnecessary violence, so he sent me to deliver his message rather than venturing here himself."

The tension ebbed from Raphael's face, but he did not lower his wings from their defensive position as he said, "Very well. You may relay your message."

I drew the letter from where I'd concealed it in my boot and stepped forward, walking on legs that felt weaker than a newborn foal's.

Raphael's face was impassive as he took the small, and now

grubby, strip of parchment from my unsteady fingers. Perhaps he'd been hopeful in that moment, holding the unopened letter from his wayward brother. I like to think so, to imagine that, in those brief seconds between him taking the letter and opening it, he felt some fondness toward Ramiel.

But, as he read, his impassiveness quickly sharpened into anger.

And his malice was directed at me.

Raphael lurched to his feet, his wings stretched to their fullest width, and closed his hand around my neck.

"Lass!" Quinn yelled.

"Silence," Raphael snapped. His unyielding grip ground against my throat, blocking the air from my lungs. I gasped, clawing my nails into his hands, but he refused to release me.

"So." Raphael strode across the room, dragging me alongside him. "My brother has sent his human *whore* to do his bidding."

"My lord...*Raphael*..." Quinn began.

"*Silence*! Unless you wish to join your whorish friend?" Raphael lifted me off the ground and shook me so violently, my teeth sank into my tongue. Blood pooled in my mouth and dribbled onto my chin. Tears scorched my eyes.

"Byron!" Raphael called toward the door. "Can you step in here, please?"

My stomach turned to rot as Byron entered the room.

The puckered burn scars imprinted upon his flesh looked, if possible, more terrifying in the bright light of Raphael's room than they had in the dim glow of Lamex's hut. It was easier to see just how disfigured he was, with much of his left ear and his nose having melted away and the webbed skin above his eyelid drooping, giving him a permanent scowl. His hair had grown since last I saw him, although the golden strands only clung to the right side of his scalp.

I must have made a sound of distress, for Raphael gave me another agonizing shake.

Byron's expression darkened upon seeing me, but he remained composed as he turned to Raphael. "Yes?"

"Was it you who told me of Swindon's destruction?" Raphael asked.

"That was Jakub," Byron said. "But we all received the same reports."

"The town burned?"

"Yes."

"Survivors?"

"Few. We also received word from nearby Kilerth that they had to dispose of several corpses who returned to the city bound to their mounts. They assume the deceased riders were sent as a warning."

Raphael placed me back upon my feet, drawing my head back until I feared he would wrench it from my shoulders. "Is this the girl believed to have destroyed Swindon?"

"The very same." Byron's mottled lips curled over his teeth, his expression both sinister and gleeful. "That is also the girl who started fires in Darfield nearly two years ago and took the lives of dozens of soldiers as they traveled through the wood."

"Thank you, Byron," Raphael said, but he did not loosen his hold on me.

"Raphael," Quinn interjected, "she...she committed the crimes. I'll not deny that. Neither will she. But the humans she killed were seeking to harm her. She was *defending* herself."

"Yet she does not defend herself now," Raphael said. "And her life has come under threat."

He tightened his grip until my lungs spasmed, and dark pools of shadow covered my vision. I had mere seconds before I expired.

And my fire had forsaken me.

"She can't control it," Quinn insisted.

"She controlled it well enough to see Swindon burned to the ground," Raphael rebutted.

"That wasn't *control*. The fire consumes her when her emotions are high. She couldn't stop it. What happened at Swindon wasn't Lass's fault—"

"Lass?" Raphael asked. "I was told her name is *Lasair*, unless Lass is one of the ekenames humans insist upon using."

"She was Lass first. *Before* Seruf claimed her." Quinn's fear-bright eyes flickered on the fringes of my blackening vision. "Raphael, my lord, *please*..." his voice dropped to a whisper. "Do not kill her before she's had a chance to speak in her own defense."

Raphael held me until I was on the very cusp of losing consciousness. "Very well."

When he released me, I crumpled. The air scorched my throat and seared my lungs, and I could not draw a proper breath. Each inhale incited a violent bout of retching. Perhaps it was fortunate I'd been ill that morning, for I had little sick left to soil myself with.

"Lass..." Quinn knelt at my side, his hands hovering above my shoulders.

"You are a Healer, correct?" Raphael asked him.

"Yes—"

"I'll ask you to refrain from using your ability for the moment."

"My lord—"

"*Raphael*. I'll also ask you not to question me. Considering you brought this whore to my room, you are as reprehensible as she."

"She's not a whore." Anger seeped from Quinn, but his hands, when he pressed them to my back, were gentle.

"According to my brother," Raphael said as he lowered himself back onto his rigid chair, "that is precisely what she is. So tell me, Lasair, what have you to say about the contents of this letter? Would you like to argue your innocence?"

"I—" Speaking ravaged my damaged throat. "I-I can't."

"As I thought."

"I cannot speak to what's in the letter because I did not read it. I *cannot* read it."

This, it seemed, was not the answer Raphael had been expecting. His face softened with surprise. "Indeed? Is your accomplice also illiterate?" His eyes swung to Quinn. "If so, I'll need to have a discussion about how my hybrids are schooled."

"He is not," I said before Quinn could respond. "But I would not allow him to read it. Ramiel said the letter was for your eyes only. I may be a despicable creature, but I'm not without honor."

Raphael's brow rose and he leaned forward, resting one elbow on his knee in a posture meant to look careless, even though his wings remained ~~taught~~—taut. "So, neither of you saw the contents of this letter?"

"No," Quinn and I said as one.

"Well." Raphael flattened the parchment against his other knee.

"It hardly seems fair to deliver punishment when you have not been informed of your crimes. Allow me to enlighten you. '*Dearest Brother*,'" he read, in a voice so like Ramiel's, it made those hateful goosebumps appear on my skin. "'*I understand there has been some trouble in your ranks of late due to the unfortunate events at Darfield. I'm sure you will not believe me when I say I did not want Ellard to Fall, but I could not sit idly by and allow him to endanger one of my own. For the anguish my actions have caused you, I apologize.*

"'*Regarding other events: I'm sure by now you've been made aware that Seruf has created a hybrid, something I strongly disapproved of. You know how impulsive Seruf can be, brother. I'm sure you won't be surprised to learn she was heavy-handed in creating her pet. The wretched girl child was given far too much power but has contained it well, given her circumstances. I am working on a theory that may help her finally gain mastery over her abilities, but it will take several months to discover the results of my experimentation.*

"'*In the meantime, the girl has proved useful to me. She's formed a strong dislike for your precious humans—this was not my coercion, I assure you. They brought this upon themselves by treating her with hostility. It will take very little coercion to convince her to kill them, and I have set her on a path that will awaken her vendettas against them. By the time this letter has reached your hands, the girl may have ~~desimated~~—decimated several of your human cities.*

"'*Of course, brother, had you been willing to put aside your childish temper and agreed to speak with me directly, there would have been no need for such mayhem. But, as you have cloaked yourself behind your humans, I have no choice but to tear through the fabric of that cloak. The girl is a perfect tool for such a task.*

"'*I'm sure you will be tempted to kill her upon reading this letter. I can't say I'll be particularly upset if you do, but I would ask that you spare her. As you've condemned me to a life of solitude, my asking to keep the pet who has warmed my bed these past months is hardly an unreasonable request. But if you end her life, I will find other pets, and other tools with which to shred your human cloak. If you wish to spare your precious humans their future anguish, I suggest you set aside your churlishness and agree to speak with me.*

"'*Until then, I bid you not to become too attached to your human companions.*'"

I felt nothing as Raphael finished reading. No sorrow, nor anger, nor hatred. No sense of betrayal or anguish over the ~~callis~~—callous way Ramiel had spoken of me. I was...*empty*. I did not even realize I'd begun to shiver until Quinn wrapped his arms more securely around me, as though trying to share his warmth.

"Now." Raphael waved the parchment through the air. "As I'm sure you understand, I cannot ignore the contents of this letter." He stood, crossed the room, and knelt before me.

Quinn's breathing became unsteady, but his hold on me did not loosen.

When Raphael spoke again, his voice softened. "Given your reaction upon hearing my brother's words, I believe you are innocent, a pitiless, foolish child, easily swayed by my brother's charm. For that, I am sorry. But as you have aligned yourself with my brother and allowed him to claim you as his own, I will not allow you to stay in Sakar. Nor will I kill you. I *dislike* the act of slaughtering humans."

He stood and walked a slow circle around Quinn and me. His shoes, a silly shining leather so very similar to Ramiel's, clicked upon the burnished stone floor. "Lasair, for your crimes, I banish you back to Uchen. You will depart immediately and be escorted by members of my army. They will be instructed not to harm you unless you harm them. You are to *remain* in Uchen for the rest of your days, however long they may be. If you are ever seen crossing into Sakar again, you will be killed. The Healer shall be punished for the part he had to play in this." These last words were spoken not to Quinn and me but to Byron. "Four days will be enough, Byron. And then he will be free to resume his duties."

A whimper escaped me.

I knew the wicked torture Byron inflicted, and I could not bear the thought of condemning Quinn to that fate.

"And, Lasair." Raphael's shining shoes nudged my arm. "When you return to Uchen, I'd like you to tell my brother that I have long been willing to put this quarrel to bed. But it is *he* who cannot look past his own pride. I will speak with him only when he has put aside his experimentations and shown genuine remorse for the crimes he has committed."

With that, Raphael returned to his chair with a lazy call to, "Take the punished away."

Quinn and I had only a moment—not nearly enough time to say all the words we so desperately wished to speak to each other—before soldiers entered the room and tore us apart.

Neither of us could ignore the cruel irony of the situation.

Had I been less prideful and allowed Quinn to read the letter, we might have been spared this tragedy.

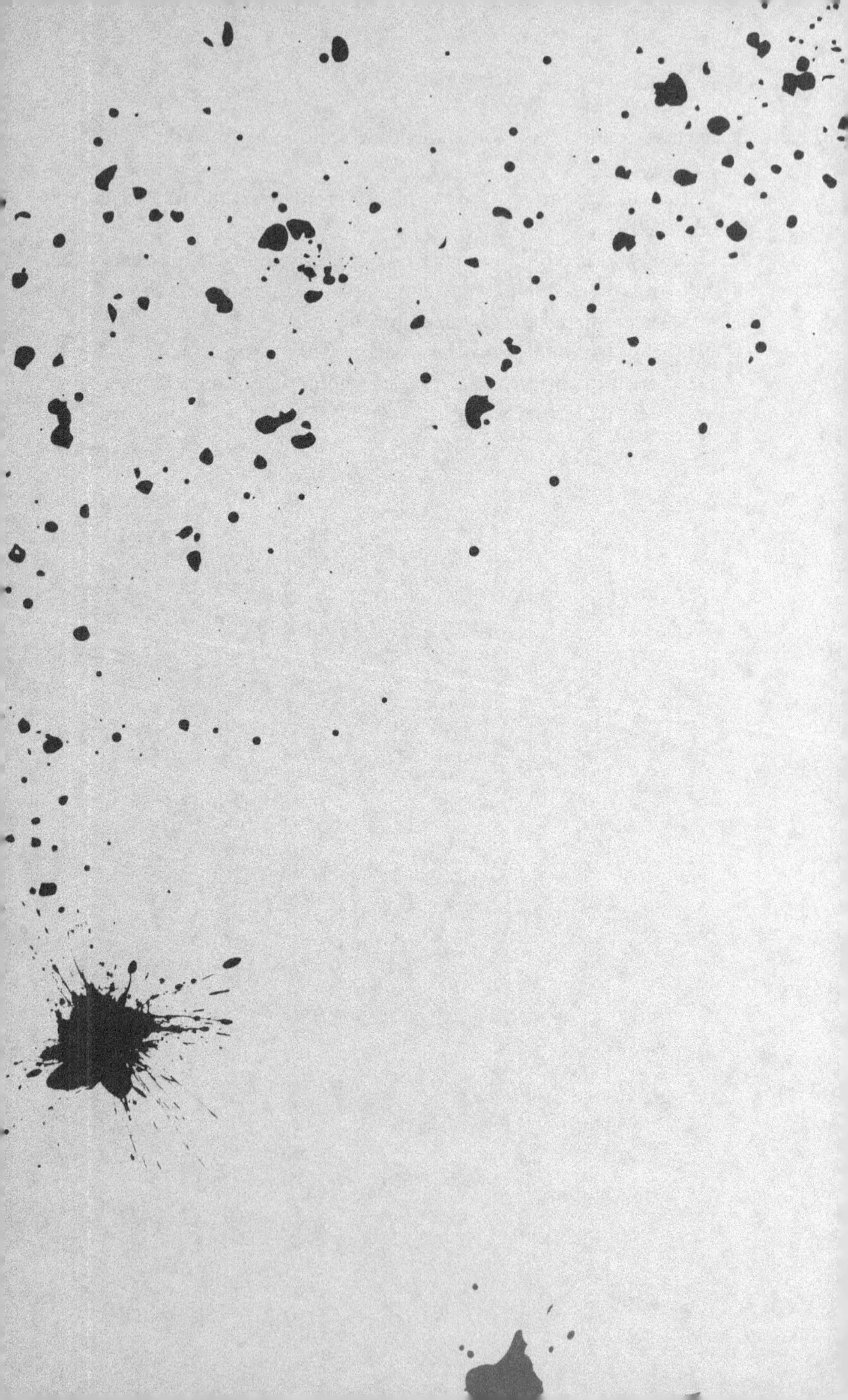

Betrayal

I have little memory of the journey to Uchen.

I was paired with a young, fast horse, accompanied by a dozen soldiers who dictated a brutal pace, and was too mournful to notice the passage of time. The ride from Niall to Muirin seemed to take only moments, even though I knew the horses would have needed days, perhaps weeks, to cover the distance.

My vessel remained tethered where I'd left it—evidentially, 'twas not uncommon for vessels to sit abandoned on Muirin's shore—and the soldiers stayed at my side until I climbed onto the deck and began the voyage across the sea. Then the rollicking waters buffeted my vessel about, leaving me too ill and weary to care about my mournfulness.

When I finally broached Oakwell's shore, three Wraiths escorted me across the land to Dunbar. They regarded me with reverence and carried no weapons, but I still recoiled, my stomach turning over itself in rage. Throughout the long trek, I beseeched my flame to emerge. I *wanted* its ravenous hunger, its *destruction*. I desired nothing more than to watch those Wraiths writhe beneath the flame's scalding embrace.

The fire, infuriatingly, did not come forth. But my fury continued to swell.

Ramiel did not greet me when we arrived at his dwelling. Nor did he visit me that night. I went to my room alone and spent the moonlight hours wallowing in my grief, ~~despairaging~~ disparaging my still rollicking stomach and stoking the embers of my anger.

The next day dawned dreary, the sun shrouded behind several dense and dark clouds. It was the perfect atmosphere for the events about to unfold.

* * *

I was ill when Ramiel arrived in my room at midmorning. My retching had, fortunately, eased, but my body was weak and my mind unsettled.

Ramiel did not seem to notice. He was as pristine as ever, clad in his usual layers of tunics, although his shining shoes were speckled with dirt, and he reeked of blood.

"Are you still abed, Lasair?" he called to me.

I was, indeed, reclining in bed, curled around my lightly roiling belly.

"It is not like you to sleep so late, but I suppose the journey was taxing, yes?" He sat on the edge of the mattress and reached to caress my hair.

I flinched. Not because I feared his touch. Rather, I was fearful of the odor rising from his clothes, which threatened to re-anger my stomach. "You've been with the Púcas," I said. They were the only creatures who left such a pungent aroma.

"I have." Ramiel smiled. "Specifically, I've been with the filly. She's grown splendidly while you've been away. Come." He stood and moved to the window, beckoning for me to follow. "See what a beauty she's become!"

I went, more to distract myself from my turbulent thoughts than out of a true desire to see the filly.

Through the misting rain and wispy morning fog, I glimpsed her standing alone in the big enclosure. She had grown in my absence, developing wonderfully long legs and an artfully refined head. But she was lonely and pacing, calling plaintively to the other Púcas, who kept their distance and ignored her cries.

"The Púcas don't accept her," I muttered.

"They tolerate her well enough," Ramiel said dismissively. "I believe she carries a different scent that makes the Púcas wary of accepting her into the herd. But no matter...With as nicely as she's developing, I'll continue my experimentations. One day, she'll have a herd of her own."

Experimentations.

"I will speak with him only when he has put aside his experimenta-tions," Raphael had said.

"I am working on a theory that may help her finally gain mastery over her abilities, but the results of my experimentation may not be known for several months." Ramiel's own words, spoken from his brother's mouth.

"Little one," Ramiel chuckled, "are you aware you've ensnared a bit of cloth in your hair?" He reached for the lilac fabric.

I withdrew so violently, I struck my head against the wall.

Ramiel paused and ruffled his wings. "Are you alright? You do look peaked..."

"The filly is unhappy," I said, ignoring his query.

"On the contrary, she's thriving."

"Physically, perhaps, but she's isolated and lonely. And she did not *ask* to be an experiment! But because you've deemed her to be one, you've doomed her to a life of solitude."

"Ah." Ramiel tutted. "I suppose, based upon your sudden hostile expression, you were made aware of the contents of my letter? Apologies, little one. That was not meant for your eyes—"

"It was a letter written about *me.* I deserved to hear the vile things you had to say."

Ramiel's smile was thin. "Vile? I sang your praises."

"'*The pet who has warmed my bed,*'" I spat his words in his face. "'*A tool with which to shred your human cloak.*' Those are not praises! And you *lied* to me! You sent me to Sakar to anger your brother— and *kill* his humans. You never intended to make peace with him."

"Little one, I did not lie to you. I *do* wish to speak with my brother, but he has steadfastly ignored me for *years*. I had to do something to garner his attention."

"So you sent me to Sakar hoping I would kill his humans because you knew that would provoke him." My flesh felt uncomfortably tight, as though it had shrunk in size and was stretched thin over my bones.

Ramiel crossed his arms over his chest, raising one hand to stroke his chin. "I sent you to deliver a letter to my brother. That is all. But I can't say I *didn't* want you to seek vengeance on his humans. They are despicable, fear-driven beasts. All humans are, but *they* were the beasts who dared to use their teeth on you."

I pivoted from the window, clutching a hand to my stomach. A bitter, ashen tang enveloped my tongue—a memory of the tastes and scents I'd experienced while walking the ruined streets of Swindon.

I *had* sought vengeance on the people of Swindon. I had gone into their town *intending* to hurt them.

"Little one, you're getting yourself upset over a minor infraction," Ramiel said. "They're humans. Like all beasts of the earth, they live only to reproduce and die. Any you killed will be easily replaced..."

I thought of Belanna and Braxton, the boisterous twins who had so easily given me their trust and friendship.

And my mind, of course, lingered for a long while on Quinn. It dwelled on the echoes of his smiles, the infectious tenor of his laughter, the way he'd teased and prodded his way through my thorns, and how gently he'd soothed the ravaged and bitter parts of my heart.

"They're not." My tears tasted like the sea as they slid onto my tongue.

"I'm sorry?" Ramiel pried.

"They're not easily replaced." I opened my eyes, meeting his impassive stare. "Humans are all the things you accuse them of being —all the things *I've* accused them of being. But they are not *objects* to be disregarded and supplanted. They're unique creatures; no two are entirely the same. And they have far more emotional depth than other beasts..." Again, my mind wandered to Quinn and the last seconds we'd spent together before Raphael's soldiers had pulled us apart. He'd murmured something to me then, words I had been too grief-stricken to comprehend at the time but which were strikingly clear in the aftermath. *"I love you."*

I'd not believed those words when he used them in his song, but I no longer questioned their validity. He'd proven them to me, time and again.

But he had no cause to believe I returned the sentiment, not when I'd oft greeted his advances with guarded hostility. During my journey to Uchen, I had anguished over my surliness and lamented that he'd seen naught but my pride and bitterness. I'd simply known no other way of being at that time of my life.

Yet he'd loved me anyway.

I *ached* to return to him, to remedy the mistakes I'd made and prove to him that his feelings were not one-sided.

"Emotional depths?" Ramiel's ~~dervisive~~—derisive laugh drew me from my reminiscing. "I think you've spent far too much time with my brother, little one. He's corrupted your mind."

"Perhaps he's *un*corrupted it."

Ramiel's brow rose. He began to contradict me, but I spoke first.

"I was naught but an experiment to you, wasn't I? The same as the filly and the other Púcas...You don't see us as living things. You certainly don't consider us your equals. We are the tools you use to achieve something. Once we no longer serve a purpose, we are discarded and replaced by another tool. You do not care if we are hurt or if we harm others." There was a sour flavor blossoming across my tongue, as though I was trying to speak around a mouthful of cinders. "I dislike and distrust humans, and I wanted to live a life apart from them. But you saw my abhorrence and you *used* it. You showed me the violence at Detha and spoke ill of the humans, calling them beasts, savages, and dull-witted creatures. And you told me, repeatedly, that I was better than them, likely so I would not feel sorrow for taking their lives. It worked. I did not despair over those I killed at Swindon. Does this make you happy to hear? I *relished* their passing. Their pain. I was more beastly in that moment than they'd ever been toward me. And perhaps I would've continued the path of destruction you wanted me to forge had it not been for—" I paused, unable to say Quinn's name with Ramiel watching me so closely. "Had it not been for your brother."

Ramiel flicked a loose thread from his tunic, looking poised and unbothered against the accusations I'd hurled at him. "Do you realize," he drawled, "that your fire emerged and disappeared thrice while you were speaking?"

The ashen taste on my tongue worsened as I looked at my hands. They were trembling but bare, until...

The flame flickered above three of my fingers, curling itself in a brief, seductive dance, before it faded into a wisp of smoke.

My stomach lurched so suddenly, so violently, I had no chance of making it to the privy.

Ramiel did not react when I spewed sick over the floor. He offered no words of comfort, nor did he attempt to reach for me when I became too weak to stand. He watched me fall and *laughed*.

"Judging by your expression, this was not the first time your fire emerged without you noticing. Tell me, little one, when did these oddities begin?"

My hand, when I raised it to wipe my lips, was swaddled in flame once more. I had an urge to scream, or better yet, rise to my feet and smear my sick over Ramiel's contemptuous face.

But I said nothing. And my limbs were so shaken, I did not trust myself to stand.

"You spent nearly two full moons in Sakar," Ramiel said. "I'd wager the peculiarities began shortly after you arrived, am I correct? There's no need to look at me in such a manner, little one. I'm only theorizing."

I knew not how I had looked at him. Perhaps my expression had been one of hurt, or wrath, or terror. Perhaps even dread.

Ramiel unfurled his wings, using the tip of the left to whisk a tear from my cheek.

"It would seem I am correct in my assumptions. This is *excellent*." He smiled.

And I wondered how I'd ever found his eerily bright eyes and flashing teeth charming. He'd never looked human, but his malicious grin gave him a more monstrous appearance than any Wraith or Púca had ever possessed.

When he stretched his wing toward me again, I ground my teeth into it, gaining some satisfaction from his discomforted grunt. Although I had not the bite to draw blood from a Celestial, I pulled several of his feathers loose.

"I'll forgive you for that." Ramiel withdrew his wings, tucking them against his back. "*Only* because of your condition. You see, little one...Seruf is heavy-handed and impulsive. In making you, she gave far too much of herself. This weakened her immensely, although she is loath to admit it, and it ensured you would never gain full mastery over your power. The fire coursing through your veins was not meant for humans, and you have entirely too much of it. You were doomed to spend the rest of your days enslaved to the flame you hate so much. But I believed there was a way to dilute your power— something Seruf had not considered. And so..." He crossed the room, carefully avoiding the puddle of sick on the floor. "I decided to breed you."

He said this in the same blithe manner a cattle herder might use when deciding to replenish his stock.

"*Breed me?*"

"Yes. It's perfectly logical when you consider it. The babe will absorb some of your fire. Not immediately; you'll need to birth it first. But once you have, you'll find it much easier to control your ability."

"I...*no*. I will do no such thing."

"You already have." Ramiel stroked my hair, ignoring my hiss. "I am limited to the resources this world provides me, which do not include adequate methods of predicting a pregnancy. But given the time that has lapsed and the changes already happening to your fire, I believe you *are* with child." He leant close, clutching his hand over my mouth when I attempted to turn my teeth into him, and whispered, "Have you had your bleed cycle during these last two moons, little one?"

My heart sprouted thorns, and its every thrum ~~puforated~~— perforated my innards.

Young and naive as I was, I wasn't entirely unwise to the ways of the world. I'd seen many an animal give birth and had witnessed the act that conceived the babes—animals were hardly discreet with their sexual ~~prolictivities~~—proclivities. As a child, I'd also overheard the talks of women and wet nurses. When I questioned Terrick, he never denied me an answer, although he likely would have preferred to *not* discuss intimate details of the female body.

I knew what Ramiel was asking, and I was certain of the answer, even as it pained me to consider it.

"Oh, hush," Ramiel soothed when I began to cry. "This is not the betrayal you think it is, little one. I am *helping* you."

He removed his hand from my mouth and bent his head to press a long, lingering kiss to my lips.

A few months prior, I would've mistaken the act for tenderness. Perhaps even love.

But now I knew better. He used those lips as a weapon, both to bind me to him and to silence my anguished weeping.

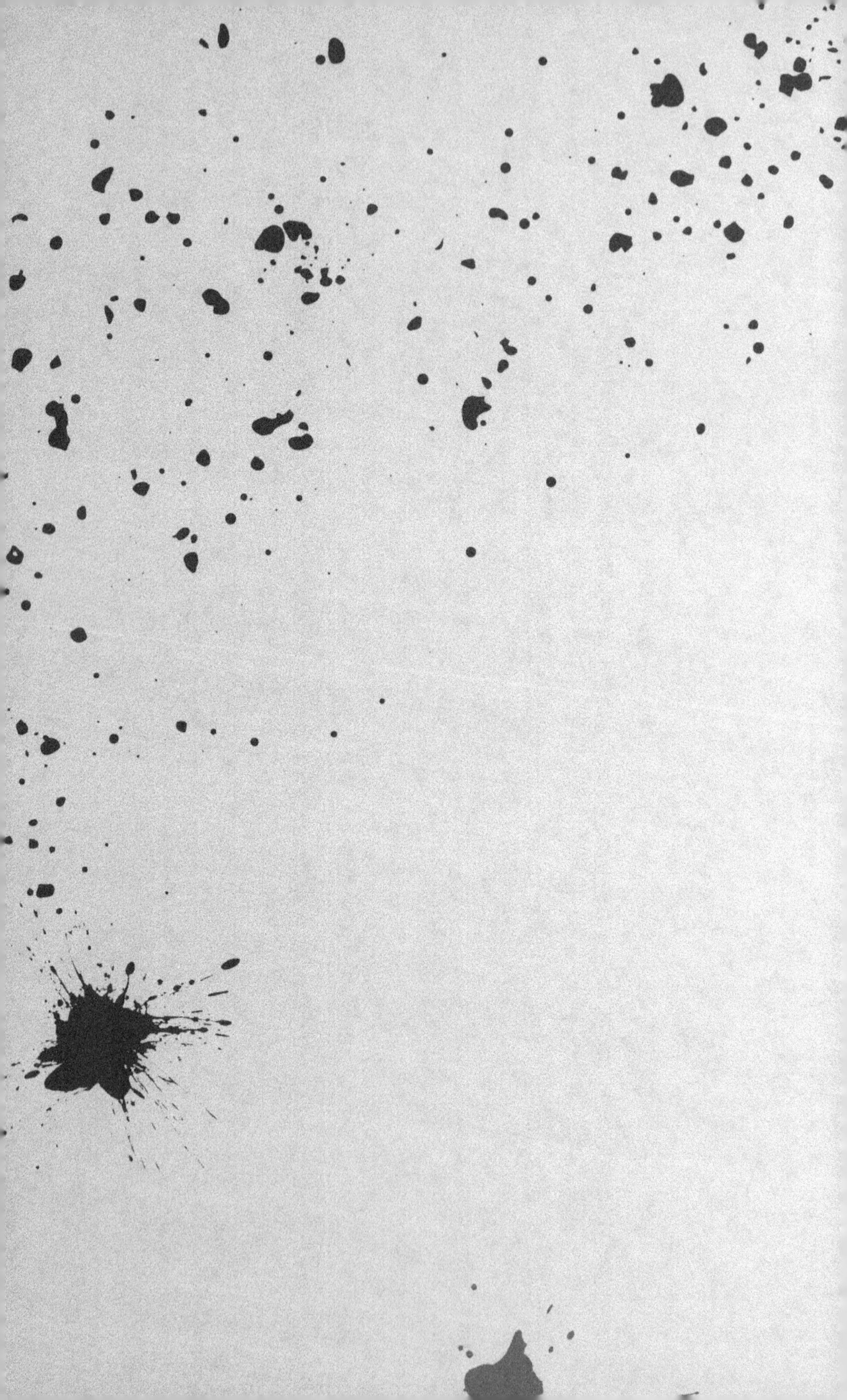

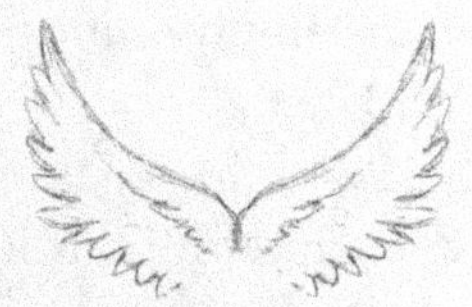

Time had once again become a fickle beast.

While the weeks I'd spent with Quinn had passed entirely too quickly, the weeks I spent confined at Dunbar seemed to not pass at all. I could hardly discern when one hour ended and another began. If not for the window in my bedchambers, I would not have noticed the days passing.

I watched the sun and moon rise and fall with bleary eyes. Sleep seldom visited me. Truthfully, it felt too strenuous, the endless cycle of closing my eyes, facing the nightmares, and awaking to find that nothing had changed.

Everything seemed exhausting. I once sat on the floor for a full day because the thought of rising left me winded. It was only my bladder, which had filled to the point of discomfort, that finally set me on my feet. And then I remained by the privy for several more hours because I could not summon the strength to walk again.

The fire, at least, provided entertainment during my confinement. Not that I was amused by its sudden appearances and disappearances, but its striking visuals eased the monotony of the day.

Until the fire also found too much tedium in its existence.

After several days, perhaps weeks, of watching the fire break into spontaneous dances over my skin, I saw it no more. It had not vanished—I would never be so lucky as to have it leave me completely—but it had retreated to sulk silently beneath my flesh.

And the monotony endured, uninhibited.

I spent a month in that room, but I aged a lifetime.

I was a far cry from the young, robust girl who'd leapt down the waterfall with Quinn.

In the early days of my imprisonment, Ramiel attempted to cajole me into accepting my fate.

"This is a *good* thing, Lass," he would say. "Linger not on the pregnancy. It lasts only a few months, but it will buy you a *lifetime* of freedom from your power."

At first, I would attempt to argue. "Hybrids do not pass their abilities to their offspring," I said on one such occasion.

"The other hybrids are too limited to pass their abilities." Ramiel knelt before me and raised his fisted hand. "Most hybrids are given this amount of Celestial blood." He unfurled one finger. "They pass *some* of it to their offspring, but it's not enough to be noticeable. Now you, little one, were given this much Celestial blood." He opened his four remaining fingers. "You will pass a substantial amount. And if your first offspring doesn't take enough, we'll try again."

"I will *not*."

He chuckled. "~~Indignancey~~—Indignancy doesn't become you, little one. It was only a suggestion. You'll likely not need to bear more than one offspring. The babe you're carrying is mine, after all." He pulled me in for a kiss, despite my best attempts to break his hold. "It may prove to be a more powerful hybrid than even you."

When I refused to soften toward his rationalizing, he stopped visiting me.

And I stopped speaking.

I saw no one else. Food, water, and other supplies were left at my door three times a day, but I rarely rose to collect them. Occasionally, a Wraith would shout through the door, "Oi! You still breathing in there?" and would persist until I answered with a bitter, "No."

And, oh, there were times aplenty I wished to cease breathing. I *ached* for death, but I never sought it. For whenever I glimpsed the lilac ribbon I kept carefully plaited into my hair, I thought of Quinn. And whenever I thought of Quinn, I yearned for life.

That is the confounding thing about the human species, is it not? No matter how we suffer or how bleak our prospects, no matter if our lives are mere ashes in the wind, the desire to endure still burns.

* * *

Another day faded into a grimy mist of boredom.

I'd been reclining sideways on my bed, watching as the waxing moon cast dark pools of shadow in the corners of my room. When a dark figure arose from those shadows, I thought myself dreaming, especially as the figure hovered in the blurred edges of my vision.

I turned my head and blinked sluggishly.

A male Celestial stood beside the open door to my room, donned in black garments, with his windblown mane of dark hair sprawled about his shoulders. His wings, which draped around his sides like a cloak, were a drab shade of steel. The only splashes of color about him were the rich, forest-green feathers at the tips of his wings.

I could not discern his face, not when he was bathed in darkness and standing so far away.

"Lass?" the Celestial asked as he shut the door behind him.

"My name is Lasair here," I said with more bite than I'd intended.

"Very well, *Lasair*." He strode toward my bed.

As he came into focus, I found myself struck by how...*ordinary* he was. He had not the beauty of the other Celestials, for his squared face was grim and harsh, nor did he possess the same elegance, for he was small and ~~sinuwe~~—sinewy.

"Who are you?" I asked.

"My name is Cheriour."

"You are not a Celestial of Uchen."

"I am not." He drew a square of parchment from his belt and handed it to me.

I did not take it. "You'll be killed for coming in here. As soon as Ramiel—"

"Ramiel is detained in Norhall," Cheriour said. "Likely not for much longer, but we will have enough time to travel to Sakar. *If* you desist arguing with me."

For the first time in days, *weeks*, the fire pricked my flesh. "I enjoy arguing."

"I know. Your friend has informed me of that. But we haven't the time. I've come to help you, Lasair."

"I...My friend?"

Cheriour silently attempted to hand me the parchment again.

I reached for it but paused when I saw the word hastily scrawled across its front. One of the few words I had the ability to read at the time.

Lass.

It was Quinn's writing.

I drew my hand back. "Is that a letter?"

"Yes."

"I cannot read."

"I am aware. But I wanted you to see it. I can read it to you."

"I'd prefer you *not* read it." It would sound unnerving to hear Quinn's words spoken in this Celestial's dull, tired tone.

"Very well." Cheriour dropped the letter onto my lap.

I clutched it so tightly, the parchment crinkled beneath my fingers. "Why are you here? Surely you did not travel to Uchen, knowing you would be killed as soon as another Celestial laid eyes upon you, to rescue a human whore at the bidding of a human boy?"

"I am not here at the boy's bidding. Although he was *quite* persistent." The corner of Cheriour's mouth curled into a faint smile. "No, Lasair—"

"Lass."

"*Lass*," he repeated, showing no annoyance that I'd asked to be called by a different title yet again. "I am here because of Raphael's suspicions. Which I now know to be true." His eyes fell, only for a moment, upon my rounding midsection.

My cheeks heated, and I folded my arms over myself, although I made no effort to move into a position that would better conceal my condition. "Raphael banished me here. Why would he now send another Celestial to retrieve me?"

"I wasn't sent at Raphael's bidding either," Cheriour said. "He believes that even if you *are* with child, you will not carry to term. He's likely correct." At this, Cheriour crouched beside my bed, leveling his eyes with mine. They were kind eyes; not as warm and emotional as a human's, but not as coolly impassionate as the other Celestials. "There are precious few instances of humans carrying Celestial offspring," he continued. "On the rare occasion it has happened, neither the mother nor the child survived."

This revelation should have shocked me, but I felt nothing as I said, "Why would you care whether I live or die? I'm just a naive human child, easily discarded and replaced, am I not?"

"You are an innocent," Cheriour said slowly, "who does not deserve the fate you have been given. You are faultless for everything that has happened in your life. The faults lie with the Celestials. Me most of all."

I scoffed. "You most of all? You and I are not ~~acquaintees~~— acquaintances. How can you assume fault for anything that has happened to me?"

Cheriour exhaled and tapped a finger against his pursed lips. "Thirteen years ago, Ellard, the guardian of Darfield, received a visitation from Seruf. He did not detain her or report her visitation to Raphael because of their bond. Ellard would have never denied Seruf protection. But he confided in me that she'd asked about hybrid creation. And that she'd become enamored with a child. He feared what she planned to do with this child. I traveled to Uchen that evening to stop her."

At this, I lifted my head, gazing into his eyes, marveling at how lush and green they were and realizing, with a cold rush of incredulity, that I had seen them before.

They'd stared down at me on the day Seruf turned me into her hybrid.

"I failed." Cheriour's eyes lowered away from mine. "I can't reverse what was done to you. But I can allow you to live your last days with a loved one. And if your babe survives..." A muscle tightened in his jaw. "It's best for it to be out of Ramiel's reach."

* * *

We flew to Muirin. An utterly loathsome way to travel—worse, even, than a vessel—for it was far too swift and disorienting for a human.

Even when we landed, my stomach continued to roil. It was quite fortunate I had not eaten that day. Otherwise, Cheriour would've worn my sick.

But then Quinn yelled my name and stumbled down the narrow cliff passage toward me, and my discomforts were forgotten.

I squirmed in Cheriour's arms until he deposited me upon the stony shore, and then I ran. I did not pause to consider my changing powers or what would happen to Quinn if the fire decided to reawaken again. The sight of him filled me with wild, reckless joy. I could not, *would* not, stay away from him a moment longer.

"Lass!" Quinn laughed when I flung my arms about his neck. His arms engulfed me, one twining around my lower back to draw me close to him, the other cradling my head. Perhaps it was the warmth and security of being enfolded into such a tight embrace, or perhaps it was the prospect of touching him, feeling his heart thumping beneath my ear, after I'd spent weeks convincing myself I'd never see him again...

Regardless of the reason, I was overcome with tears.

"It's alright, Lass," Quinn murmured.

I buried my face into his chest to stifle my sobs.

"I don't like this, Cheriour," a deep voice spoke from behind me. "If you remain on these shores for too long—"

"We won't, Hurleigh," Cheriour said. "I'm giving the child a moment to recover. Before I bring her and the boy inland."

"*Recover.*" The other voice laughed harshly. "She'll not be recovering from her condition."

I craned my head, drying my tears on Quinn's tunic, and glimpsed the strikingly handsome Celestial who had spoken. He stood atop the sea, his bare feet skimming the surface of the water, while his magnificent green and blue wings arched toward the starless night sky. Naught but a set of black trousers clothed his large body, but his near nakedness did not soften the harshness of his appearance.

Behind him, the sea swelled into a towering pinnacle, a wave larger than any I had ever seen.

I must've made a sound of distress, for Quinn's fingers dug into my back.

"This is foolhardy, Cheriour," the seafaring Celestial said. "She belongs to Ramiel. He *will* come to collect her."

"Ramiel will not dare to cross Raphael," Cheriour rebutted. "Once I bring the girl and the boy inland, they'll be out of his reach."

"Raphael will *not* protect Ramiel's whore."

"He will," Cheriour said firmly. "I need you to hold the sea only a few moments, Hurleigh." He turned to us. "Have you everything you need, boy?"

"I do," Quinn said, "just atop the cliff—"

"Go collect it. Quickly."

Quinn nodded. But when he moved to pull away from me, I had a difficult time releasing him.

"Oh, Lass." Quinn carefully slid out from beneath my grasp. "A few weeks ago, you struck me with your thorns whenever I got too close. Now you won't let me go. And you once said I possessed no charm..." He smiled, but it was flat and dull, unlike the careless grins he usually offered me. And his hand, when he wrapped his fingers around mine, was wracked with tremors. "It seems I *have* succeeded in charming you."

"I kept a distance only to refrain from harming you," I said. "But as you've proven you've no regard for your own safety—"

Quinn pressed his mouth to mine, stealing my words. This kiss was brief, lasting the span of a single heartbeat, but it left my lips aching for more.

"I know, Lass," he said. "I *know* you want to protect me, but please don't push me away anymore. I'll gladly risk the flame to keep you by my side." With his other hand, he wiped the tears from my cheeks, pausing to stroke my hair and the lilac ribbon still plaited through the strands. And then he coaxed me to follow him up the winding cliff trail.

"Did Cheriour read you my letter?" he asked.

"No."

"No?"

"I would not allow him to. I—I wanted to hear the words spoken by you." The letter, strapped to the inside of my boot, chaffed my skin as we climbed the cliffside, but it was more a comfort than a pain.

"Ah. Well, it contained a grand retelling of how I discovered Cheriour and swayed him to help." Quinn winked. "But I will regale that tale to you once we've taken refuge in the woods."

My stomach turned to rot. "We're returning to Niall's woods?"

"No. I—I am not welcome in Niall anymore. Or in any city, for that matter."

"You were *banished*?"

"*No.*" The word hissed between his teeth. "Healers are far too valuable for banishment. They'll not kill me, either. I will be imprisoned if I'm captured, nothing more. But fret not, Lass, I will not be captured so easily. I may not be much for soldiering, but I'm skilled at fleeing and hiding."

"And you were given this sentence because you sheltered me at Niall?"

"No, I've already paid for that infraction." He pressed his lips together.

My heart bled for him, knowing the pain he had likely suffered at Byron's hands. "So you were *tortured* for aiding me, and now you face imprisonment for helping me yet again..."

"I face imprisonment," Quinn said adamantly, "because I abandoned my post at Niall. Something I would have done regardless of whether you needed my help or not." He lifted our twined hands and kissed my knuckles. "My hands are ill-suited for soldiering, after all."

We crested the cliff just as my legs had begun to tremble with exertion, and my eyes fell upon the town. Several people remained outside their homes, even though the night would linger for many more hours. These were the watchmen who lived their lives beneath the moonlight, guarding both the townspeople and their livestock. They regarded us with abhorrence as Quinn released my hand

and bent to retrieve the packs he'd placed upon the cliff's edge. Quinn smiled at them and hummed a cheery tune that seemed at odds with the direness of our situation.

Below us, the sea roared like a restless, wild animal preparing to ravage the lands in search of something to ease the unyielding gnawing at its belly.

The tremors began from deep within me as Quinn secured a bag to his back. And they refused to ease, even when he closed his hands over my arms, attempting to warm me. "Lass?" Uncertainty wavered his voice.

"We truly are fools, Quinn. Ramiel...he won't...You know of my condition, do you not?" My words were barely more than a whisper.

"I'm aware." He fought valiantly to keep his gaze from my midsection, but his eyes swept briefly over the soft mound concealed beneath my white tunic. "And—I'm sorry, Lass. It's—what he did to you..." Quinn's eyes shone with unshed tears. "I'm *sorry*." He drew me to him, pressing his fluttering lips to my brow, the lids of my eyes, my nose, and my cheeks. Each soft kiss was punctuated by a whispered, "*I'm sorry, Lass.*"

I pressed myself against him, seeking comfort in his warmth, even as every fiber of my being warned me I would find no solace tonight.

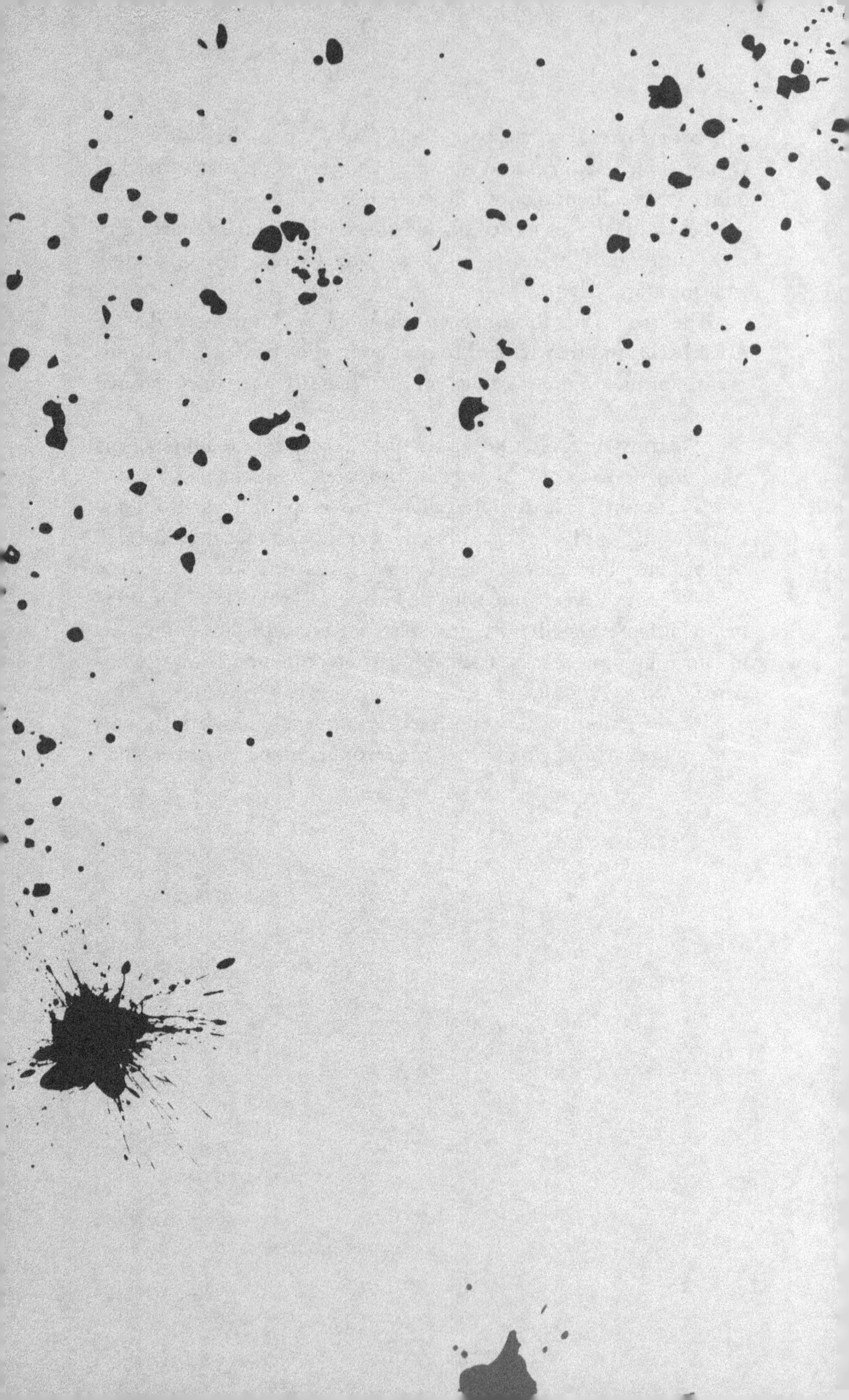

Flame

Ramiel's arrival was a mere flash of white against the blackness of night. So brief and inconspicuous, it might've simply been lightning. But the ~~cadance~~ cadence of the ocean changed, rising to a near deafening roar.

My dread worsened. The feeling inside me was akin to the sensation one would get if one were walking across a smooth surface and suddenly stepped into an unseen rut.

I drew away from Quinn, clasping my hands together to still their trembling. I knew. Before I glimpsed him through the looming darkness, I *knew* Ramiel was there.

"Lass?" Quinn asked.

I gasped as a wave nearly the size of Niall's castle swelled. It traveled *away* from the shoreline, rolling outward into the sea, where Ramiel hovered, his wings outstretched, a gleaming sword clutched in one hand.

Beside me, Quinn's breath grew ragged. "It's alright, Lass," he murmured. "Hurleigh protects this shore. The Conqueror won't come inland."

The Conqueror. At that moment, Ramiel's appearance befitted the title the humans had given him. He looked wrathful, beautiful, and unwavering. His eyes had already found me on the cliff's edge, and the fury darkening his gaze caused my heart to stutter.

The mountain of water hurtled toward Ramiel. He did not move or lift himself out of its path. He merely watched me and raised his sword, pointing its tip at Quinn.

The wave swallowed him.

Below us, the Celestial Hurleigh ~~wayded~~ waded farther into the sea, his green and blue wings twitching as though fighting the urge to take to the skies. Cheriour stood back, his steely wings raised above his head.

Both waited.

The wave swelled and faded. Ramiel emerged, unfurling his wings from where he'd wrapped them around himself.

Below us, Hurleigh retreated, his feathers twitching more violently.

"Hold, Hurleigh," Cheriour called.

"We two cannot hold him," Hurleigh said.

"We can. He cannot last; he's been isolated from the City for too long."

"Ellard thought the same." Hurleigh's wings raised themselves to their fullest height. "And he is mortal now."

"Ellard," Cheriour said, "tried negotiating with Seruf and lost sight of Ramiel. We *can* hold him, Hurleigh. Stay with me."

A second titanic wave battered Ramiel.

This time, he faltered, disappearing into the bowels of the sea.

I held my breath, hardly daring to hope but still finding myself ~~boyed~~ buoyed by optimism.

Ramiel appeared once again, more slowly this time, and he looked shaken as he curled his chin into his chest, struggling to maintain his composure.

He was *weakening*.

But not as quickly as Hurleigh's resolve.

Upon witnessing Ramiel's second emergence, Hurleigh turned away from the sea. "I'm sorry, Cheriour. But I won't give him my Essence." He ruffled his wings and disappeared.

* * *

I should pause for clarification.

Cheriour's plan, while not without risk, had been sound.

Hurleigh controlled the sea. Had he stayed his course, he would have incapacitated Ramiel. He wouldn't have killed him, for a Celestial could not die from something as simple as drowning, but being thrashed by waves was as exhausting for the Celestials as it was for humans. Eventually, Ramiel would've been forced to retreat, lest he found himself weakened and at the mercy of his enemies.

A weakened Ramiel also would not have *dared* to risk his brother's wrath by pursuing me inland. Cheriour knew this. He could have succeeded in his quest to free me.

But Cheriour was a limited Celestial with no powers of his own to use against Ramiel. He relied on Hurleigh. *I* relied on Hurleigh.

And we were both foolish for doing so.

* * *

It is easy to sense when one knows defeat is near at hand.

Although Cheriour stood stoically at the beach, holding a blade in each fist as he readied himself for the attack, his wings quivered, and his shoulders hunched. It was the posture of a being who had lost hope but was not yet ready to concede defeat.

He did not waver. Even as Ramiel rushed to the shore, brandishing his ~~lumanous~~—luminous sword, Cheriour stood fast, raising his own blades in defense.

They collided, the clanging of their weapons louder than any clap of thunder.

The sound alerted the people of Muirin, who awoke from their peaceful slumbers to find themselves trapped in a terror.

"It's the Conquerer!" some cried.

"Where is Hurleigh?" others moaned.

"Lass." Quinn touched my arm. "We must—ach!"

I startled when he drew away with a cry, staring at the blisters coating his palm.

My fire had returned, once again curling itself around my flesh.

"Quinn—" I began.

"It's alright, Lass." He smiled, even as his fingers trembled. "It's naught but a minor burn. But we must go..."

"*Go?*" Fear bittered my laughter. "It's too late for that, Quinn."

"Ramiel won't—"

"He *will*. Did you not see the guardian of Muirin flee? Do you not see the battle unfolding below us?"

The two remaining Celestials warred on the beach. It was a spectacle quite unlike any human fight. Ramiel and Cheriour tumbled about the sand and sky together, often locked in a tangled embrace, turning the sharp feathers of their wings into each other. When they drew away, they struck each other with their blades. Radiant silver fluid spilled from their wounds, and each came away from their scuffle nursing injuries. But Cheriour, sporting a large laceration across his chest, was far worse off than Ramiel, even as he stalwartly attempted to hide his pain and continue with the fight.

"Lass, we have time," Quinn insisted. "We can make it—"

A bout of screaming swallowed his words.

The humans of Muirin, driven near mad with panic, had hastily begun evacuating. Fear made them violent. They fought amongst each other: petty squabbles over food, belongings, and which direction they might take out of town. They dashed about blindly, hardly caring if they trod on their kin. Several people cried as they found themselves trapped under the horde. No one offered to help them stand.

Quinn ran from my side when an aged, stooped woman collapsed beneath the weight of dozens of fleeing humans. He split the crowd, bellowing, "Stand aside! Give her a chance to breathe, for pity's sake!" as he lifted her from the ground, guiding her into the open door of one of the moss-covered dwellings. As she sobbed, he crouched beside her and healed the angry marks the mob had inflicted upon her flesh.

On the beach, Cheriour's left wing crumpled against the ground, broken and bleeding from the blade Ramiel had embedded into its joint.

Ramiel lifted his gaze to the top of the cliff, and the vicious glee in his eyes turned my stomach to rot.

He would slaughter Cheriour, and then turn his rage to the citizens of Muirin.

"Lass..." Quinn sprinted back to my side. "We *must* go."

"*You* must go," I turned away from the cliffs. "Now. I'm destroying this city."

Quinn faltered. "Lass...what?"

"I'm destroying the city," I repeated. "If I do not lay waste to it, Ramiel will, and he won't spare those who dwell here, whereas I care not whether they live or die. If you can convince the humans to stop fighting amongst each other and seek refuge elsewhere, they will live."

"Lass..."

"I can't guarantee he won't hunt you. But perhaps...if I am thorough...if there's enough time..." My tears burned hotter than any flame. "Perhaps he will accept what he sees at first glance and won't search for the living."

"And what of you?" Quinn's eyes seemed, if possible, even bluer against his suddenly colorless face. "Will you flee with us?"

"I'll return to Uchen with Ramiel."

"No. *No*! Lass...for feck's sake..." He moved to pull me into an embrace, but the sting of my flame brought him up short. "*No!*" he cried again. "Near two years ago, I watched you leave with a Celestial, not knowing if I'd ever see you again. And now you're asking me to watch you leave with *another* Celestial?"

"I'm not asking."

He staggered back and grasped fistfuls of his own hair.

"Quinn—" I began.

"No!" he hissed. "I won't do this again, Lass. I *can't*. Two fecking years...and *nothing* has changed."

"I've changed," I said. "Two years ago, I had nothing to live for. Now I do." I tried to smile, but a pained grimace gripped my face. "You taught me I should want more from this life than to merely survive it. You reminded me what it is to feel joy. To feel *love*. I want to *live* now, Quinn. *Fully*. As we did during our time in the woods. And I will do everything in my power to find that life again. But there is no happiness for me in a world where you are not alive."

Quinn's hands ran first through his hair, then down behind his ears and along his cheeks, before finally coming to a rest over his mouth. He held them there, cupping his palms over his lips and nose as though trying to contain a scream.

"If..." I swallowed. "If I survive the coming months, I promise I will return to you. But you must leave me tonight, Quinn. You must stay alive. *Please.*"

Tears welled in his eyes. The sight of him standing before me, pale and in clear distress, was thrice as painful as receiving an arrow to the heart.

But I had not the time to comfort him.

Ramiel's triumphant yell rose from the beach.

"Go, Quinn," I said. "*Now.*"

"*Please...*" he said in a broken whisper.

I strode past him, raised my flame-wrapped arm, and touched the first house I encountered. The moss-coated wood made a cheery crackle as it burned.

"Seruf!" someone cried when they saw the flame. "Seruf's here!"

"No." Quinn's eyes were glassy and rimmed with red as he turned to the mob, "The Firestarter is a hybrid of Sakar. She is here to help. Her fire will shield us. But we must *move*. Don't—for feck's sake, don't try to bring your belongings."

A woman had begun to collect spools of fabric from inside her dwelling and had overfilled her arms. She dropped the fabric and tripped herself over it.

"People and animals *only*." Quinn helped the woman back to her feet. "Anything else will only be a burden."

I traversed the town, lighting the empty buildings ablaze.

Quinn strode through the city streets, brandishing his arms, shouting instructions, and occasionally singing in his warbled tenor, as though seeking to irritate the particularly stubborn folks into moving. And he was quick to quiet the cries of outrage people expressed when they saw their homes destroyed. "It is a dwelling," he would say. "Mere bits of wood and moss, nothing more. You can build another..."

"Me mam built that house!" a woman shrieked as a structure collapsed with a resounding rumble.

"Is your mother still alive?" Quinn asked.

"No. The old hag died years ago."

"Then stop your fussing and *move*. For feck's sake! All this belly-aching over a ~~gastly~~—ghastly shack..."

A laugh burst out of me. The comment wasn't particularly humorous, but it was so very much like Quinn to say such a thing in his vibrant, prideful tone. So very much like him to drag a smile onto my lips, even as I otherwise felt wretched.

Even as I sobbed.

The tears persisted as I moved from dwelling to dwelling, running my hands along the walls and furniture, lingering inside each home until it had been sufficiently destroyed.

People still screamed as they watched the flames crawl toward the heavens.

"Keep moving!" Quinn's voice was faint now, but I clung to it for as long as I could. And I mourned when I reached the outskirts of the town and realized I could no longer hear him.

I stilled then, straining to hear the last threads of human conversation, but they were gone. I was surrounded only by the malicious hissing and crackling of fire, the mocking whistle of the wind as it twined itself around the ruined city, and the pained creaks and groans from buildings on the brink of collapse.

Until I heard his voice.

"This is quite impressive, little one."

Ramiel stood behind me. He bled profusely from several large wounds, and his right wing lay twisted at an unnatural angle against the ground. The limb had been badly broken, and he seemed to be in quite a bit of pain as he limped toward me, breathing raggedly.

"They committed a crime." I pleaded for my voice to remain steady. "They aided the Celestial in stealing me away. You punished the Celestial. I punished the humans."

"Indeed. And did you *punish* the human boy you embraced on the cliff's edge?" Ramiel's brow rose.

"The boy was a fool who believed himself in love with me." My stomach swelled into my throat. I bid it to lower and settle. "He is gone now."

Ramiel's mouth curled. "You are a vicious little one. Well done, Lasair. Although, I'd appreciate it if you refrain from putting your life in such peril while you are carrying *my* child."

I had an urge to strike him then, to dig my nails into one of the many punctures in his flesh. But I did and said nothing as I followed him down the narrow cliff path.

He had not even glanced upon the ruined houses, nor searched for the bodies. He was not hunting the humans. It was a victorious moment. I told myself this repeatedly as I stepped onto the beach. The townspeople were safe, albeit without a home. *Quinn* was safe.

But the Celestial who'd attempted to rescue me was not.

Cheriour lay on his side, dangerously close to the rising surf. His clothes were ragged, with hardly enough fabric left to cover his body. Blood—*red* blood—oozed from his numerous wounds, staining the water around him. His wings had been torn from his back and sliced into several pieces. I trod on one such piece, and my ~~rebelelous~~—rebellious stomach surged when I saw the spattering of gray feathers clinging to bloodied bone.

A wave rolled onto the beach, gently cascading into Cheriour. He screamed as the salt of the sea burned his raw wounds.

"Yes, being mortal is quite painful, isn't it, brother? Or so I've been told. I cannot speak from experience, of course." Ramiel's joyous laughter chilled my bones.

Cheriour weakly rolled onto his stomach, bracing his hands near his head. And upon seeing his back clearly for the first time, I could not contain my strangled sound of revulsion.

Small, bony fragments protruded from his shoulders—the remnants of his wings. These were jagged, as though it had taken several attempts to rip the wings free, and still oozed small particles of light. The rest of his back was badly torn; much of his flesh hung in long, wriggling strips.

He lifted his head, turning to me when I gasped. Although visibly in a great deal of agony, his eyes were still calm and kind.

"Leave him, little one," Ramiel called. "We'll need to take a vessel back to Uchen, I'm afraid." He flinched when his damaged wing spasmed.

I ignored him and moved closer to Cheriour.

"Lasair..." Ramiel warned.

"I need to douse the fire before I board a vessel." I knelt and extended my still flame-swathed fingers toward the sea.

A wave rolled onto the beach, swallowing my hands in a gentle embrace while simultaneously lashing at Cheriour's back.

"They've escaped," I hissed to him, using his shouts to mask my voice.

Cheriour paused, his eyes searching mine, and yelled again when the wave returned to the sea.

"Muirin is destroyed," I whispered, "but its people live. If you have the strength to reach them, Quinn will help you. He's a Healer."

"Lasair!" Ramiel bellowed.

"The flame will not leave!" I said. The wave had already extinguished the fire, but as my back faced Ramiel, I hoped he would not see my lie.

As another wave approached, Cheriour grunted, drew himself onto his elbows to protect his wounds from the surf, and rasped, "I'm sorry."

I touched my hand to his bloodied knuckles. There was so much I *wanted* to say. I wished he had not put his life in peril to help me, but I was grateful for the last moments he had allowed me to have with Quinn. I prayed he would find the strength to leave the beach and seek help.

But I had not the time to speak my mind. With the wave already receding, and Ramiel growing impatient, I could only utter, "I'm sorry too."

And then I left him.

A year and a half ago, I had abandoned the land of mortals because I was frightened and knew not where I belonged. I'd been hoping, foolishly, to find my place amongst the Celestials.

Now I knew where my heart resided. And although I climbed onto the vessel of my own accord, I did not willingly leave the mortal lands. I merely allowed myself to be stolen away.

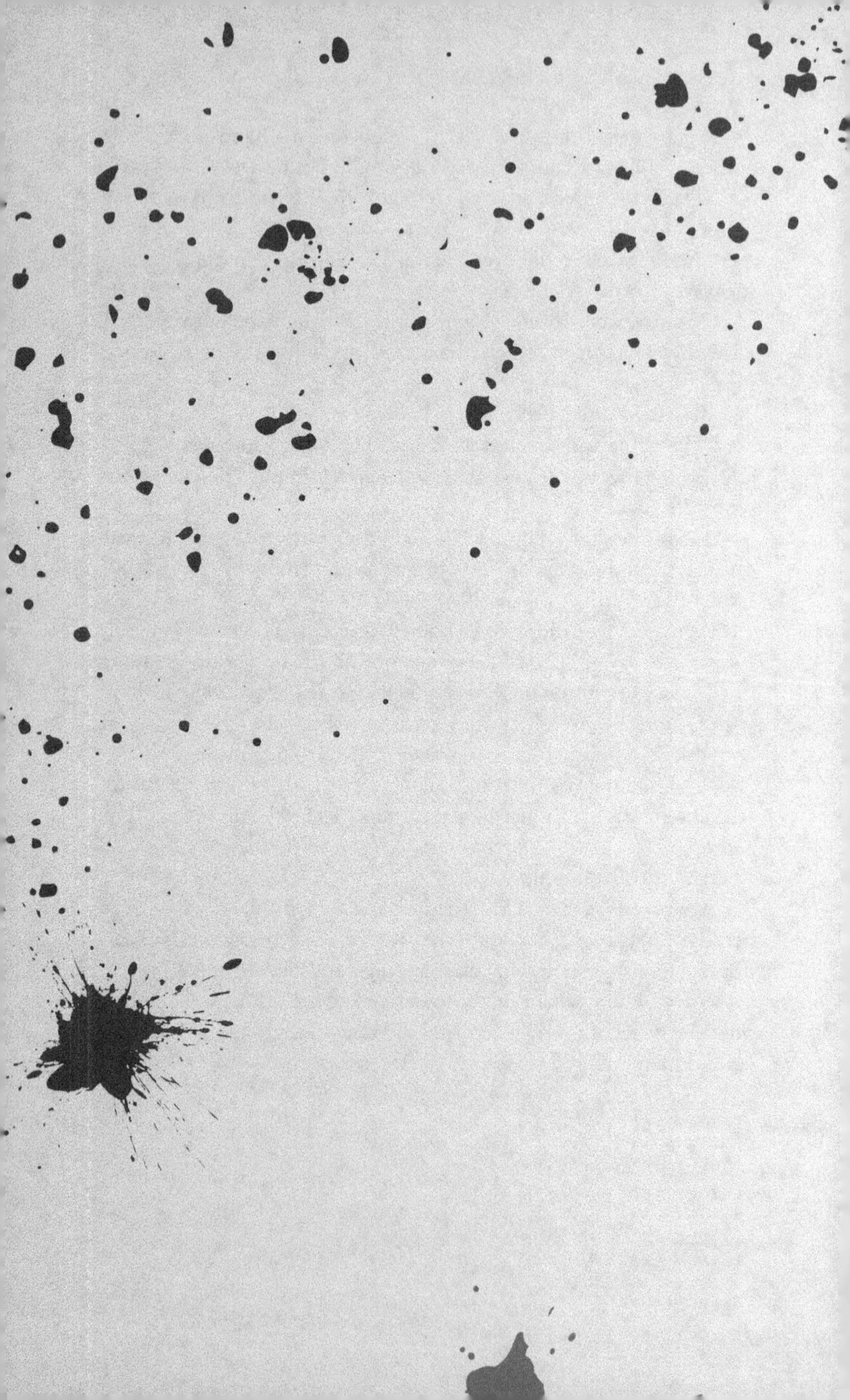

Oath

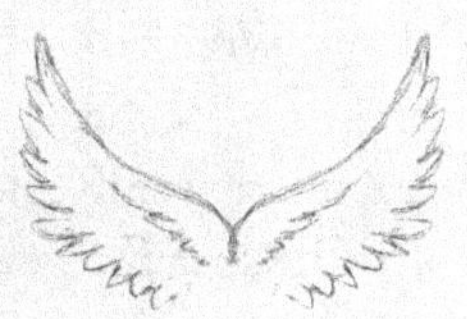

As soon as our vessel arrived upon the shores of Uchen, and my stomach had settled at the promise of steady land once more, I found I could no longer contain the rage and hurt.

Ramiel reached for me.

The early morning sun glowed upon his head, turning his chestnut hair crimson, a shade eerily similar to blood.

I lunged at him, clawing my fingers into his wounds. When the flame flickered over my fingertips, I grasped onto his face, wishing I had the power to kill him.

I didn't.

But my fire caused him great pain. I *relished* his outraged yells.

It took five Wraiths to restrain me, and they did so violently, ~~bludgining~~—bludgeoning my body until I was too dazed to stand.

"*Enough*!" Ramiel called. "Bring her here. Now."

The Wraiths grasped my arms, forcing me to remain on my feet, and dragged me to Ramiel's side.

"That is quite enough, little one." Ramiel gingerly touched the blistered skin on his cheek—a wound that was, frustratingly, already healing.

Pain seared my skull when I lifted my head, but I kept my chin raised, refusing to lower my gaze.

He laughed, coldly and without humor. "And here I thought

you'd be *grateful* I allowed those humans to live...*tsssk*, don't look at me like that, little one. It was a clever idea to create a ruckus as a distraction, but my eyes are sharper than a human's. As are my ears. I *know* you helped them escape."

He strode toward me, malice shimmering in his normally impassive eyes. It frightened me. So much so that I flung myself back, struggling to break free of the Wraiths. They held fast, laughing as Ramiel struck his hand across my face. The pain was blinding; for a full moment after the impact, I saw only blossoming spots of darkness and feared my vision to be lost forever. But it returned, albeit slowly, as Ramiel snatched my chin in his palm.

"Little one—"

I spat.

Ramiel clenched his fingers around my chin. With a soft crackling sound, my jawbone splintered. The pain was shocking. I wanted to scream. But, with the way he held me, all I could do was whimper.

"I saw how you embraced that boy," Ramiel hissed. "You claimed he was besotted with you, but I believe it is *you* who is entranced by *him*. Your attachment to him, silly as it may be, is the *only* reason I allowed him to live. I am not a monster, Lasair, no matter how much my brethren try to paint me as one. But if you have another outburst like this"—he gestured to his blistered cheek—"I will return to Sakar to collect the boy, and you will watch as my Wraiths feast upon his flesh."

My yell was muffled, but it ached as it tore out of my chest.

"Compose yourself, Lasair." Ramiel violently ripped his hand away from my chin, rattling my freshly shattered bones. "I am being perfectly reasonable. If you would cease throwing your childish tantrum, you would see that."

"Reasonable?" Speaking caused me great agony, but I forced the words from my broken mouth. "As *reasonable* as you were when you killed that Celestial—your own kin?"

"I did not kill him," Ramiel said. "I made him mortal. And he was well aware of the consequences of stealing from me."

"*Stealing* from you? I am not an animal you can claim ownership over—"

"That is *precisely* what you are," Ramiel said. "All humans are dim-witted, savage beasts who require a master to direct their ferocity. Raphael has his pets. I have mine." He waved a proud hand at his Wraiths. "And you, Lasair, are tethered to *me*. I've been quite generous in allowing you the full length of your bindings, but, as you've seen fit to use the extra length to cause mayhem, I'll not be so lenient again. Return her to her chambers," he said to the Wraiths. "Ensure the door is properly bolted, and have bars fitted to her window. I'll not risk another Celestial wandering into her cage again."

"You should take heed," I hissed as the Wraiths pulled me away. "Even the most tightly restrained beasts have been known to bite their masters."

"Perhaps." Ramiel rubbed his still-healing cheek. "Although, I doubt you'll live long enough to figure out how to sink your teeth into me."

* * *

The words scrawled across the parchment meant nothing to me. There were hundreds of them, and I could only discern four...one of which being my name.

At the same time, those words meant everything. They had been written by Quinn's hand. Words intended for *me*.

He had not, of course, expected me to be able to understand them, hence why he'd asked Cheriour to read the letter. But as I sat alone in my bedchambers, clutching that parchment with trembling fingers, I vowed I *would* learn to read them.

Until then, I would keep the letter safe. From Ramiel, who would no doubt destroy the parchment if he ever found it, but also from myself.

I had wept in relief upon returning to my room and discovering that my boots, and thus Quinn's letter, had remained intact. My flame oft delighted in destroying the things I held dear, but it had shown mercy and spared Quinn's words. And I would not further test its ~~leinency~~—leniency.

My fingers ached and bled as I clawed at my bedpost, prying the ornate top from the shaft—not an easy task, as the Celestial metal was expertly crafted and unwilling to yield. But yield it did, and the inside contained a narrow crevice that would adequately house my parchment, just as I'd hoped.

I touched my lips against the letter before I folded it and pressed it into the post shaft. "I *will* see you again," I promised. "Whether in this life or the next."

TO BE CONTINUED...

Acknowledgments

Listen, if you've made it to this point of the book, I just wanna give you the biggest, mushiest bear hug, LOL. There were millions of other books you could've spent your time with—and all of them probably would've been cheerier than Lass's story—but you stuck with my girl. So thank you. From the bottom of my heart. I know Lass's story is quirky, and it's where my grimdark elements grimdark the hardest. But there's a happy ending in her future...I promise!

And I do have to get sappy, so buckle up for a hot second!

I wrote this book in tandem with Ashes of the Earth. For me, Addie and Lass's stories are twined around each other (maybe now you've started to see what I mean) and I work on them together. So that team I had for Ashes of the Earth? They helped me get through this book as well. And neither book would've gotten done without them.

So thank you. To my author friends, Adina, Brindi, and Devon for supporting me through this. To my fearless editor, Meg, for braving these chonky-ass manuscripts. To the beta readers, Stephanie, Alix, Jayden, Jasmine, Marje, Gloria, and Hannah, who helped me whip these second books into shape.

And to my readers...y'all get the biggest thank you of all. (Like I said, I wanna give you a big ole bear hug!).

We'll meet again with the final books in the Across Time and Across Time Companion trilogies!

Until then...

Happy Reading!

About the Author

As a child, Stephanie E. Donohue roamed Narnia with the Pevensie siblings and rode the Hogwarts Express with Harry and his friends. She never tired of discovering new and magical worlds through the pages of a book. And, when the yearning to explore still wasn't satiated, Stephanie turned to writing. With a pen and a few sheets of paper, she learned to craft new worlds, and vibrant characters to explore with.

That passion has never died. Stephanie still enjoys writing stories that take readers on exciting, and sometimes dangerous, adventures.

When she's not writing, Stephanie can usually be found cuddling with her two cats, obsessively re-watching The Office, or rocking out to a Pound Fitness class.

Other Books by Stephanie E. Donohue

Standalones

Windsong (2022)

Bewitched by the Sea Monster (2025)

Across Time Trilogy

Fires of the Forsaken (2023)

Ashes of the Earth (2024)

Embers of the Damned (2026)

Across Time Companion Trilogy

Hunted by Fire (2024)

Betrayed by Ash (2025)

Cursed by Ember (2027)

She just wanted a gosh-darn pizza. The apocalypse had other ideas.

Addie did not have "getting plucked from the 21st century and thrown into the apocalypse" on her "things to do after work" checklist. Yet here she is, trapped in the hellscape known as Sakar—a world torn apart by a Celestial war. Now she's dodging soulless Wraiths, getting chased by venomous horses, and trying her darndest to avoid a meltdown.

Thankfully, Cheriour, the gruff and grumpy commander of the human army takes her under his wing. He's blunt, brutal, and socially awkward. *Totally* not Addie's type.

So why does she find him so infuriatingly attractive?

As Addie's connection with Cheriour grows so does the danger. Wraiths threaten to eliminate the last dregs of humanity and secrets about Addie's past are about to surface that might just make her the key to saving everything... or destroying it.

Darkly thrilling and laced with biting humor, *Fires of the Forsaken* is perfect for fans of *Game of Thrones, Deadpool* and *Supernatural*.

Earth's last hope has anxiety, a lethal power, and absolutely no idea what she's doing.

Addie is having a colossally bad year. She's stuck in a bullshit biblical war, her friends keep dying, and her newfound power might be slowly eating her alive.

At least she has Cheriour, the gruff, battle-scarred commander of the human army, who is secretly a teddy bear hiding beneath a grumpy face. But even their budding relationship is threatened as the war rages.

With Wraiths scavenging the ailing country of Sakar, and the Celestials tightening their grip, Addie must lead a desperate mission to save what's left of this world. But the deeper she dives into the secrets of Sakar—and the reason she was brought here—the more she realizes some truths should stay buried.

Gritty, emotional, and packed with sharp humor, *Ashes of the Earth* is a thrilling grimdark romantasy perfect for fans of *Game of Thrones*, *Deadpool* and *Supernatural*.

9 781967 709083